THE WATCHMAN

WITH

A HUNDRED EYES

For Chief Randy Unmul, Springfield PD

Richard Sand

A Lucas Rook Mystery

Library of Congress Cataloging-in-Publication Data
Richard Sand, 1943-

The Watchman with a Hundred Eyes /
by Richard Sand
Library of Congress Catalog Card Number: 2005929926

p. cm.

ISBN 1-930754-77-9

First Edition

10 9 8 7 6 5 4 3 2

Printed in the USA

Interior design: Jennifer Adkins

Durban House Publishing
7502 Greenville Ave., Suite 500
Dallas, TX 75231
www.durbanhouse.com

Also by Richard Sand

Tunnel Runner
Private Justice
Hands of Vengeance

Non-Fiction

Protocol—The Complete Handbook of
 Diplomatic, Official, and Social Usage

For My Little Brother

My thanks to Martha Rudnicki, Deen Kogan, and Jaye Davidson, wherever she is.

"Beauty is bought by judgment of the eye."

Shakespeare

He heard the screaming through the closed doors in the hall and in his head. The muffled cries of terror and of pain. Of the bleeding that had stopped and never would. Of his shame for doing nothing and wanting to do it all. The shaking cries for help. The rutting noise behind the door. Afterwards the water running and the sheets rolled neatly in a ball.

There was no one else to tell. How do you speak the things too horrible to say or even hear inside your head? The rutting noise behind the door. The unmuffled cries for help. Keep the TV on. The moving mouths whose words you did not hear, but meant you were safe downstairs. You hid behind the wooden box and felt its warmth until you heard them coming down the steps. Your sister was back in bed. Daddy smoked a cigarette and Mom was in her dress that shimmered when she walked.

Lucas Rook had helped Grace Savoy before. But that was because she lived next door and was beautiful and blind. This was different, riding with her in the limo and sitting around while they did the shoot. It wasn't his kind of work, but nothing had come from Mrs. Politte or her fancy lawyers from the job upstate. He only had one ongoing case and a few prospects, so he took the job Grace had been talking about for the last year or so.

Usually there was nothing much to do at the shoot except get her things and keep her company, which Lucas didn't mind because they knew each other and the pay was good. A couple of times he got off his chair and had a conversation with somebody hanging around the shoot, particularly one creep who showed up in a raincoat. That ended up with a soliloquy in the alley.

Rook stepped over the low wall between their patios and opened the slider. Grace was at her dressing table. Her hands were shaking as she lit another cigarette.

"I've only got half my face on, Lucas Rook," she said. And then she started to cry.

"You okay?" he asked.

"Grace Savoy is beautiful." She dabbed at the mark on her face. "You can hardly see it now, can you?"

"What happened, Grace?"

"I wanted to put it down the incinerator chute, you know, a proper cremation, but I didn't have the heart. Would you do it for me, Lucas?"

Rook could see the dead bird in the wicker trash basket.

"It flew from the patio. I could hear it flapping against the windows. And then I tried to help it out and it was screeching, but I couldn't."

"Is that what…"

"It flew up into my face, Lucas, and I…" She started to cry again. "I tried to, you know, get it away, and I just killed it."

"Finish your make-up, Gracey. I'll take care of this." He started out into the hall.

"I can't work today, Lucas Rook. Not with this mark on my face. They'll pay you anyway. I'll see to that."

"What kind of bird was it?" she asked when he got back. "What kind of bird did blind Grace kill?"

"A cardinal," he said. "You know, the red kind."

"That's the male," she said. "You'd think the pretty one would be the girl, but sometimes Mother Nature gets it wrong." She dabbed her blind eyes.

Lucas put the wicker basket back underneath her table. "I'll be next door for a while, Grace, if you change your mind about work. Then I'll be going out."

"My uncle Bert was killed by lightning," she said, but Rook had left.

Lucas Rook waited for a half hour, reading the Post and doing the exercises for his bad leg. Then he went around the corner to Oren's for a plate of eggs. Jeanie had not been back to work since she had gotten sick. Sam was clearing off the counter as Rook came in.

"Cup of joe, Joe," Sam called into the back. He liked saying that. "And two fried eggs, break the yolks. Rye toast, well."

Joe Oren came out of the kitchen. A big man with curly hair and freckles. He was listing as he walked.

"Back out again, Joe?" Rook said. "You got to see that chiropractor of mine, Ray Lotka. Got hands the size of dishpans, but he makes magic with them."

Oren sat on the stool next to Lucas and fished a Flexeril from his pocket. "Good to go, partner. Got a pack of frozen peas on the spot that hurts. I'll be as good as gold, then serve them up for lunch."

Rook sipped his coffee. "How's my girl doing?"

"I'm fine," she said, coming out of the kitchen with her book bag in her hand.

"I told you not to be using the alley, Jeanie," her father said.

"Nothing can happen to me because Uncle Lucas is here."

"Uncle?" Rook said. "I thought you were going to marry me."

"That too." Jeanie took a sip of his coffee. "It's so bitter. You should put some cream and sugar in it."

"You eat breakfast, Jeanie girl? Sam will scramble up some eggs."

"Sam made me some, Daddy."

"No he did not," Sam said through the serving window. "She had a half a piece of toast and that's all."

"You got to get your strength up with all those college boys around and you been sick and all," Joe Oren said.

"I'll grab something when I get to school, Daddy. A protein bar or something." She kissed her father and Lucas Rook on their cheeks. Jeanie Oren was halfway out of the door before she came back and gave Rook another one. "Since we're getting married," she said and then she left.

"Feels like time's going out the door," Oren said. "And me, I'm just spinning on this stool. She's done school, she'll move out. Then I'm going to hand this place to Sam or close it up."

"And do what, Joe?" Lucas asked.

"Come over to your place and stare at the wall. Maybe team up and catch the bad guys if there's any left over."

"There always is," Rook told him.

Rook paid his bill and walked over to Jimbo Turner's. The shineman was brushing off the coat of somebody who didn't care and doing his little dance.

"A pleasant morning," Jimbo said. "Cheap cocksucker," he added when his customer was gone. "And I mean that true. Now he's a big somebody, but I knew him when the tough ones made him suck their dicks. 'Bucky' they called him because of his bad teeth, and now such a fine man he is."

Rook got up on the stand.

"What's new on these mean streets?" Jimbo said. He looked in close at Rook's shoes because of his failing eyes. "They need some black to keep the cordovan just right." He handed up the *Daily News* and dropped a match into the polish can.

"You doing good, Jimbo?"

"Except for they wanting to tax my stand, I'm doing just fine for a diabetic, old white shineman. Especially you going to bring me that sweet white corn and them Jersey tomatoes like you said."

"That I will, Jimbo, that I will. And I'll be talking to somebody about their taxing you like I said I would."

The shineman rubbed the soft polish in with his fingertips and hit his brushes together clickety-clack. "I know that," he said.

When Jimbo finished his shine work, he offered his shoulder so Rook could get down. Getting down was hard from the way they had broken his leg before he got the last of them that had killed his brother. The Rook brothers had gone through the academy together, Kirk and him, twins who got their gold shields on the same day. Jimbo used his whisk broom like an artist before Lucas went back up the street.

Rook's office address of 166 Fifth Avenue only meant something if you were from out of town. The elevators were always breaking down and tenants turning over. The dental lab was replaced by a company that put together toys and dolls, so you could always find a jiggling eye or a plastic arm here or there. The two Asian tenants were still at it, but the closest thing to a karate fight was the Japanese pissing in the Korean's mail slot while he was on vacation.

The photographer who never went out was still in the office next to Rook's, crashing things and yelling words that made no sense. The super's son was showing up more and more because Manny was stuck in the bottle again.

Lucas went upstairs and straightened up a bit. He had a borough councilman coming in with a job for him to do.

Rook looked at the clock. His appointment was forty-five minutes overdue. Politicians were always late, overscheduling like doctors and sneaking away to do whatever. He'd give it an hour. If the meeting turned into anything, he'd tack the time on somewhere in the bill.

The phone rang as Lucas was leaving the office. It was Councilman Garner. "I'm sorry I'm late. Traffic is rough."

"Thought you politicians could part the Red Sea," Rook said. "You want me to wait?"

"Could we meet at my office at two-thirty? I just got out of session."

"Sure, sure," Rook said. Things were never what they seemed with pols, but that was true with everybody Lucas worked for.

Lying to hide their stupidity or their own crimes or some little secret for somebody to get ahold of.

The phone rang again. "We'll be working after all," Grace said.

"I got things to do, Gracey. My day's all…"

"It's a vodka spot. I'll be wearing white fur and hardly anything else. We'll be shooting at night."

"I got a four o'clock."

Grace Savoy lit a cigarette. "We won't be working until nine. I need you there. That man might come back. The one in the raincoat."

"No he won't."

"You can slather me with make-up, Lucas."

"Slather? Sounds like something you do with barbeque sauce."

She exhaled her menthol smoke. "Sounds nice to me. I'll see you around seven."

"Eight, Grace," he said. "And be wearing something when I get there."

Rook called Sid Rosen to tell him he'd be going out around noon. Ride Kirk's Avanti. He did that once a week to keep the motor running and whatever.

"You coming over, Lucas boy?" Sid said. "Bring some cans of dog food for old Bear here. Chicken only though. Beef makes his ears itch."

Lucas moved the papers around again on his desk so he could see the calendar. "Makes his ears itch, Sid. Is that right?"

"Gives him yeast. And a half-gallon cherry vanilla ice cream. Whatever's on sale. Except Ben and Jerry's, the pricks support Mumia. Murdering cocksucker never did deny it, killing Danny Faulkner. Shot the poor bastard in the face."

"Only thing he ever denied was his name, Sid. Then again,

'Free Mumia Abdul Jamal' sounds better than 'Free Wesley Cook.'" Rook stretched his bad leg. "That book you lent me, Sid…"

"If you're not done with it yet, you can bring it by next time."

"Good, Sid. I appreciate it." Finished, he hadn't even started.

Rook went by once a week to see Ray Tuzio in the nursing home. Ray had taught Lucas about the streets. Him and McCullagh. But Tuze didn't have anybody else unless you were counting Big Jim McGloan, who shared the airless room with him at the Police and Firemen's Home.

At first, Rook went on Tuesdays so his old partner would know to expect him. But then more and more he could see that Ray Tuzio couldn't tell one day from another. And it was a good idea to change-up when he was coming so the home wouldn't treat Tuze like a dying dog when they thought nobody was showing up.

There was a deli around the corner from Rook's office. Foxes only tried to rob you on every other item, so he walked over and got the dog food and ice cream and some donuts to take out to Tuze. And two cakes of Camay soap. Tuzio always told him when they started and ended their shift, "Watch their hands and wash yours." The soap was starting to accumulate in Ray's room, but the staff would steal it quick enough when they figured no one would notice.

When Lucas got to the policemen's home, Jim McGloan was sitting on the bed, so thin you could see his blue veins through his skin.

"They took Tuze out, boy-o. Took my partner here out to get a tooth yanked. Pull 'em all out, I says. Not about my partner's here, but mine. A man's teeth are his own business, you know."

"He's doing alright, Big Jim?" Rook put the bag down. "Donuts are store bought. You see he gets the soap, and he has any trouble with that tooth or whatever, you call me."

"Got his back." McGloan lay down, then he sat back up. "Time's the baddest perpetrator of them all," he said.

Lucas Rook rolled up ten minutes early to Councilwoman Garner's borough office on Northern Boulevard. Only somebody who had never worked the streets didn't get to the scene early. You didn't, meant you left your brain in your desk.

The only parking space on the block put him too close to the fireplug and likely as not the PBA emblem on Kirk's Avanti was not going to prevent a parking ticket. Lucas looked at his watch. Time to swing around the block a couple of times for a spot to open up and look things over. Always swing around the block once unless you got an "officer in distress" or the like.

The first time around there was nothing. The next pass-by a creep had his eyes on this fat Latin lady's handbag. Lucas pulled alongside of her and asked directions. The booster moved on.

A red station wagon pulled away from the curb as Rook came around to the front of the office again. As he pulled up to parallel park, a blue Caddy tried to jump the spot.

Lucas backed up. They both rolled down their windows.

"Fuck you," said Artie Carlin.

"You too," Rook answered.

"I didn't know you cared," Artie said. He put another two pieces of Juicy Fruit into his wide mouth. "I'll take my usual spot at the hydrant."

"Fixing tickets is a crime," Lucas said.

Carlin pulled by. "I don't fix them. I just don't get them." He parked up the street and then came back. He smoothed his hair piece as he walked.

"I got a feeling it's going to be just me and you, Artie. A call would have been nice."

"You know the way the Councilwoman is. Busy, busy." Carlin unlocked the office door and looked at his watch. "Right now she's either meeting with the mayor, visiting a house-bound constituent, or getting a pedicure."

The walls of the outer office were covered with campaign posters even though the election was more than a year away. The photos did her justice: part housewife, part movie star. Part somebody you wouldn't want to play cards with.

They went into the back. Artie's office was next to hers. "You want coffee, Lucas, there's a Starbucks around the corner."

"Only if it's eight bucks a cup and they got goat cheese croissants with little doilies on them." Lucas looked at his watch. "What's up, Artie? You running numbers again?"

"Numbers? I wish. We got a 1.8 billion, that's with a 'b,' dollar deficit even with Albany kicking in the other half and the sales tax going up to 8.625."

"You talking to me?" Rook said. "You're boring me to death."

"It's called fecal gravity. Shit rolls downhill." Artie Carlin wrote down a name. "She wants you to look at this guy. He shows up at a fundraiser and writes too big of a check. Then he wants to talk to her about some development plan, turning a shirt factory into condos. Too much, too soon."

Rook looked at the name. "Especially when the check's from somebody's name ends in a vowel." He took one of Artie's cards from off the desk and wrote down Jimbo Turner's name and the location. "Friend of mine, Artie. Getting hassled about his not having a license for his shoeshine stand."

Carlin put the card into his shirt pocket. "Done," he said.

Rook had hoped that the councilwoman would have had something for him more than check a guy out. But she was a "comer," so it paid to handle it. It also meant that helping Jimbo Turner had to be between Artie Carlin and him. Otherwise, checking out the guy with the scary check earned him zero.

"Do that thing for me, Artie," Lucas said.

Carlin patted his shirt pocket. "Done," he said again.

There was a parking ticket on the car behind Rook's. He took it up the block and put it on Artie's windshield and then drove back into the city. His cell phone rang. It was Angela Garner.

"I got hung up," she said.

"Didn't know you were into that scene," Lucas said.

"You'll be the first to know. You talk to Artie?"

"We're good."

"Good," she said. "We should get together."

A taxi veered into Rook's lane. He had to turn the Avanti hard. "When you got a minute."

"It will take more than that," she laughed.

Lucas stayed in the curb lane. The fiberglass coupe was running hot. He would tell Sid Rosen when he got back. As he approached the 59th Street Bridge, the clock in Rook's stomach went off. All of them who worked the street were like the crocodile in Peter Pan. It was time to Code 7.

Rowland's Luncheonette still had a soda fountain where you could get a real egg cream. Lucas had never tried to get a meal on "Masterbadge." Maybe he got dessert or some take-out on the arm, but otherwise, he paid his way.

Toots Rowland was sitting by the door in his luncheonette chair with the red cushion, not knowing where he was, but not disliking the state of his life. Yetta worked the register, looking a little too happy.

"Toots," she said. "Lucas Rook's here to see you."

Rowland's response was to fart.

Lucas sat at the counter. "Half the world would agree with

that," he said.

Yetta's nephew poured a cup of coffee and handed over a menu.

Rook had a meatloaf platter. The mashed were from a mix, but the peas weren't mushy so it was alright. He paid full boat. Toots Rowland farted him a goodbye.

Traffic was backed up once Lucas hit Manhattan, and even with his shortcuts and backways, it took him twice as long as it should have. Sid Rosen was in the back of his garage hoisting a tranny from a Chevy Cavalier.

"How ya doing, Lucas boy?" He pulled on the winch without looking up.

"She's running hot, Sid."

"Anything over 100,000 miles, it's going to happen no matter what. Pretty soon they'll be making cars the way they do those disposable cameras. I'll take a look. Meanwhile, I'll be out at the auction next week. My man says he got two Grand Marquis set aside. It's about time we retire your Crown Vic."

"You see something good at the auction, grab it."

"I won't get no rice-burners, Lucas boy," Sid said. "They can't be trusted." He wiped his hands off and took a paperback from his desk. "I know you didn't finish *Nostromo* yet. Maybe you've had enough of Mr. Conrad." He handed over a Kurt Vonnegut, *Cat's Cradle*. "'Be careful who you pretend to be.' Clever guy."

"Burned his house down with Pall Malls."

"I did not know that, Lucas. I surely didn't." He went back to working on the transmission. "I see something good at the auction…"

"Right, Sid. You need me or whatever, I'll have my cell. You look after that dog's ears."

"Won't give my German Shepard police dog no beef products, that's for sure."

Rook grabbed a cab to his office. His bad leg was bothering him. All them horse pills, glucosomine, whatever, were a crock.

For a change, it was the freight elevator that was down. Two deliverymen were trying to get a box of doll parts into one of the passenger elevators. They were arguing with the super. The bigger of the two was wearing a red bandana, pirate-style. "I only get paid if this goes up, it goes up," he said.

"Like I told you," Manny said. "Freight goes in the freight elevator."

"It's going up," the big man said.

Manny took a pipe wrench from behind the radiator.

"We could wait, Mel," the other deliveryman said. "Let's grab a smoke."

"We could wait, but we ain't. It's going up or somebody's going down." He pushed his sleeves back and made his tattoos dance.

Rook came in, walking slow. "Everything okay, Manny?"

"Take a hike, crip," Mel told him.

The super held his pipe like he meant to use it. "I got this, Lucas."

The big man took a half step forward. Lucas kicked Mel hard in the shin and then brought the heel of his right hand up under his chin. The pirate went down. Rook bent over and pulled his ankle gun, hiding it from everybody but Mel.

"You act up again," Lucas said, "you cause my friend here any more trouble, I'm going to shoot you." He pressed the barrel to Mel's teeth. "Otherwise, we're fine. Now have a nice day."

Rook waited until the deliverymen set their box aside and left. Then he rode the elevator up to his office. The usual odd noises came from the office next door. The photographer who never came out was saying, "Turning, turning," over and over.

He looked through his mail. All crap except a thank-you note from Mrs. Politte for the job he did for her upstate with her personal check for $500. Her note said, "I hope you will buy yourself a nice suit as a special thank-you from me." For beating Calvin Treaster to death with a pair of baseball spikes. Fair is fair.

Lucas checked his messages. Another reminder from Dr. Brown that he was overdue for his cleaning, a recording from the NRA, and a call from Dwight Graves to tell him that Hy Gromek had died. "He never made it to retirement," the message said. "Funeral is tomorrow."

Gromek dressed like he was in a Hollywood movie. Hy was a good cop, even though he got cute on the case where Sid Rosen took the beating. A good cop'll work anybody except his partner. Rook poured himself a cold beer. "At least he didn't die in the street," he said out loud.

Lucas Rook went back to the St. Claire Hotel. Tony was packing up at the inside desk. Leo came in to replace him. He had a big plastic bag with him and made a point of showing it off.

"What's in the bag?" Tony asked.

"Rabbits, Anthony. Big, fat, juicy rabbits."

"You're shittin' me, Leo. You surely are."

"No I ain't," Leo said. "Bought them down in Chinatown, hanging by their furry legs."

Leo reached into the bag. "Damn," he said, shaking it hard, "Bambi here's trying to escape."

Tony jumped up, but when he saw Lucas smiling and Leo laughing so hard, he realized he had been had.

"Gotya, gotya," Leo said, spitting the way he did when he spoke. "Gotya good. I surely did."

Tony got ready to leave, making a great show of taking his *New York Post* with him. "What goes around comes around," he said. "Ain't that true, Mr. Rook?"

The elevator doors opened. Grace Savoy was there with her guide dog. "Going out, Lucas," she said. "Unless you want to do the honors."

"Not picking up any shit in a napkin, Grace."

"No, dear. I just went. And besides, I meant take me out."

Rook looked at his watch. "Weren't you supposed to be

shooting tonight?"

"Shoot's cancelled. The art director got the union up his ass, which I thought he'd rather enjoy, but it isn't working out that way. In any case, you and I are going out the town. It's your particular combination of aftershave and man smell."

Lucas Rook rode upstairs to the tenth floor. The retired orthodontist who collected butterflies was just coming out of his apartment. He had a *vanessa cardini* on his shoulder. "Lovely evening," the dentist said, "lovely."

"Dr. Haimowitz," Lucas acknowledged.

Rook opened his apartment door like it was someone else's place. His living space was dark. The recessed ceiling lights were out, and the only light came from one standing lamp and its reflections in the mirrors.

The bathroom door was closed, as he had left it. Lucas made his routine check of his apartment before he settled down. He put his .45 on the mantelpiece, poured himself a cold Yuengling and checked the messages on his answering machine. Two calls from Grace an hour ago and one from Sid Rosen saying that he had his eyes on a black-on-black 2000 Grand Marquis. Real clean.

Rook took his beer and went out onto the patio. The hawk that came by was late as the day went up and the night came down.

Detective Gromek's funeral was going to be at Riverdale Chapel at ten. Then the graveside ceremony with the precinct and the boys from Downtown with their white gloves on. Gromek's partner would be in ceremonial blues. All together they wouldn't dress half as good as Hy did.

Lucas checked his closet. His dark suit was clean. He owed Hy that. Pay his respects and sign the book.

There was a knock at Rook's door. Grace was dressed in green silk and not much of it. Her hot pants were nothing more than panties.

"I'm ready." She had glitter on her cheek.

"I should be so lucky."

"You'd be disappointed," she said. "I'd only suck you dry, come a thousand times, and beg you to fuck me in the ass. But now it's time to work."

"I thought the union, whatever."

"That shoot is out, but my agency wants me at the next location. I think it's for pig's knuckles or something. It's at the Cloisters, and even a blind girl can see that's not safe."

Rook got his slapjack, his slicker and his gun.

"Plus, Lucas, that man in the raincoat…"

"Grace, that was only once and he's not coming back."

"Are you sure?" She walked close to him, smelling like musk and mint.

"You keep coming on like this, it's going to be me in the trenchcoat."

Her car was waiting downstairs. Grace reached out and touched her driver's afro. "Hi, Kenny."

"Hi, Miss Grace," the driver said. "I don't know the gentleman."

Lucas handed up his card.

"The chess piece, Mr. Rook. Nice touch."

"Out Broadway to 187th", Gracey told him.

"The long way?" Kenny asked.

"I like the way the night sounds," she said.

They rode through the New York night. Fading comedies, busy bodegas. Nations of blue-black illegals selling knock-off Burberry and Rollies. West on 187th and another on Fort Washington Avenue to Fort Tryon Park in the heart of the 34th.

Lucas knew the precinct well. When he and Kirk first got split up, he went up to Washington Heights while his brother got sent across town. It was the Wild West back then. Mike Buczek getting killed in the line of duty and all that. Now Jimmy Kehoe ran a tight ship. The statistics said crime was down three quarters.

The Cloisters were five medieval French quadrangles enclosed by vaulted passageways. There were kleig lights set up at two of them. Lawrence, the art director with the round glasses and the cravat, was smoking one cigarette after another in the doorway from Moutiers-Saint Jean. On either side of the portal were stone images of King Clovis I.

"Christ Almighty," Lawrence said. "Did anybody scout this location? There's a fucking Virgin on the tympanum. Tympanum, that's the semi-circular area over the doorway, for those of you who give a fuck. You want me to be showing a hint of nip under the Virgin Mary?"

The director walked over to the Pontaut Chapter House. The stone capitals had basketweaves and rosettes. The hint of color on the ribs of the stone vaults was the color of Grace's dress. He lit another cigarette.

"This is what I'm talking about," he said. "This joint is off the hook!"

"I love it when you talk 'street,' Larry."

"It's 'Lawrence,' Ms. Savoy." He took a deep drag on his Gauloise. "Now let's take a peek."

Grace walked to his voice.

"You move like ballet."

"Thank you, Lawrence," she said. "How would you like me to be?"

"Just the way you are, dear. Like an orchid in the rain."

The driver with the red afro couldn't stand it anymore. "Do you believe all this shit?" he said to Rook.

"Way too artsy-fartsy for me," Lucas told him. "But then again, nobody's paying me to be a critic." From the corner of his eye he saw a man in a raincoat.

Rook started over, but the man moved on.

"Let's not upset Ms. Savoy, Kenny. Don't you think?" Lucas said.

"I think you're right. Worry and gratuities are strangers," the driver said.

Lucas walked toward the shoot, but Lawrence waved him away. "You're ruining the light," he said. "Do you mind?"

Rook went into the shadows.

"Lovely," the director said. "A driver, a bodyguard, your whole entourage is here and we're not even shooting."

"I cannot stand this undercurrent, Larry," Grace said. "I really can't. And I'm getting tired."

"Twenty more minutes, my diaphanous angel. I promise."

The twenty minutes spread into an hour and a half. "It is time to leave," Grace Savoy said very loud.

Kenny brought the car around. She insisted they stop for take-out Mexican on the way home and tipped her driver fifty dollars.

"We're all alone, Lucas," she said, half flirtatious, half bored to death. "Would you like to come upstairs?"

"That's where I live, Grace. We're neighbors, you know."

They rode up to the 10th floor. She asked him in.

"I've got an early day tomorrow," Rook said. "I got to get my beauty sleep."

He went back to the St. Claire. Lucas checked his apartment, then sat in front of the television with a cold beer. He drank another, then dozed.

Lucas awoke an hour later. Then took his .45 and went in to bed.

That night he dreamt that he was in a long tunnel. His twin brother, Kirk, was at the other end, saying something in a hollow voice.

Lucas made salami and eggs in the morning, frying the slices of deli meat until they puckered into red discs. After breakfast he put on his dark suit and the black tie. It wasn't his first cop funeral and wouldn't be his last, but it was all different since he had seen the white gloves lowering his brother into the ground.

Lucas checked his watch that he wore like he was left-handed. He'd get up to the funeral parlor, do the receiving line and be out of there. There would be police politics going on, but he'd be in and out fast. He grabbed a taxi to the Upper West Side.

"Riverdale Chapel?" the cabbie said. "My cousin married a Jewish girl they laid out there. She got breast cancer." He jogged in and out of the adjacent lane. "Couldn't believe they had a closed box. But they tell me that's what they do." He fed himself a piece of gum.

"Thought you were a member of 'the tribe' yourself," Rook told the cabbie as they pulled up to the funeral home. The driver was checking his profile in his mirror as Rook walked away.

The viewing wasn't for another fifteen or twenty minutes, but there was a line outside already. Rook didn't see a familiar face or cops' shoes. Detective Marc Nucifora came up. He was a huge man, but athletic. "You working this?" he asked.

"Hy Gromek's funeral," Lucas said.

"Don't think so, Rook. They got two of them this morning,

but I think they're both females. Ladies, I mean. Me, I'm working this creep, he's boosting hearses."

"Maybe he needs a hearse for himself."

"You got that. Shitbird deserves whatever he gets." Nucifora adjusted his tie. "I'll go inside and see who they're laying out. I'm supposed to be an employee of this joint."

The mourners' line moved forward. Lucas listened to the small talk. Nucifora was back in a minute wearing a yarmulke. "I'm supposed to be putting the flags and stickers on the window. The two they got laid out, they're both not men. One lady's named 'Leibowitch', or something like that. Not 'Fat Fuck Leibowitch'. We should be so lucky. The other's Tennenbaum. I asked about Hy Gromek. They said they got another funeral parlor up in Forest Hills."

Rook slid out of line. No way he was going to make Hy's send-off. He'd mail a card, give something to the Benevolent Association. He went back downtown and went over to Joe Oren's for a cup of good coffee and a slice of coconut cream pie.

The big, freckled man was coming out of the kitchen with a platter for himself. "You got your funeral clothes on. Anybody I know?"

"Not me and not you, Joe."

"I hear that. You want to join me?" Oren pointed to the plate of meat loaf. "Eat my own cooking so it got to be good, even them frozen peas."

"Cup of joe, Joe. Slice of coconut custard if you got it."

Jeanie Oren came out of the back. She had her hair all curled like her father's. "You like it, Lucas Rook? I'm going to be quite stylish since we're going to be getting married and all."

Her father put his fork down. "I don't know what scares me more. The 'getting married' or the 'and all.'"

"I made the coffee fresh and the pie," Jeanie said. She went back into the kitchen to bring it out.

"I know she didn't," Lucas said.

"She looks like 'Annie,' don't she?" Joe Oren said.

Jeanie sat down at the counter with Lucas and hummed while he ate.

"I know 'The Wedding March', too, Lucas Rook," she said.

"Gotta go," he said.

A gypsy cab slowed as Rook was walking west from Penn Station. The driver opened the windows on his Town Car. "You want a ride, you surly prick?"

Lucas recognized Tom Bailey from Safe and Loft even with his full white beard.

"Thought I was Santa Claus, right, Rook?" Bailey said. "Working without a medallion here. Can I run you someplace?"

"Over to the St. Claire, Tom. How you been?"

"Some up, some down. Good thing we smackin' them towel-heads good so someday gas goes down. I got a nephew over in Iraq. Name is Kirk, like your brother."

"How's the wife, Tom?"

"She's good. Getting some surgery though. Elective. I don't get it. She said them lines at the corner of her eyes making her look old. I says you look fine to me, which gets me nowheres. Going to cost me three grand. Three grand so she looks like a doll or something. For six she gets new knockers, which I'm working on." He ran a yellow light. "How you doing, Rook?"

"I'm doing." They rolled up to the St. Claire. "What I owe you, Tommy?"

"On the house," Bailey said. He handed over one of his cards. "You ever need me for whatever, Rook. You know I can still drive. I can still work a case too. Just call me up."

Lucas put the card in his shirt pocket. "I just might do that, Tom. Take it easy."

"Any way I can get it," Bailey said. He pulled across the street to a short lady in a long, dark coat.

Leo was reading the *Post* when Rook came in, so Tony and he must have gotten over their last dispute.

"Man was by, looking for you," the deskman said without looking up. "Didn't leave his name." Leo spit when he said his s's and t's. "He said he'd call you on the phone."

"You're a regular concierge. I appreciate it," Lucas said.

The lady who looked like Martha Raye got on just as the elevator doors were closing. She smelled like mothballs and stale cigarettes. "Getting off at three," she said as if she had never seen him before. "Women's undergarments," she said as the door opened. "Next stop, Hardware."

Lucas gave his apartment a walk-through before he put his .45 on the mantelpiece. His answering machine was flashing, and he could see another dead bird on the patio that probably flew into the glass doors running from that hawk.

There were three calls. One from Carlin saying that the first matter they had discussed had been resolved, but thanks anyway. And also that he had personally taken care of that other thing. There was a message from Grace doing heavy breathing and saying that she was going out, and an automated call from a dating service.

He poured himself a cold Stella and checked the TV listings. Tomorrow he'd stop by Jimbo Turner's stand and tell him that his tax thing was over. *Tears of the Sun* was on at nine. "Cowboy the fuck up" should be on the back of the dollar bill.

Lucas started the tub and got some Epsom salts and his .38. The phone rang. It was Warren G. Phelps, Esquire extraordinaire, able to put a rabbit in a hat and pick your pocket at the same time.

"Didn't know you had to put in such long hours, counselor."

"I'm in Hawaii, Lucas."

"Things are tough all over. Give me a second." Lucas put him on hold and went to shut the faucets off.

"I'm on trial," Phelps said when Rook got back on the phone.

"I hope they find you not guilty, counselor. You got something for me?"

"Everything's still quiet with the U.S. Attorney's Office." A little reminder of who's boss. "A new client I referred you went by your office and then the St. Claire."

"I missed him. What's the deal?"

"Since their person missed you, they've arranged a business lunch at the 'W.' You should be hearing from them tomorrow."

"I'll remember where they came from, Warren."

That was the fealty Attorney Warren G. Phelps was looking for. "And remember to drink like a fish, eat like a pig and double-bill them for everything, Lucas."

"You taught me well, counselor," Rook said. Things were picking up. He decided to go out.

Lucas took a quick shower and put on a pair of black slacks and a loose sweater. A lot easier to conceal his .45 than wearing a shirt outside his pants, which was the easiest giveaway a guy's a cop.

Rook went around the corner and up the block to the new Italian place that had opened. The bartender that used to be at Monte's was supposed to be over there.

Maggio's was noveau, which meant small portions and shit he never heard of. The maitre'd tried to sit him outside.

"I want bus fumes with my macaroni, I'll let you know," Lucas told him.

Pachetta worked behind the bar. All these years he still had the look he'd be grabbing at your little sister if you turned your head.

"What do you say, what do you know?" Pachetta said.

Rook sat down. "Menu looks like I should've eaten before I came over."

"Let me get you some gnocchis. She makes them herself. Broccoli rabe's good."

"I think I rousted him once. You got Stella on tap?"

Pachetta drew him a beer and put his order in. "What d'ya hear, what d'ya know," he said again when he got back.

"Whatever," Rook told him.

The food came fast. Good, but the serving was only for somebody with a staple or two in his stomach. Rook ate and went back to the St. Claire.

Tony was working the desk. He did not look happy. "I was just getting ready to take the wife food shopping and the boss calls. Leo, he got to go home. His old lady is sick."

The Martha Raye lady was getting off the elevator as he got on. "Main floor," she said. "Men's clothes, shoes and small appliances. Everybody out."

Lucas went upstairs. There were two messages on his machine. Another one from the dating service and one from Grace, whistling like a bird. "My funeral ode," she said.

Rook poured a beer and sat down to end his day with Bruce Willis. "Cowboy the fuck up."

Lucas showered and dressed while his percolator did its work. Sometimes the newspaper was outside his door, sometimes it wasn't, depending on whether Tony or the spitter was at the desk and if the retired dentist was on vacation or not. Nothing there, so he drank his first cup in front of ESPN II. Muy Thai, nothing like kick-boxing from Thailand to start the day. The next thing he knows, there's a 30-0 fighter in full drag and a promo for a movie. "Beautiful Boxer: Parinya fights like a man so he can live like a woman." There goes breakfast.

He put on another cup of the "free" coffee he had gotten in the mail. Free and they sent him a coffee maker that he didn't order and monthly bills for all of it. The French coffee pot went back to them in pieces, and the next bill would get the same attention as the five before it.

Rook went out and over to Sid Rosen's garage. There was a light in the shop and Rosen already had a car up on the lift.

"Early to bed…" Rook said.

Rosen finished the quote, "…early to rise, makes a *good* man healthy, wealthy or whatever. Wise enough to get you this Grand Marquis before the auction. It's clean as a teenager's tubes after his first blow job."

"That clean?"

"As I can remember a million years ago, Lucas, boy. I change the oil and tweak the suspension, it's all yours."

Lucas sat down at the wooden desk and stretched his leg. "What's this going to run me, Sid?"

"I made a killing on your Crown Vic. This Merc's two years newer. Garage rates going up in November."

"Bottom line."

"Eighty-five more a month for everything. Less, if you do something with the Avanti, taking it out to my house. Garage it there or whatever."

"Eighty-five it is."

Rosen let the oil out. "Driver only took it back and forth to his office. You going over to Joe's, get me a hot tea and bagel with a shmir. Something soft for my dog. You know, scrambled eggs, hamburger, whatever. He lost another tooth. I found it under my desk."

"Thanks for the information, Sid. I'll see you in a while."

Lucas went around the corner to Joe Oren's. The counter was full. More upscale spillover from the Soho spread-out, which meant pretty soon there was going to be a new menu.

The only open booth was for four, so Lucas waited in the doorway. The man at the end of the counter got up. He had taps on his shoes. Rook took his spot.

"Cup of joe, Joe," said Sam, who was working the counter.

Jeanie Oren came out of the back in a waitress uniform. She had a blonde streak in her hair. "I heard Sam say cup of joe, Joe, I knew it was you, Lucas Rook."

"Miss," said the man on the next stool. "I said 'soft' and these eggs are not soft."

Jeanie took his plate. "I'll speak to the chef," she said.

"You mean hash slinger, don't you?"

"I don't think that's appropriate," Jeanie said.

"That's the problem, miss. You don't think."

Lucas turned towards him. "Watch your mouth or pay for your coffee and leave."

"Who do you think you're talking to, fella?" said the man.

Rook put a heavy hand on him. "Your new dentist. Now beat it."

The man put a five on the counter and left.

"You are the shiznit, Uncle Lucas."

"Whatever that is, Jeanie. And if it's 'Uncle' again, I guess the marriage is off."

She shook her head. "I don't like boys anymore."

He put his cup down. "Jeanie, you're not…"

Jeanie Oren started to laugh. "You mean…I'm not a lug or anything."

"Lug?"

"Lesbian until graduation. I'm not."

Joe Oren came in the front door. "Who's not graduating?"

"I'm graduating and I'm not a lesbian."

Joe's face got red. "Who said you were, Jeanie?"

She laughed so hard she had to sit down on the empty stool. "Nobody, Daddy. Everything's fine."

Lucas had two fried eggs with the yolks broken and rye toast. He ordered the bagel and cream cheese for Sid, and Joe gave him some ground turkey that was even beyond the chili pot.

Jeanie Oren stood on her tiptoes and gave Lucas his kiss on the cheek as he left. "I'm still available," she said with her little laugh. She smelled like soap.

Rook dropped the food off at the garage and called over to Betsy Ross. He hadn't been to the Garment District since he did that job for Macar, grabbing up the insider who was pilfering cashmere coats because he could not resist the ponies. Big surprise.

"You open, George?"

"Seven to six. That you, Mr. Rook? You come over, I'll fix you up."

George Sarkissian had a bad kid. First time he jams himself, Lucas gets him some rhythm. Second time a stern lecture. Third time, the kid beats on his own father, for which Rook gives him a tuning-up.

No way you could cab into the Garment District without sitting in traffic for a half hour watching the meter roll. Rook got off at 32nd and 10th and walked a block up and then east to 8th Avenue.

Despite the recent attempts to convert the valuable Manhattan real estate to other uses, the Garment District was still the hub of the clothing trade. Trucks double-parked, racks of goods cornering like race cars. Hasids, Asians, Spanish, all hustling to make a buck.

Betsy Ross was a third floor walk-up over Stanley Pleating and Stitching. George was working the steam press, angling the pants so he could get a perfect crease with his good eye. He got up as Rook came in. "Welcome, welcome," he said. "Anything you want."

"Looking for a suit. Got a fancy lunch today."

"Got a couple of 46's end of the run. Very nice goods. Fit you perfect."

"Leave enough room."

Sarkissian shook his head. "I know, I know, so they don't see."

Lucas tried on the suits. They fit perfectly across the chest, and nobody could tell he was carrying. "The pattern of this gray one, George."

"Right, too busy. I got a nice 44, they run big."

Rook tried it on. "Good," he said.

"You wearing this today, I'll do the cuffs while you wait. No extra charge."

The hemming took Sarkissian only a few minutes. He handed the navy suit over. "I'll send you the bill," he said.

Rook could see the outline under the tailor's vest.

"Since when are you carrying, George?"

Sarkissian looked away. "A man should wear a gun for if his

own son shows up." He shook his head. "What a life."

Lucas went slowly down the steps. His leg throbbed and the ribs he'd broken in Oneonta ached. He got a cab a block over and took a hot bath and four Advils before his lunch.

The restaurant at the W wasn't called Sheila's since she had left to open an art gallery. The help was tripping over itself trying to be "haute" something or other. A pretty, but serious woman came up to Lucas Rook. She was dressed in a black pantsuit and had a half dozen silver bracelets on so there was a clinking sound when she extended her hand.

"Mary O'Reilly. Warren described you perfectly," she said as she shook Rook's hand firmly. "He said you looked like a cross between Robert Urich and Richard Boone."

"Ms. O'Reilly," Lucas said.

The host took them to their table.

"You can call me 'MJ' since we'll be working together. Do you prefer Lucas?"

"Rook is fine," he said.

The waiter came, a nervous Antonio Banderas type. Rook ordered a Stella and MJ a Vigionier. She waited until Antonio left before she spoke.

"My company has worked out the details with Warren. If you haven't gotten the retainer agreement and check, it will be hand-delivered today. We pay handsomely. One hundred ten dollars per hour, plus expenses. We fight hard. We win."

Rook sipped his beer. "Who's we?"

"SDA. We're Fortune 500. Perhaps you're familiar with our range of subsidiaries."

He looked at her.

"There's been some publicity recently..." She sipped her white wine. "Our cemetery and funeral division and the SEC. Everybody's looking for an Enron everywhere. So what we don't need is bad press." She took another sip. "We own a funeral home here in Manhattan, one in Queens and three more on the Island. Somebody is causing quite a stir, desecrating our commitment to the dearly departed. The 'Hearse Ghoul' they're calling him."

"And what do you want me to do, Miss O'Reilly?"

"Find him," she said. "And put a stake in his heart."

7

No cop believed in coincidence. But this wasn't that, his going to the wrong funeral parlor and now he's working a case there. It was a "financial upturn" as Sid Rosen would call it.

The follow-up meeting with SDA at their corporate headquarters was tomorrow at eleven. By then, he'd have done enough spade work to show he meant business and enough billing so that he wouldn't come up empty-handed. Rook went back to the St. Claire and changed out of his suit. Old friends or not, he was less likely to get any good information looking like a suit.

The chapel he had seen Nucifora at was in the 20th precinct and Rook still knew the duty sergeant and some of the boys at the squad. The captain was a prick, but if that was still a problem or whatever he could still reach out to Larry Smith at Patrol Command.

Last time he was up to West 82nd Street, Jim Mullen was working the desk. One of the old timers who knew what to pass by and what to clamp down on. He also was the unofficial precinct historian and kept a big book on everything important that happened in the precinct's 1.1 miles, from John Lennon getting whacked at the Dakota Hotel to whatever weird shit that went down at the Thanksgiving parade or spilled over from the Park.

The desk sergeant was not Jim Mullen, unless Mullen had

had a sex change and spoke Spanish.

"Can I help you?" asked Sergeant Navarez. She had fancy make-up, but a hard face.

"Friend of Jim's."

"Excuse me," she said.

"Detective Stevenson, Bud. tell him it's Rook. He's expecting me."

"I don't…" Her phone rang. She shook her head and handed Lucas the receiver. "It's for you," she said.

"You coming up or what, Rook?" Bud asked.

"Thought you'd be out for donuts or whatever, Bud," Rook said. "Here tell your desk sergeant to let me pass."

Lucas handed the receiver back to the desk sergeant and went up to the squad.

Stevenson was working one of those hand spring exercisers with one hand and doing the crossword puzzle with the other. "Four letter word for nasty sonofabitch making it big in the private sector, R-O-O-K," he said.

"Detective Stevenson, how's the 20th been treating you? Still tapping every sweet thing over at Julliard?"

Bud Stevenson put down the paper and switched hands with the exerciser. "I've run my bow across more violins than I care to mention. You still seeing that college prof, Rook? Caitlin, wasn't it?"

"Catherine. She had the good sense to throw me out." Lucas went over to the coffee machine and poured himself a cup. "Glad that some things haven't changed, the coffee still tastes like crap. Jim's off, Bud?"

"Way off, Rook. The big C came up and got him fast."

Rook sat down. "I was over at Hy Gromek's send-off. Not going to be any of the old timers around."

"We're the old timers now, Lucas. You notice our new sergeant downstairs? She got no husband and three kids, which she occasionally brings one or two to work, and had two drug collars and one conviction and she's got stripes on her arm. But what brings you to the happy 2-0?"

"Same job Nucie's on over at Riverdale. Somebody boosting the hearses."

"Today's your lucky day, Lucas Rook. You buy me something cold and wet other than a dog's nose and I'll tell you all about it. '*Philtrum*–the midline groove in the upper lip that runs from the top of the lip to the nose.' Good puzzle word."

They went down the back stairs. A uniform was coming up with a birdcage in his hand. "Don't even ask," he said.

McLaughlin's was two blocks away, but Stevenson took the unmarked anyway. "Ms. Puerto Rico didn't ever ask that you check your weapon, did she, Rook? Last month, plainclothes from Manhattan South walks right up into the squad with a bazooka, a fucking bazooka, and she doesn't say a word. And that's no *peccadillo*," he said.

The taproom was in the middle of the block with no parking whatsoever. There were cars double parked on both sides of the street and up on the sidewalk. The locals knew not to complain, and the building supers knew to call over to McLaughlin if somebody had to get out for a real good reason.

The place was crowded.

"Pitcher," Stevenson told the barkeep.

"Hey, Dobie," Rook said.

"That's Obie, his brother over at Miata's is Dobie. They're dead ringers."

"You're shittin' me."

"Nope, Lucas Rook. I shit you not."

They took a table in the back. The beer came fast.

Stevenson picked up the menu. "Crabcake sandwich is good."

"Two," Lucas said.

Bud called over to the waiter, an ex-counterfeiter with bad skin.

"Computers put him out of business," Rook said. "I remember him. Busted him myself. The shitbird was even floating paper from the joint."

"Now anybody's got half of a computer's doing it. Read in the paper some 8th grader out west passed twenty thousand dollars in bad checks after seeing that movie with Leonardo DiCrapio." Stevenson finished his beer. "I bought him in that movie alright, but no way in *Gangs of New York*." He poured them each another. "The funeral homes. The 'hearse ghoul' we're calling the weirdo behind he's boosting hearses and doing himself, whatever."

Stevenson took two big bites of the crab sandwich. "You working for the insurance company, Rook? That's primo dollars."

"Working for the funeral parlor, Bud."

Stevenson dipped one of his fries into his tartar sauce. "Careful, careful. They tell you their whole story?"

"They never do."

"You got that right. State's Attorney General jammed them up. Anti-trust or whatever. Something that they got agreement with the Jews that the temples make it look like they're the official Hebrew funeral parlors or whatever. And they were supposed to be using the old bait and switch. State Attorney makes them roll back the price on their boxes and change the names of their locations.

Bud Stevenson took another bite of his sandwich. "Tells you something about dying, don't it, Rook?"

Lucas dipped one of his fries into the sauce. "Tells me my rates just went up," he said.

SDA was located on E. 42nd between Second and Third Avenue. Rook took a cab uptown and then through Times Square, Rudy's monument. Used to be you want to grab a CI or find one of the local pervs, you knew right where to find them. The mayor cleans up 42nd Street and the slime just spreads out.

The outside of the building had a black granite veneer. The atmosphere inside was part corporate, part mortuary.

"May I be of service to you?" asked the dark-haired woman behind the ebony desk. Rook guessed that her accent was Canadian and her glasses phony. Her nameplate said, "Ms. Marble."

"I have an appointment with Ms. Reilly."

"And who might you be?" she asked.

"My name's Rook. Your name really Marble, you're working here?"

She looked at her computer screen. "You will be seeing Mr. Sirlin. He will be with you shortly."

Lucas took that to mean he should take a seat. There were a number of slick brochures, all making death something other than the bag of blood it was. Rook was just getting irritated by the wait when Hugh Sirlin came out. He was a fit-looking man in an expensive suit, Bali shoes. A two-hundred-dollar black tie.

"Sorry to keep you waiting," he said. His handshake was a bit too strong. "One of those days."

They went back to Sirlin's office. The wall behind his desk hinted at the Vietnam Memorial. Rook didn't like that at all.

"You come highly recommended by Attorney Phelps."

"I appreciate that, Mr. Sirlin."

"Call me Hugh," Sirlin said. He passed over a prospectus. "We were founded in 1960 by Cecil Matman. Since then we've grown to three thousand locations in North America, Germany and Argentina while maintaining the highest quality of care and professionalism, assisting families in transition."

"That's a lot of funerals, Hugh."

He handed Rook another booklet titled "Respectful and Seamless Transition."

"It's much more than that, Mr. Rook. Pre-need arrangements, grief services, Internet accommodation, asset management."

Sirlin poured himself a bottled water. "Two billion in annual revenue. While death rates have been dropping, our annual sales are quite successful."

"And the trouble with the Attorney General's Office?"

"You do your homework." He poured a glass of sparkling water for Rook. "Actually, there was very little fallout from that. A 'seamless transition' you could say. Which makes the present circumstances all the more intolerable. We require your swift and discreet services. Not only is some cretin making off with our vehicles, he is depositing his sperm on the deceased. We don't need that to become known."

"That's enough to keep you in the headlines and the tabloids forever," Rook said.

The SDA executive sipped his Pellegrino.

"Your history with the State Attorney, Mr. Sirlin, that complicates things. My fee needs to be adjusted."

"I'll follow up with Warren."

"His fee for reviewing the paperwork is from your end," Rook told him. "Or we can do this on a handshake."

Sirlin reached into his ebony desk for his checkbook. "This should make up the difference. There will be a substantial bonus if this matter is resolved within the week."

"Any particular reason for that deadline?"

"We've a Title 78 shareholders meeting."

"I'll get this up and running," Rook said.

Sirlin handed over the check. "Put a stake in his heart," he said.

8

"Put a stake in his heart," Sirlin had said, same as his girl. Maybe it was their team cheer. Maybe she reported back everything she said. Or SDA ran tape. "Put a stake in his heart." Put a steak in my fridge. No way he wouldn't grab up the freak getting off on the corpses. The sicko was going to do more, not less. They always do.

Do it clean and don't permanently piss off anybody that mattered. And if the hearse ghoul booked, the boys at the 20th could take the credit. He'd take Sirlin's bonus.

The job had its sex to it, which they all did. Pursesnatching, embezzlement, they all had to do with getting off one way or the other. This job, the perv was *doing* it, so there'd be the DNA. The sciences boys would be a help. So would his CI's into the sex scene. Swing by the Stroll. Jumpy was a shoe sniffer. Pay Dr. Hepburn a call.

Eng's II was a decent Chinese restaurant near the Riverdale Chapel, and it would be a fine thing to have some spare ribs or whatever and a cold Tsing Dao while the client's meter was running.

Lucas went into the restaurant. The place was empty. Not surprising since it was well past lunch and before dinner.

"You got a problem with that?" said a buxom blonde in an Oriental outfit. She leaned in towards the Mandarin queen at the cash register, who flitted between her zen indifference and her glittering diamond bands. "You got a problem with that, Mrs. Yep, you can kiss my fine Irish ass."

"A line forming?" Rook said.

"Everything is just fine, sir," said Mrs. Yep. "We would be happy to serve you. Valerie, show the gentleman to a table."

Valerie saw who it was. "Buy a girl a drink, Detective Rook?"

"I think I can do that, pretty girl."

She leaned in close. "Buy me two and you can bend this fine Irish ass over the kitchen sink."

"I think I can do that too. Since when you been working here?"

"Since The Famous closed down. Working here sucks."

The Chinese queen turned her diamond bands and looked away.

"Her husband's got a baby's dick," Valerie said as she brought over the menu.

Rook had pork lo mein and egg foo yung. The cold Tsing Dao was perfect.

"My shift is over, big boy," Valerie Moon said. "Buy a girl a drink."

They went around the corner and grabbed a booth.

"Still the charmer, Miss Moon."

"You ain't changed a bit, Lucas Rook. The bluest eyes and the darkest look."

Their drinks came. She had a Chivas and water. Lucas sipped a Jamison. "You eat?" he asked her.

She looked at him across her glass. "Let's go home," she said.

Rook drove her car across to Fort Lee. Last time he was over there was for Gary Seidman's retirement, twenty-five years and glad to go.

Valerie lit a cigarette and looked out the window. "Had to sell the house. It was too much. Him in the ground and the boys gone."

"They alright?"

"They're alright." She pointed him to turn. "So am I. How's by you?"

"Doing good. Mining the streets instead of sweeping them."

"Come on over here, Lucas," said Valerie Moon.

They made love when they got to her apartment. Then she made fresh coffee.

"You'll call me?" she asked.

"That I will, Miss Moon. That I will."

Going into the funeral parlor made him think about when Kirk died. Ann said she wanted it all in addition to the police escort and service. You'd think that would be enough, the motor-cycles, dress blues, flag on the coffin. But she insisted on the wake and the whole nine yards. Lucas saw that the casket was closed. He wanted the world to remember who Kirk was. They could look at the picture on the coffin, not his broken brother inside.

"Welcome to Riverdale Chapel. I'm Ellis Rayvitch," said the tanned man in the black suit. He offered a well-practiced hand-shake and understanding eyes. "I'm…"

"Hugh Sirlin sent me," Rook told him. "About your problem."

"Of course he did, Mr. Rook. I was expecting you. You thought…"

"Right, right."

"It must be habit. My wife says I order a pizza, it sounds like 'Sorry for your loss.' Let's go back to my office."

Rayvitch took them down the walnut hall and into a large and somber room. He took off his yarmulke as if he was shedding a hundred pounds. "You're here about the desecrant."

"If that's what we're calling him."

"It's an industry term."

Lucas stretched his leg.

Rayvitch looked at his watch and took a box of cigars from his desk and offered one. "I smoke only after I've seen all my appointments. You don't talk to somebody about a twenty-thousand-dollar funeral and smell like a cigar."

Rook took the five-dollar smoke for when he went over to the 20th Precinct. "Twenty thousand?"

"Some more, some less. You can get a nice service for somewhat less than ten." He turned the air cleaner on behind him and lit up. "It's always a shock and a sin when someone desecrates the deceased."

"What's the motivation, Ellis, sex, brutality, what?"

"Both. Sometimes it's just vandalism. Sometimes it's overwhelming grief." He took an appreciative puff. "How dare you die on me?"

The funeral director put the cigar in the ashtray. "My dentist says I shouldn't smoke, but I love the aroma of a fine cigar. We had one incident here before. We caught one of the technicians. Turns out that was his thing. He could only function if they were perfectly still."

"And cold?"

Rayvitch took another puff. "Anyway, that was five or six years ago."

He got up and opened the cabinet behind him. "My cardiologist says I should drink."

Lucas accepted a glass of port.

"We have had the usual post-interment issues as well, Mr. Rook."

"Graverobbers, Mr. Rayvitch?"

"More often than not, it's tipping over tombstones. But nothing since we installed our new security. Twenty-four hour video, lights." He took a sniff of the smoke rising from his cigar. "Tasteful, though." He finished his port more like it was a draft beer than something that cost twenty-five dollars a glass. "Now let me show you around."

The place was bigger than it appeared from the outside. The building was deep and the operation spread into the properties on either side. The funeral director took Lucas through the two slumber rooms, a smoking parlor, florist and headstone sales. There was a large display area for casket sales, from simple wooden boxes to bronze works of art for the cold and dead.

They stopped outside a large interior office under construction. "A video studio, state of the art. Online, virtual, the latest, with access to whatever setting and music you could wish for. Departure of the dearly beloved by a mountain stream accompanied by Celine Dion. Always tasteful."

A man with a red beard came out of the cold room. "Ellis," he said. "The problem has not been fixed. Thermostat's still on the fritz."

"I'll attend to it," said Rayvitch.

They walked by the embalming room. The curtains were drawn across the glass window. Lucas pointed in that direction, so that the funeral director walked over and pressed the intercom button.

"Slide one curtain," he said.

The embalmer complied. He had a corpse sitting up against an inclined backboard. On the table next to it was a roll of plastic wrap and a bottle of superglue.

Rayvitch gestured for him to close it back up.

"I hate to ask," Lucas said.

"Quite the contrary. The decedent is in a semi-sitting position, the 'semi-Fowler position' for dealing with a significant edematous case. Severe swelling, we deal with by this rather effective drainage method accompanied by a combination of Xoros and Tri San."

"And you do what with the Saran wrap and the superglue?"

"The 'blow-out patch method,' actually, to deal with rips in the skin. Quite effective."

Rayvitch went to a second embalming room. A gowned man

was disinfecting the pumps, ejectors and foul stink.

"Busy place, Ellis," said Lucas.

"Busy and thorough," said Rayvitch. "We observe all the protocols here. The equipment is all Pflager, top of the line, aspirators, vein directors, refrigeration, gurneys, everything."

"One would think you'd have closed circuit video for quality control," Rook said.

"If we had appropriate internal surveillance, we probably wouldn't be talking right now. But the right to privacy is paramount here, Mr. Rook. And after all, the dearly departed can't give their consent. Personal dignity is our primary concern."

"I'm sure, Mr. Rayvitch. I'm sure. I'd like to look at your personnel records. Involuntary terminations, any complaints from disgruntled customers."

"Let's go to my office, Mr. Rook. We're a small shop here. No human resource person or anything. The buck stops with me, you could say."

When they got back to his office, the funeral director poured himself another drink and relit his cigar. "The police have already looked at those records, Mr. Rook."

"That's fine, Ellis. Then you won't have any problem with me doing the job Mr. Sirlin's paying me for."

"I'll have to call Corporate," Rayvitch said.

Lucas looked at his watch. "I'll be back tomorrow. And don't worry, Ellis. You'll find my work dignified."

Lucas cabbed back to his office.

"A bouquet like cedar," said the driver.

Lucas looked at the ID posted in front of him. "I know you, Ernesto Canales?"

"No, but perhaps you should." He tapped a hello on his horn to a cab that went by. "You appreciate a fine cigar as the one in your shirt pocket, perhaps you might be interested in some excellent Cubans."

"Perhaps I'm ATF, Ernie, and you just jammed yourself up."

The cabbie changed lanes. "How about those Jets?" he said.

There was a silver truck double-parked in front of Rook's building and traffic was backed up. The waiting time started to click on the meter.

Lucas handed over the fare and a tip. Ernesto gave him two blank receipts and a blank stare.

Rook got out and walked to 166. The tough guy deliveryman was there.

"You ain't shit," he said, puffing out his chest.

"You are," Lucas told him.

"Christ, Mel. I need this job," the sidekick said.

"He needs to get his ass kicked. He surely does. And I'm the one to do it." The pirate wheeled a box of plastic doll parts towards the service elevator.

Manny was standing by in reach of his lead pipe. "Everything's under control," he said.

"10-4," Lucas answered. Citizens loved police talk.

The passenger car came down with the girls and their cigarettes. Bernie from the wholesale watch place was in the back. He nodded to Rook as he lit up. Lucas had busted him once for switching knock-off watches for the real ones that came in for repair.

A mailcarrier got on. Not the usual jack-off, but a blonde wearing her hair down. A nice rack. "Morning," she said. "Regular's got his day off."

"So I get my mail through the slot? You got it now, I'll take it."

"I can't do that, sir," she said. "It's against regulations."

Lucas gave her a little salute. "You got one of the mailing tubes or whatever, just knock."

"Have a nice day," she said as she got off on the third floor. She knew her job. You stop on every floor, people get pissed. Get off at three, walk down a flight. Ride up to five.

There were the usual noises from the photographer. "Put a lid on it," Rook said. "You don't want me coming in there."

The loony started making his bird calls. Rook banged on the wall. "I come next door, I'm going to pluck your feathers."

As he unlocked his office, the super got off the service elevator. "Mel said he was going to get you good. I thought you ought to know."

"I don't think so, Manny."

"I got your back."

"I appreciate it. Going to buy you another pair of fuzzy slippers, Manuel. Christmas is coming up."

Lucas checked his answering machine. Gavilan calling to ask if he got the poster, another reminder that he was a member of the New York Bar. Who could forget his brother-in-law, the dentist, blowing his head off at the breakfast table and lawyer

Gavilan not missing a beat. Him and his "assistant." Ricky and Lucy, each one of them gets a twelve out of ten on the smarm meter.

A couple of calls. Another solicitation from the dating service and Ellis Rayvitch from the funeral parlor. Rook called back.

The answering service answered in a lilting English voice. Then Rayvitch picked up.

"Bad time, Mr. Rayvitch?"

"I had an appointment. Eighty-one-year-old woman walked on to the FDR in rush hour."

"I'm sure you'll have her looking like Jackie Kennedy in no time."

"Family and the grief counselor are coming in. Part of our comprehensive services."

"You called, Ellis."

The funeral director drank his port. "Ms. O'Reilly will be speaking to you about the personnel files."

"It's SDA's dime," Rook said.

Another call came through. It was Ms. O'Reilly. Rook let Rayvitch know who it was and took her call.

"Mr. Sirlin suggested a follow-up," she said. "Perhaps we could do a dinner meeting."

"What do you have in mind, Ms. O'Reilly?"

"Lobster and a cold beer would be excellent."

"You twisted my arm," Lucas said. When women in her position ordered beer they were telling you they were self-assured, which either meant they were going to bust your stones or you had a real shot at fucking them.

"Cano's at eight," she said and hung up.

Rook went by Jimbo Turner's for a shine. Jimbo was up on his stand, finishing a tomato sandwich. He turned the bread as he ate so none of the juice ran down.

"Man thinks you eat a tomato sandwich, you're a poor man,"

he said. "They be wrong." He took another bite. "Slice it up thick, good piece of onion, man's as rich as a king."

"I'll swing on back, Jimbo."

The shineman folded a piece of wax paper around his meal and came down off his stand.

"Even a king's got to have commerce, Lucas. Especially when someday it's going to bring him some of them fine Jersey tomatoes he's been hearing about."

"Just waiting on the weather, Jimbo. All they got is them hothouse kinds."

The shineman ran his fingers over the leather, then applied a coat of wash. "I'm eatin' on a batch that came in from Chile. It's winter there when it's warm up here. Not the same as no Jerseys though."

The shineman used his rag. "You know Hy Gromek passed on. And Mims too." He spit. "Not right to say their names in the same breath."

"I knew about Hy. Good cop. What's up with Mims? Somebody displeased about his shystering them up?"

"Nothing so what'shisname. Car accident is all. Up on the FDR. Some crazy lady…"

"Walked in front of him."

The shineman rubbed the polish in with his fingers. "You heard about it?"

"Didn't know it was that scumbag, Mims. Couldn't happen to a nicer guy."

"The lady, old lady I hear. She must have wanted to do herself in. Didn't know she was doing the world a favor while she was at it." Jimbo made a little sign of the cross and went back to working on the shoes.

"What do you hear? What do you know, Jimbo Turner?"

"Same old, same old, Mr. Rook, except Hy and Mims." He went to the brushes, clickety-clack.

"You get anything about some perv up at the funeral parlor

on the west side, you let me know."

"Ain't heard nothing on that. I do, you do."

He squirted two drops of water from an old hand-lotion bottle and snapped the rag before shining the shoes so they looked like glass. Then he offered Rook his shoulder so he could get down okay and took out his whisk broom. No dance necessary for Lucas Rook. Lucas handed over a fiver. "That tax thing is gone, my friend. You get anything else about it, you let me know."

"I appreciate that, Mr. Rook, I surely do. Next three shines is on me."

"Fair enough," said Rook.

He walked on over to Sid's garage. There was a sign on the door: "Back in a half hour."

Lucas glanced at his watch and went by Oren's. Joe, Sam, and Jeanie were at the prep table in the back. Jeanie had a black porkpie hat on and they were playing cards.

"Where'd you get that hat, Jeanie girl?" Rook said.

"Pull up a chair, Lucas Rook. If you got the cash and if you got the nerve."

"Jeanie here's the Manhattan Kid," said Joe.

Jeanie pushed her hat back. "Made six dollars already and my cards just warming up."

"Too rich for me," Lucas said.

Sam got up. "Throwing chicken cutlets on the grill. Breaded 'em up myself."

Rook pulled up a chair. "Sounds good. Coffee hot?"

"Cup of joe, Joe," Jeanie said with her little laugh.

Sam poured three and a half cups and Joe Oren filled his daughter's the rest of the way up with milk.

"Olé," she said. Nobody got it. "Geez, guys, I just made a joke. Ole?, au lait. You get it?"

His daughter drank her coffee and milk fast, making a slurping sound that got everybody laughing.

"I'll be by to pick you up at nine," Oren said.

"That's okay, Daddy. Jamal's going to pick me up and we're going to stay at his place."

Her father's face reddened. "What?"

"Got you!" she said as she went out the door.

"Got you good," Sam said. "That she did."

"Give me a heart attack worse than you be eating my food every day. You know I cook my eggs in bacon fat, that's okay for coming once, twice a week, not every day."

"Don't eat no pork," Sam said. "That's dirty food."

"Coffee to go and a piece of whatever pie," Rook said.

"You going over to the garage, ask Sid when my Mark's going to be ready."

"Who said that's where I'm going, Joe?"

"You're not the only sleuth around here, Lucas Rook. Besides, you order 'whatever' pie, I know you talking about Rosen."

"I got some chicken necks for the dog of his, I'll wrap them up," said Sam.

Rook told them thanks and walked back over to Rosen's. The sign was gone, but the bay door was still down. Lucas went around to the side. Sid was sitting at his desk with his glasses up on his head.

Rook put the bag down. "Coffee and coconut pie's for you. Chicken necks for Bear."

Sid took the coffee out and drank it black. "No good with the necks, whatever. Bear, he ain't here no more."

"With your wife?"

Sid took a bottle of Wild Turkey from his desk. "Died in his sleep, Bear did. Climbed up in my bed and died in his sleep." He lifted up a toast. "'When you're dead, you're dead. That's it.' Marlene Dietrich said that."

Lucas sipped his bourbon and waited for his friend to go on. Sid drank his down and poured himself another. "Then again, maybe she missed something," he said.

Rook went to Wingy Rosenzweig's. The first cab stopped for him, then drove off, Ernesto Canales with an unlit fine cigar in his mouth, probably figuring Rook was ATF after all. Lucas jotted down the cab number. When he got around to it, he'd make a complaint to the Taxi and Limousine Commission about something or other.

The hack in the second taxi was a short bald man with an Eastern European accent. He rode the streets hard with the meter off. "First Slovak cowboy you ever met, huh?" he said. "Ten bucks."

"The ride is six."

"Eight," the driver said.

Lucas handed over the six in the same hand he held his old NYPD badge.

"No tip? I made good time for you."

Lucas handed over another single. "That you did," he said. "You fucking your boss, that's your business."

There was a new wrought-iron door at the front on Wingy's brownstone, and the big iron flower pots were chained down even though they must have weighed a couple of hundred pounds. Somebody was fucking with Wingy, which was not a good idea.

Lucas went up the steps and rang the bell. A stranger's voice answered the intercom. Strong, black. "Rosenzweig residence. Do you have an appointment?"

"It's Lucas Rook."

He was buzzed in. Another camera on the stairway and a new door at the co-op. Wingy opened the door. He wore a Hawaiian shirt as always, never trying to hide that flipper of his and always looking like he was on holiday. "You like the new set-up? I got everything here, surveillance this, surveillance that. You wipe your ass, I got a picture."

The doorbell rang again. "Perfect timing." The recording of the strong black voice played and the video screen showed the delivery man announce himself, then put the Chinese food in the dumbwaiter. Wingy opened at his end and sent a twenty down.

"Why all the Fort Knox?" Lucas asked. "Somebody try to hit you?"

"Tried. Figured they'd hit me up for my pharmaceuticals."

"Not a good idea, I take it?"

"I don't think so," Wingy said. He took out two Lennox settings and poured out the Sum Gum Lo Mein and the chicken and cashews. "Always order for two. Chink food's better reheated anyway. Beer's in the fridge."

Lucas got out two bottles of Kirin.

"And what are you drinking?" Rosenzweig asked.

Rook brought two more and they sat down to eat.

"You looking for something or somebody, Lucas? The way you're coming up the steps, you could use some Celebrex, good drug no matter what the lawyers say."

"I'm good. Things get crazy, I take some Tylenol or whatever."

Wingy twirled a forkful of lo mein. "You drinking, you watch that Tylenol. Kill your liver as bad as a .357. Advil, Ibuprofen eat a hole in your stomach and you bleed out. Class-Threes, the way to go. Perc's, Oxy-whatever got a bad name unless you're too stupid to know any better." He took a long, cold pull on his beer. "Or maybe you're here to pay Wingy a social call?"

"That too, partner. And always a home-cooked meal."

"Ain't had one of those in years." His eyes looked over at the picture of himself and his late wife waving goodbye in their Hawaiian shirts.

"So what brings you to my abode? If it's not out-of-date pharmaceuticals and if it's not to play gin rummy, you're looking for somebody."

Lucas took another fork of the chicken and cashews. "Right you are, Mr. Rosenzweig. As perceptive as usual."

The intercom rang again. A tall black woman in a short red skirt appeared on the monitor.

"Come back in an hour," Wingy told her.

The woman left without an answer.

"Don't let me put a wrench in it," Lucas said.

Rosenzweig started his second Kirin. "Friends first. She massages my prostate. Thirty minutes later, it's no matter to me. She got a sister."

"Maybe next time, Wingy. You heard about this perv boosting hearses over at the Riverdale funeral parlor? Doing his nasty on the dearly departed."

"Actually, I have not. Only knew one necrophil myself. Came here for anti-fungal and Flagyl Metronidazole, but that was three, maybe four years ago." He served Rook the rest of the lo mein.

"You got a name, Wingy?"

"My professional ethics aside, my late customer dispatched himself. Maybe he was into that auto-asphyxiation jerk-off thing." Rosenzweig finished the chicken dish. "There's a joke in there somewhere. Maybe you could try some support group or whatever."

Rook stretched his bad leg. "Probably. They got them for everything else."

"You going to eat and run, Lucas? You got that runnerish look about you."

"Going to see a snitch, Wingy. Next time I drop by, I'll bring some corned beef specials."

"You find a deli not run by spics or gooks, you bring me a half pound of tongue, sliced thin."

Lucas finished his beer. "I'll do that."

"And real rye with seeds. Not that prepackaged crap."

Wingy Rosenzweig buzzed Rook out and watched him go down the steps. Then he washed the Lennox and sat for a while, looking at the picture of himself and his wife waving goodbye in the tropical sun.

Lucas checked his watch. Run out to see Tuzio or pay a visit to Jumpy Ames, maybe both and then get ready for his meeting with Ms. O'Reilly. He thought about calling her back and reminding her to bring the personnel files, but that would probably piss her off. Businesswomen were like that.

He went back to Rosen's garage to get his new Merc. The bay was closed and the side door locked. Lucas left a note about Joe Oren's Mark and rolled out in the Grand Marquis, which Sid was considerate enough to leave up front.

The car ran clean and smooth and the fuel gauge hardly flickered on the way to see his CI. There were the expected number of SUV's parked outside of the bowling alley, men who worked with their hands pretending they were cowboys, soccer moms that they were Captain Kirk.

Rook went into the bowling alley to see Jumpy Ames. The same ugly woman who tried to bust his balls last time was behind the counter. A team from a dental lab dressed in orange and black were sizing up their enemy claims adjusters.

"You with the Pirates?" the woman behind the desk asked. Then she recognized who it was. "Mr. Ames is not here."

"I'm flattered you remember me," Rook told her. "When will his eminence be returning?"

"Not for a long time," she said. "He's as blind as blind can be, poor man. And now if you'll excuse me."

"Sure, lady. You better get over there before that costume party on lane 6 throws a hissy fit."

Rook went out to Brooklyn. The great borough that brought the world PeeWee Reese, Gil Hodges, and the Duke also brought forth Jumpy Ames. Over the bridge and a ten-minute ride.

Lucas pressed the buzzer for 3F.

"Who is it?"

"CB, that you? How's it baking?" Rook asked.

To no surprise, CB didn't answer, but let him in.

Khali Fuller, known to his associates and fans throughout the criminal justice system as "Chicken and Biscuits," had been partnered up with Jumpy since they'd shared accommodations at Albion, courtesy of the New York State Penal System. Chicken and Biscuits was doing another piece for his ten thousandth smash and grab. Jumpy was doing his first hard time. Whether it was Fuller liked to have his prison issue sneaks sniffed or that Ames didn't give a rat's ass that his cellmate kept his ears stuffed with toilet paper, they partnered up.

"I don't do crimes no more," Chicken and Biscuits said when he saw Lucas Rook.

"Glad to hear that, CB. Where's your running buddy?"

"Don't do no crimes. Got my cases all settled up. State of New York and me is squared, except the State of New York gave me Hep C and I'm just waiting on the paperwork to get my suit case filed."

Rook went into the little sitting room. The sofa was being used as a bed. No pillow case. A pair of army blankets.

"Where's Jumpy?"

"He lying down like I ought to be."

Lucas found his CI in the back room. Jumpy was sitting in a straight backed chair looking out the window.

"Heard your voice, detective. You'll pardon me I don't get up and shake your hand."

"Hospitality wasn't your strong suit, Jumpy. Unless somebody dangled a sweaty pair of size tens at you."

"Ain't much for you busting on me, Rook. Other than watching the shadows that come up this time of day, I don't give half a fuck. Doc says another six months, whatever, I'm blind as a bat."

"You waxing your carrot too much, Jumpy boy. Your momma told you, you do yourself like that it would make you blind."

Ames turned in his chair. "Leber's Hereditary Optic Neuropathy. Big words for I'm going to be as blind as a bat."

Lucas walked closer as he spoke. "So maybe whatever got you so depressed you're back to doing bad things, Jumpy?"

"Don't matter you tune me up, Rook. Don't matter at all."

Rook grabbed him by the ear. "Lost all my sympathy somewhere, Jumpy."

"Jesus Christ! I don't do nothing except listen to the TV is all."

"You got yourself off on dead folks, Jumpy. Huffing their cold feet, then doing your thing." He grabbed his CI by the nose.

"No, no."

"You know anybody got that kind of appetite?"

Ames shook his head. "I do I'll tell you. I'll do that for sure, and I'll ask CB too."

Lucas Rook took a ten out and put it in his informant's hand.

"Here's twenty bucks, Jumpy," he said. "Buy yourself a fancy pair of shades."

Places to go. Shitbirds to see. One of the maxims of expert policework. Jumpy Ames wasn't going to give him anything, but one of New York's ample supply of dirtbags would give something up. There was enough time for another descent into the slime before he got himself all pretty for MJ and that lobster and cold beer.

Jerry Reifsnyder was busy with a customer, taking in a used '52 Bowman series. "Your 'Wally Moses' got rounded edges, no way they're sharp. Your number 105 could be a reprint."

"Alright about the edges," the customer said. "But no way about the reprint. That's bogus you talking to me like that."

A fat white man came in and asked about Labron anything. Lucas Rook kept his back to the counter and looked through a stack of old magazines. A couple more *Boy's Life* than maybe should be there.

When it was just him and Jerry, Rook went up to the counter. Reifsnyder turned pale, then tried a joke. "You looking for *Gangbusters*? Maybe some Paladin stuff?"

Rook gave him the stare. "Maybe you got 'The Scoutmaster and the Eight-Year-Olds.' Maybe your travel kit, you know, clothesline, Vaseline, and a lollipop."

A geek came in for the latest X-Men.

"Closed," Lucas said.

"But…"

"For inventory," Jerry told him. "Just a half hour."

"That's right. It will only take Mr. Reifsnyder and me a couple of more minutes. You come back, you get that X-Men for free." He took Reifsnyder into the office and closed the door.

"I don't …" Jerry tried.

"Have any more copies of Timmy and Lassie play hide the bone?" Rook looked at his watch. "I've got about ten minutes before I either thank you or break your nose again. Sit down."

Jerry did.

"Now get back up. I just wanted to make sure we knew who was boss here. I ask you a question, you answer it. I tell you to eat one of these porno mags, you do it."

Reifsnyder nodded.

"How's the smut business?" Lucas asked. "The hard-core stuff?"

"They buy, I sell. The First Amendment still allows that."

Rook took a copy of *Blue Boy* off the pile next to him. He rolled it neatly into a tube and then jammed it into Jerry's solar plexus.

"Wrong answer, Jerry. Let me be more specific. I'm not here to buy any pictures of your dick in a chicken. Who you got in here coming in for necrophilia stuff?"

Reifsnyder tried to catch his breath.

"You mean tapes, videos, whatever?"

Rook sat down and put his feet up on the desk.

"Right. Unless you got some of the stiffs stashed away."

"*Necrobabes* is the best seller of 4208."

"What's that mean, Jerry?"

"It's all code. '4208' is the Texas Penal Code for 'Abuse of Corpse.'" He tried to get the curl out of the *Blue Boy* magazine. "Like 'Moon Priestess.' Penthesilea was one of the Moon Priestesses of Athene. Achilles killed her and then…"

"Speared her twice, did he, Jerry? So who's your best customers?" Lucas pushed his sleeves back a bit to remind Reifsnyder that he would tune him up bad.

"I don't know them except by what they tell me and what they buy. You know, Joe probably isn't Joe. You know what I mean."

Lucas looked at his watch. "You wanting to give me a blow job when you're done jerking me here, Jerry?"

Reifsnyder stepped back. "I only got a couple of regulars that come in regularly for that kind of material. A lot just get it off the Web, Perv Scan and whatever. They don't give me their right names anyhow and everybody pays cash."

"Let me decide what's important, okay, pal?"

Jerry looked out the gated window and back again. "One calls himself 'Ted'. Maybe for Ted Bundy. He kind of looks like him. I read he liked to do it to them after they were dead."

"Teddy did like to stick it up their ass when they were nice and cold," Rook said.

Another customer came in.

"I got to get out there, he'll rob me blind."

"Then you better start talking."

"There's somebody collects quality hardback editions, especially relating to Bluebeard."

"The pirate?" Lucas asked.

"No, Gilles de Rae, a French count. They said he killed a couple of hundred boys."

"You got an address?"

"A phone number. I'm supposed to call and leave a message when something comes in."

"Give it to me, Jerry, and then you go sell the chump one of the footballs you've been signing in your spare time."

Reifsnyder wrote down the number and handed it over.

"Pretty good memory," Lucas told him. He leaned in close. "Remember this, you call Bluebeard or Teddy-boy or talk about our little conversation, them balls you're peddling as autographed out there, going to be the only ones you got."

Captain Hook's alarm clock told Lucas it was time to hit the Arby's he had driven by on the way in. Hand-cut roast beef or whatever on bread that wasn't pumped with air. The turkey looked good. The girl behind the counter looked better. Maybe twenty, skin like milk, just the right amount of lip gloss. Her hoop earrings were big enough to shout "slut."

"Can I take your order?"

"I bet you could," he said, but she ignored him.

Rook ate his lunch wondering whether the new generation still had young girls who loved cops, particularly in the back seat of their cruiser. He got Dr. Hepburn's machine when he called from the car, even though he had tried the private number. The recording was a hoot. "I'm sorry I can't take your call right now, I'm with someone who thinks he's me. Please leave your name and number, and remember I don't take insurance."

Charlie Hepburn called back in moments. "Sorry, I was busy double-billing a schizo. What's up, detective?"

Rook slid through a yellow light. "An enigma wrapped in an annuity."

"Sounds like me. This personal or professional?"

"The latter, Charlie."

"Good. Then I've got time to see you." The shrink lit a Lucky. "Give me a hint so I can get a head start on the Internet."

"Necrophilia."

"*Arrenderi monte,* Lucas."

"With a side of ravioli."

"Those who have broken the highest taboo. I'm pretty jammed up with heart-broken housewives and self-doubting accountants." He exhaled a breath of licorice smoke. "But for you, I'll make time."

"You mean for my client."

"Whatever." He took another drag. "See you soon."

Dr. Hepburn's office was on the Upper East Side, but since SDA was going to be paying, it didn't matter that the parking lot would be trying to give it to him like Ted Bundy. There was a back-up getting into the garage and a traffic control officer came over. "You're obstructing traffic." She adjusted her hat, which was tiny on her round head.

Lucas flashed his NYPD gold shield and she waved him around.

"Keep me up front," Rook said when he got in. The attendant salivated at the thought of a ten spot, then shook his head when Lucas tinned him.

Lucas walked down 1st Avenue to Hepburn's building. He pressed the buzzer and the psychologist let him in.

Charlie was riding an exercise bike with his white hair jammed into a Red Sox hat. "You mind if I pedal while we talk? Time is precious, Lucas. Besides, I have to get back the seven minutes of my life I just snubbed into the ashtray."

"I got a funeral parlor client being bothered by somebody waxing himself on their deceased."

"'...Even that coldness by which you are for me more beautiful.' That's Baudelaire," Hepburn said.

"Baudelaire? I think I busted him once."

"I get to write a report? Maybe testify? That's where the cabbage is." The shrink fished another Lucky from his shirt. "Short version: more than half of necrophiliacs work in the funeral business and 90% are male. No surprises there. Most are heteros, but more than half of the necrophiles who commit murder are gay. Most violations are right before burial. Nice way to say goodbye. Shall I go on?" He lit up.

Rook jotted some notes on the narrow reporter's pad he took from his jacket. "You're talking, I'm writing."

"The mean age is 34, 60% are married, most simply wanted an unresisting partner. My favorite is Carl von Cosel. Fell in love with a TB patient. Kept her corpse as his wife for seven years. Her parts rotted out, he fabricated new ones."

"That's love, Charlie. Tell me about Bluebeard."

Hepburn took another drag and began pedaling slowly. "Gilles de Rais. Friend of Joan of Arc. He disemboweled a couple hundred boys and deposited his sperm into their wounds. There's Erich Fromm's *The Anatomy of Human Destructiveness*, which outlines more specific character traits. At our next meeting I'll enlighten you. Now you'll have to excuse me, I've got a patient coming in any minute. You tell me who to bill, I'll send you a preliminary report."

"You going to change your outfit there, Charlie?"

Dr. Hepburn looked at his appointment book. "Nah," he said as he took another drag.

Lucas Rook put on his grey suit and a black turtleneck. Leave the jacket open because he had put on a couple of pounds and she could get a look at his .45. He had learned enough from the perv store and Dr. Hepburn to show he knew his business, but it never hurt to show you meant it too.

MJ O'Reilly was at the bar. The slit skirt showed plenty of leg. She waited with her cigarette for Rook to light it.

"I thought they don't allow smoking here," he said.

MJ held his hand as he offered the match. "They don't." She inhaled deeply.

The bartender looked at her.

"Is my table ready?" she asked.

The host came over. "I'm sorry, Ms. O'Reilly, smoking is prohibited."

"I'm not smoking," MJ said. "But I am waiting."

"I'll see about your table," the host said.

She snubbed out her cigarette. "'He who controls the checkbook controls the game,'" she said. "SDA owns a permanent reservation here."

Their table was next to the window so they could see the traffic going by.

"Do you have something for me, Mr. Rook, or does that Smith and Wesson mean you're not glad to see me?"

The somalier poured her a glass of Vigonier and offered one to Lucas. He ordered a beer.

"Making things go bang is a hobby of mine, Mr. Rook. But then again, when it comes to business, the fucking you get is rarely worth the fucking you get."

Their waiter came over. A striking woman in a tuxedo. Her red hair was in a crew cut: no eyebrows, white lipstick. "Merle is pleased to serve you," she said with the smallest bow. "Will madame be having her usual?"

"Madame will," MJ told her.

"And you, sir?" Merle asked.

"Caesar salad, easy on the dressing, heavy on the anchovies. Petit filet, the garlic sauce on the side."

Merle nodded and left.

Adam's apple a little too big, wrists a bit too thick. Boy trying to be a girl looking like a boy. Rook said, "I love New York."

MJ sipped her wine. "Tell me about having sex with some-body who's not just acting dead, Mr. Rook."

"There was the X-ray guy, fancied himself an inventor," he told her. "He worked at a TB clinic. This lovely girl comes in, she's dying. He falls in love with her. And they live happily ever after, man and stiff, until he gets busted."

She crossed her legs. "Romantic, don't you think?" MJ took another sip of her wine. "I'll be right back," she said.

Ms. O'Reilly was back being the business bitch when she returned. "And how do you find Mr. Rayvitch? Is he cooperative?"

"He is."

The server arrived. "Madame's skate wing with capers." She presented the plate. "Caesar salad, dry, ample anchovies." The accent was on the "an."

"Everybody's got an act," MJ said. She sliced her appetizer delicately. "I assume sleuthing is what you do best?"

"I find the bad guys."

"And 'grab them up'?"

"And 'grab them up.'" Lucas took a forkful of greens with the salty fish.

MJ called for Merle to refill her wine glass. "I didn't mean to be a smart ass. I do tthat," she said. "There's the smart ass me, the corporate me, and the corporate, smart ass me."

Lucas let it pass.

She took another sip of wine.

The rest of the time was a dinner meeting. She asked again about Rayvitch and reiterated Mr. Sirlin's desire to have the matter concluded expeditiously. "If this goes well," she said, "we can almost assure you that in addition to being bonused, you will be placed on our 'Preferred Vendors List.'"

"I appreciate that, Ms. O'Reilly."

Their coffee came. She waved off the dessert cart. "Are you running his DNA from the mess he is leaving?"

"I don't think that's necessary. I've met with the local precinct and I have a profile."

"Can you share that with me, Mr. Rook?"

"I'd like to do a little of what we sleuths call spadework before I do that."

"How exciting," she said. "But do move quickly."

MJ O'Reilly hailed a cab outside of the restaurant and gave the driver her address on the West Side. She cracked the window and lit her cigarette. When they got to her building she lit another. "Would you like to come in for a drink?" she asked.

"I don't like to mix business with pleasure, Ms. O'Reilly. It's not a good idea. You can wind up losing both."

She stopped and took a deep drag and turned away as she exhaled. "I do understand," she said. "Although, I thought you gave me more credit than that."

"Coffee would be good."

"Coffee it is, Mr. Rook. And perhaps I can answer any other questions you might have about SDA."

There was no doorman for her brownstone and the security

system was ticky-tac. At least she had a peephole and a police lock and deadbolt on her door.

"They should at least put in a card swipe system. They're not all that expensive now," he told her.

MJ nodded. "We're going to. The company owns a bunch of buildings and we're getting to it."

There was a small elevator, and Rook could smell her perfume. She hinted at moving closer, but didn't. Her apartment was modern black and white. There was no television, stereo, or books.

"I'm going to change into something more comfortable while the coffee's brewing," she said. "Nothing from Frederick's of Hollywood," she added with her first smile of the night.

His cell rang. It was Grace Savoy.

"I thought I heard something, or dreamt I did. I don't remember which," she said.

"I'm with a client. Is everything okay? What was it, Gracey?"

"Maybe I was dreaming," she said. "I thought it was the bird I killed. The red one, you said. Flying over from your place, trying to get out. Then again, I can hear a pigeon fart a mile away. Will you come over when you get home? I'll make some franks and beans."

"I'll check on you when I get back. Put your alarm on."

MJ Reilly came in. She was wearing jeans and a sweatshirt. "Sorry to interrupt," she said. "Another client?"

"Not at all," he lied.

She sat down. "What would you like to know?" she asked.

At their hourly rate, he didn't care what she said. Lucas got her to go on about what she knew about the company, including the corporate structure, Mr. Sirlin and Ellis Rayvitch. Sirlin was the consummate corporate honcho and Rayvitch had been married twice and was now seeing a Hunter student less than half his age.

Then Rook got MJ talking about herself. Her father was military. Her mother spent most of her life in a wheelchair from muscular dystrophy. She had a sister who was a "stay at home" married to an insurance man.

She lit another cigarette. There was a tiny tremble to her hand. "Oh, it's late," she said. "Thank you for coming up. I'll see you out."

Rook walked up to Central Park. Haven for nannies and other people's kids in the daytime. Furtive gay sex and muggers in the night. Catherine Wren and a man in a derby hat drove by in a carriage. It was so absurd, Rook almost waved. He thought he saw her turn towards him and touch her gloved hand to her face.

When Lucas got back to the St. Claire he checked the place and then crossed over the patio to Grace Savoy's apartment. Her lights were on, but she was sound asleep with the stereo on. When he went over to turn it off, her guide dog got up and then lay back down.

Rook went back to his apartment and wrote out some notes. A lot of hours to bill. A lot of money. He drank a beer and went to sleep.

Lucas had a bad dream. He was in a hearse. His brother was waiting for him. Kirk was so cold that he glowed with it. And all his teeth were stone.

Joe Oren came in from the kitchen. He was listing a little to the left, which usually meant that his back was out. Today, it meant something else.

"You okay?" Lucas asked him as he ate the last of his scrambled eggs.

Two Wall Street types in running shoes came in for their coffees to go. Joe attended to them and motioned for Rook to join him in the kitchen.

"We grabbed up somebody broke in the place," Oren said.

"Figured you'd tell me when you felt like it why you're walking heavy and Sam got his whomping stick over there."

"I got my thirty-eight-ounce Luke Ester bat, you're right. No way I'm winding up like him," Sam said. "Getting gunned down when he was working as a bank guard instead of being in the Hall of Fame. That's not happening here."

"Perp tumbled down the steps a couple of times," Joe Oren said. "So he won't be back. But, he does, or he got friends, I'm going to put them down, which is why I'm packing iron."

"This is our place," said the cook.

"You need me or whatever," Rook said.

"Just wanted you to know." Big Joe handed over a brown bag. "You wanted Jerseys, these ain't them, but they are as firm as my late wife's cans."

"Appreciate it," Rook said. "Make sure the shitbag falls into your place, not out."

Jimbo Turner ran a cloth over the seat of his shoeshine stand. "Now hop on up here and let me get to work. My smeller tells me you been out to Jersey for this old white shineman." He took the paper bag from Rook without opening it up.

Jimbo looked the shoes over once, then twice. "Need a little blood on them, bring them back to life." He popped a new can of oxblood polish for Rook to see. Then he took a plastic bottle from his shirt and squeezed a couple of drops on his hands. "Smells like peppermint, don't it? Well, it is. Couple of drops of peppermint oil keeps the arthritis from getting to me."

He wet his rag and wiped the street grime off. Then he smoothed in the first layer of polish, working the red-brown color in with his fingertips. "Fine day you bring me them tomatoes, Lucas Rook. Fine day indeed."

Jimbo Turner worked the brogans good and shined them twice. Then he offered his shoulder for Lucas to get down and used his whisk. Rook handed over his five, but Jimbo Turner would not take it. Instead he reached behind his stand and took out his own paper bag. It was a brand new hat.

"Like Popeye Doyle. Lucas Rook, I remember you and your brother wearing them when you was first coming up. The 'Porkpie Boys,' they called you, and what's his name, John Austin."

Rook nodded. "I appreciate it, Jimbo."

"I know you do," said Turner. "I know you do. Just like a diabetic old white shineman appreciates having a good friend looking out for him."

Lucas Rook walked over a block to get a cab. Stop at Sarkissian's to get some discount jacket or whatever for Bud Stevenson at the 20th, who called to say he had something on the jitbag who was boosting the hearses.

A taxi pulled over and then a Lincoln Town Car came alongside. Tom Bailey rolled down the tinted windows. "Run you uptown, handsome," he said.

The cab driver told him "Fuck you" with a strong accent.

"Go fuck a camel, you Al-Qaeda piece of shit," Bailey said.

The taxi pulled away.

Tom Bailey swung into traffic. "Where you headed?"

"I'm running up to the Garment District if it's on your way."

"That it is, detective. Going to pick up some Broadway producer type. Always travels with this big Doberman of hers. Towel heads nor the criminals of the Carribean won't pick her up." He tapped his horn twice and made a right turn from two lanes over. "Don't block the box, my ass."

Bailey adjusted his tie and checked himself in the rearview. "Where you going? Maybe I can beat the deal."

"Sarkissian's. Over Stanley Pleating. 32nd and 8th is good."

"No it ain't, my friend. Sarkissian ain't there anymore. You didn't hear?"

"Tell me, Tommy Boy. Got to be the kid, right? No good piece of shit."

"Terrible, terrible," Tom Bailey said. "That piece of shit kid comes back in to boost whatever from his own old man's joint. Except George is working late and it turns out he caps his own kid he thinks is a burglar."

"Bag of crap, Tommy Boy."

"Anyways, the kid gets it good and he's flat down dead, Rook. And George puts one in his own head when he sees who it is. Ain't that some shit?"

"Couldn't be worse. Then I'm running uptown."

"My schedule does not permit," Bailey said.

"Then here is good."

"Sorry to put the shitstink on your day," Bailey said. He let Rook out at the corner and drove away.

Lucas walked a couple of blocks to stretch his leg and clear his mind. Used to be a TV show, *The Naked City*, the city has a thousand stories or whatever. It does, and they're always bad.

The desk sergeant at the 20th Precinct was the same hard Hispanic with the fancy make-up. You threw one into her, she'd melt your dick.

"Friend of Bud's," she said.

"I'm flattered you remembered."

"Don't be flattering yourself," she said. "He called down not five minutes ago to tell me you was coming. Said you thought you were all that. All hard, but with big blue eyes, and that you'd be hitting on me, which ain't never going to work."

"Never's a long time, Sergeant."

She smiled, but the hardness in her face did not go away.

Rook started up the steps with Jimbo Turner's hat in his hand.

Detective Stevenson met Rook halfway up the iron stairs.

"We in a hurry or you glad to see me?" Lucas asked him.

"We're going to grab up your 'hearse ghoul.' I thought you'd want to be *contiguous*. Nucie's bringing the unit around."

Detective Nucifora waited for them in the unmarked.

"Where's your beanie?" Rook asked him.

"My *yarmulke*. Or some of them call it a *kepah*. Them days are over."

"Where you parked?" Stevenson asked.

"Tom Bailey ran me over."

"How is that lucky cocksucker? Still got a knot in his pocket the size of Gibralter?" Stevenson got in the front of the black Chevy. "Hop in the back," he told Lucas. "I'll drop you off close enough to get what you need."

Nucifora had the front seat back as far as it could go. Rook stretched his bad leg out on the seat.

"So your Hebrew days over?" Stevenson asked. "Meaning

you loan me a dollar I don't got to pay you back three?"

"For you, you only pay me back double." Nucie swung around a delivery truck. "Which reminds me, I heard on the radio something about Mel Gibson's old man and the Aryan Brotherhood or whatever."

"It's all bullshit anyways," Bud said. "Same as *Schindler's* whatever. All them movies are the same. Only two things in Hollywood is fags and *lucre*." He pointed to the corner up ahead.

Nucifora pulled their unit to the curb.

"We're going over to the Diamond Car Wash halfway up the next block. Grab us up a car thief."

"Appreciate it, gentlemen. My treat at McLaughlin's."

"You twisted my arm," Nucifora said.

Rook passed the new hat up front. "Look great with your Easter outfit, Bud."

"Appreciate, Lucas. I'm an aficionado of all things *millinery*."

Rook got out of the unmarked. "Appreciate the thirty days to word power, too, Bud. I surely do."

Lucas walked slowly up the street so the detectives could do what they had to do. There was a bodega in the middle of the block, and he stopped in for an onion roll and coffee.

The cashier was arguing with an old lady with orange hair about why an apple cost sixty-five cents.

"Didn't cost you no sixty-five cents. My father sold apples on the street for a penny."

"I put it on the scale," the cashier said. "It tells me how much."

"You got your thumb on the scale, I seen you," said the lady with the orange hair.

The cashier called for her husband, who came up from the back. "Give us a break, Mrs. Davis," he said. "One day, give us a break, *por favor*. I got other customers here."

Rook got his coffee and roll and went out and walked over to the scene and picked up a *Daily News*. He heard the sirens coming from a half dozen blocks away.

Lucas put his coffee on the newspaper box and went up the block. As he reached the corner, a guy in overalls came around the corner, doing the Jailhouse Strut in rubber boots. His cuffs were wet. Lots of cons washing cars. Rook clotheslined him.

The car thief dropped like he was shot. Lucas patted him down. A straight razor in his left sock and a reefer in his right. "Naughty boy."

The two detectives were not far behind.

"A present for you boys," Rook told them.

"This fine citizen slip on a banana peel?"

"That he did, Bud," Lucas said. "That he did."

The cruiser arrived with the siren still wailing. Rook moved across the street. A moment later, the sector car pulled up behind it. Sergeant McDermott got out and walked over to the blue and white. "Turn your siren off, dear. That's the thing that goes real loud and tells the bad guys we're coming."

The policewoman in the cruiser fumbled at the dash. "I answered the Code, Sergeant. Dispatch must have…"

He walked away shaking his head. "We alright here, detectives?" he asked.

"We are, Sergeant," Nucifora told him.

"A pleasure you could drop by to our clusterfuck," said Stevenson.

"Wonderful to have you here, gentlemen," the sergeant said. "Save me the paperwork and spare me from the bitches with badges." He got back into his unit and swung away. "Give my regards to that coincidental bystander behind the newspaper."

"Mere *synchronicity*," said Bud. "Now, let's get this maggot into the system and ingest a libation or two."

"You mind I have a chat with the slimebag before he's processed?" asked Lucas. He handed over the perp's knife and the weed. "Once the Legal Aid lawyers get ahold of our shitbird here, I get nothing."

"I'm fine you converse with our perpetrator," Stevenson told him. "Except he's still out cold."

Nucifora grabbed the car thief by his collar and put him into the unmarked. Rook got in alongside. "We running him over to Presby, Bud?"

"Only emergency room we're running him over to is McLaughlin's, partner."

"Shit bag's out cold calls for cold beer, partner," said Nucie.

"Do you concur, Detective Rook?"

"I concur, Detective Stevenson. I do."

They drove to the bar with the car thief drifting in and out of consciousness.

"So when my partner here is not wearing his beanie and going to one funeral after the other…"

"I actually met a real nice girl at one of them," Mark said. "Short blonde hair. Lives in White Plains."

"Nice girls don't five you a blow job the first time out," Stevenson said.

"They do now. After Clinton or whatever, they don't even think it's sex. Anyways, she didn't swallow."

"So when my partner here isn't going to funerals and getting blow jobs from blondes who live in White Plains and spit it out the window…"

"She used a Kleenex," Nucifora answered.

"How dainty," said Lucas.

"*Dainty*, excellent word."

"Right, like the stew, Bud," said Nucifora.

Stevenson pulled around the back of McLaughlin's. "That's *Dinty Moore*, but no matter. So when Nucie's not getting blowed or wearing his beanie, we develop they take the limos around to the same car wash every morning at eight. They're all cons working at any car wash. Everybody works there except the owner's been in the system. We take a look at who we got, and sleeping beauty here got the perfect pedigree. Did a nickel at Rahway for boosting hearses and selling them to these specialty clubs, who are ghouls themselves, driving around in hearses they paint all up with skulls and whatnot."

"Like motorcycle clubs. You know what I mean? We trunkin' him, trussin' him or bringing him in?" Nucie asked. "He's still going in and out."

"I don't want him kicking no windows out, partner. Let's trunk the scumbag. Give us time to *cogitate* on the meaning of life and I don't want him kicking my windows out."

They cuffed Willard Spangler's hands and feet and put him in the trunk.

"His sheet got anything him spanking his monkey or whatever?" Rook asked on the way in.

"Nope," said Nucifora. "We got the names whatever of them hearse clubs. One over in Lindenhurst is pretty active in receiving these stolen vehicles. 'Crypt Cars' or some weird shit like that."

The bartender tipped his hat when they came in McLaughlin's. "Table in the rear," he said.

"Thanks, Obie," Bud told him.

"I'm Dobie. Over from Miata's. My brother's out sick."

"You're sick, Obie, you try that shit," Stevenson said. "I locked you up twice already and you're the one with that little mole over your right eyebrow."

"Besides," said Nucie, coming up to the bar, "Dobie's the one that's only half a fag."

"That's not right, detective."

"Neither are you, Obie Dobie," said Bud. "Jack and water on the house for my friends on account of you trying to be who you're not."

Rook, Nucifora and Bud Stevenson went into the back. The counterfeiter with the bad skin was wiping down the table.

"Pitcher and a pound of twenties," Nucie said.

"Certainly, gents, and will you be ordering lunch?"

"Certainly will. Me, I'm having the crabcake sandwich," Bud

told him.

"Two," said Lucas.

"Pork and provolone. Mustard and onions, Raymond. And a pound of twenties."

"*Redundancy* is a sign of impending senility," Stevenson said

The beer came. Raymond hung around the table trying to pick up something he could use.

"Shoo!" said Nucifora.

"Shoo?" asked Lucas.

"Precisely and redundantly," the detective answered.

They raised their glasses. "To the good guys," said Stevenson.

"And no shit on your shoes," said Nucifora as he got up to go to the john.

"So how ya doing, Bud? Everything good?" Rook asked.

"Kids good. The wife's getting the change. One day she's freezing, the next she's burning. My wife's going through the change of life and junior over here's getting blow jobs from this blonde's spitting it out of the window." He drank his beer. "How's trading the world of shit for the world of commerce?"

"Same shit, just a different flavor. And there aren't any benefits. Blue Cross, dental, whatever."

Raymond brought over their lunch. He put the sandwiches down and announced a pound of twenties with the napkins.

"You being smart?" Stevenson asked.

"Smart enough to stay out of the joint," the waiter answered. "Not smart enough to not be wiping tables in this dive."

They finished their lunch and went around back to the unmarked. Willard Spangler was awake, but not alert. His voice was raspy from Rook's forearm to his neck.

"I dreamt I was dead," the car thief said. Then he started to retch.

"Christ!" Bud said. "Not in the back of my unit." Nucie took Spangler over to a trash can to puke, but he passed out again.

"We got to run this jitbag up to Presby," Nucifora told his

partner. "Maybe we should not have spent all this time following the false leads Mr. Spangler had given us. Otherwise, we would have taken this fine citizen directly to the ER if he had any symptoms at all."

"Drop you on the way, Lucas?"

"I'm good, gentlemen. I get a piece of change behind all this, both of you fine humanitarians are going to benefit hardily. Give me a call if this perp cops to doing himself on the dearly deceased."

"We'll talk to him hard. And thanks for the new brim, Lucas," Stevenson said. "Going to wear it forever. A chick magnet if I ever saw it."

"Take it light, Rook," Nucifora told him.

"I'll take it any way I can get it, boys," Lucas said.

"Light, tight and full of fight," said Stevenson. "The way it used to be."

Lucas went back to his office. He had more than enough information to write a decent-length interim report. Good money in that in itself.

An hour of computer research and the phone would produce three more hours of billing. And there was the trip to "Cars of the Crypt" in Lindenhurst. If that went well, Lucas would present Mr. Sirlin with the option of recovering the vehicles. Insurance concerns could mean that it was likely as not that SDA would not want the hearses back at all or even to know where they turned up.

Then there was the other half of the job. Finding the necro perv would mean checking the employees against the profile the shrink had given him. Lots of interviews. Maybe another dinner with Ms. O'Reilly and who knows where that could lead. Life was good.

14

Rook got the 10:25 train to Lindenhurst. "Forsaken Land," the name meant. Better suited for the city. The largest village in Suffolk County used the county P.D. Last time he checked, Frank Donato was the chief. No need to check in. He was going to pay Cars of the Crypt a call. Do some asking around and get in a day's good billing.

The town planners, or whoever, were working too hard on that "village" thing. They kept that terminology for whatever tax or political reason, but it was still another one of the stops away from the city. Copague, Lindenhurst, Amityville, Babylon. Peter Winkler used to live there. The famous photographer. Rook had driven Grace Savoy out to sit for her portrait. Ten grand she paid for a picture of herself that she could never see. She told him it was in a museum somewhere.

The luncheonette was still there across from the station. The girl behind the counter looked like a grasshopper. The coffee was still good but the prices were way up. There were two cabs outside the station.

"11004 Burmont," Lucas said.

"Drive or Avenue? We got both," the driver answered without turning around.

"The car place."

"Figured." He pointed to his license on the visor. "I'm a

'Burmont' too, but no relation to either. Taught mathematics for thirty-one years. You picking up? Good idea. They ship all over. My late wife, she died two years ago. Just like that, she gets an aneurysm in the kitchen. She's making chicken and dumplings and she drops dead." He stopped too short as the light changed. "We used to ship our station wagon down to Sarasota. You picking up?"

"Nope, just up from Brooklyn, doing an appraisal. Water damage. Easier, I figure, to take the train."

Burmont looked at his watch. "You want me to wait? I'm going to stop and eat. I'll be back in an hour."

"An hour's good. I'm late, you start the meter," Rook told him. "But I shouldn't be much longer."

The girl at the car place couldn't have been more than eighteen. Somebody should have straightened her teeth.

"Looking for Cars of the Crypt."

She moved her chewing gum to her back teeth. "Do you have an appointment?"

"I called. Name's Hurst. 'Hurst's Hearse,' from Cleveland."

"Around the side of the building on the left. Ask for Donny. You'll know him, he looks just like the guitar player for Radiohead." She said the rest quietly. "Except he's in a wheelchair."

"On the left. Like the guitar player for Radiohead."

"Right." She brought her gum back where she could get to working it. "Guitar player like Dwayne Large. You know, 'Large and in charge.'"

Rook went outside and moved his .45 to his belt and pushed the sleeves of his windbreaker back.

There was a decal on the glass door of a Cadillac hearse all tricked out with red flames on the side. A long hair was listening through his headphones and playing bad air guitar.

"Donny?"

"Donny who?"

"Guess I got the wrong place. Looking for a dead sled."

Donny Wagoner rolled out from behind his desk. His wheelchair and his arms were covered with death heads, grim reapers, and the flames of hell. "You a dealer or a collector?"

"Little of both. Hurst's Hearses from Cleveland."

Wagoner did a pirouette in his chair. "I don't have it. I can." His cell rang. He lit a Marlboro and answered it. "Right, right. '77 Superior Endloader. Your '96 Lincoln six-door and four grand."

"Business must be good."

"People just dying to get in line," Donny said. "Bought and sold a '34 LaSalle in a half hour this morning. Got a line on a pink Councour d'Elegance."

"Looking for something new. Very specific." Rook opened his jacket so his .45 showed. "2004 Cadillac Eagle Ultimate. Silver and black. Friend of yours from the car wash boosted it from the Riverdale Chapel. My sister was still in it."

Wagoner's eyes widened when he saw the gun. "I didn't…I mean, I don't. I'm a fucking cripple, for Christ's sake."

Lucas walked in close. "Richard Widmark black-and-white flick, he pushes an old lady down the steps in her wheelchair. I'm going to make him look like a faggot, you don't tell where that hearse is."

Rook stuck the muzzle of his .45 up against Wagoner's dick. "You feel this, cripple boy? I hope not. Because I'm going to blow your balls off you don't give me what I want."

Donald Wagoner started to shake. "Bought it quick, sold it quick. Didn't know nobody was in it, for Christ's sake. Couldn't be. It came in here. I washed it, sent it off to Jersey." He wrote down the address. "This is all fucked up."

Lucas let the hammer down easy. "We're done here, friend. Unless you're shitting me. Then watch out for them steps."

Rook went outside. The math teacher was waiting for him and finishing up a hard-boiled egg sandwich. "You get what you want?" the cabbie asked.

"Everything's fine," Lucas told him. "There's an extra five in it for you if I make the next train out."

15

It was not a good idea that security at the Policemen's Home had never been on the job. And no way was this mope any more than some politician's hand-out.

"You have to sign in," the security guard told Lucas Rook as he pointed to the visitor's badges.

Rook walked on by.

"I'm supposed to ask for I.D."

Lucas kept going. He went back to Tuzio's room. Tuze's face was still swollen. Jim McGloan wasn't there.

Rook sat down on the empty bed. "Your tooth okay, partner?"

Ray Tuzio got up and walked over to his maple dresser that stood side-by-side with Jim McGloan's. He started rummaging through his drawers. "Grab up my iron. We're going to roll."

"Let's ratchet it all down here, partner," Lucas said.

Tuzio went into the little bathroom. He came back and sat on his bed. The front of his pajamas was wet. "My face is all swole up. I should've zigged instead of zagged or whatever. Never left my feet. You lose your feet, young pup, it's all over. They put the boots to you. Take your weapon and your shield."

Ray Tuzio stood back up. "Never left my feet," he said.

The night nurse came by. No real nurse at that, by the way she looked. Best she could do was bust your balls and maybe wipe your ass.

"Are you a relative?" she asked.

"I'm his brother."

"Mr. McGloan's personal effects are in the office, which is only open until five," she said. "And you have to make the arrangements."

"When did that happen?"

"They have all that information at the office." She went on up the hall.

Lucas walked over to his partner. "When did Big Jim pass, Tuze?"

"Never saw him off his feet neither, which is why we're part-nered up."

"I guess that's right, Tuze." Rook put a pair of sunglasses on the maple bureau. "Your Aviators," he said. "Must have left them in the squad. Up on the visor or whatever."

He looked over at Ray Tuzio, who had taken him to a thou-sand danger calls. The first man through the door had fallen into sleep.

Lucas Rook stopped at the bed of Big Jim McGloan. "As right as rain," he said. "Time's the baddest perpetrator of them all."

The "nurse" was in the vestibule catching a smoke. "I want the doc to look at my partner tomorrow. His face don't look right."

"I told you," she said. "You have any questions about Mr. McGloan, the office is open tomorrow at nine."

Rook walked a step closer. "Let me make myself clear, missy. First, it's Sergeant McGloan. Second, the doctor is to see Ray Tuzio tomorrow."

She started to say something, but he cut her off. "I'll be back tomorrow. That's not done, you'll be back working the fryolator, dear."

"I didn't catch your name," she said.

"You don't want that either. The doc's not been in to see Ray Tuzio when I come by tomorrow, I'll be back here tomorrow night."

There was a bar two blocks away. Used to be a mobbed-up place. Now they made it with fifty kinds of wings in the front and skanks giving lap dances in the back.

It was Marie Cumming behind the bar. She must have put on a hundred pounds, which is why she wasn't cranking wanks in the Champagne Room anymore.

"Well, if it isn't Detective Lucas Rook," she said. "What brings you in here?"

"Here for old times. Jack and water."

She poured the bourbon out. "We got the best wings in the city," she said.

"No more interested in that than a bj in the back." He tapped on the bar and she poured him a second.

"Well, pardon me for living."

"Nothing personal," Rook said. He drank his second as quickly as he had his first. That was for Jim McGloan. This was for himself. "Take care, Marie," he said. "You look just fine."

Lucas knew that he was not anybody MJ O'Reilly was going to want to have dinner with, so he tried her from his cell. A nice voice on the other end said she was in meetings. Rook didn't leave a message and drove on back to Sid Rosen's place.

"You come in to return my book. We're charging fines, you know."

"Big Jim McGloan passed," Lucas said.

Sid put his tool down and wiped his hands off on his overalls. "Good man, Big Jim," he said. He went over to his wooden desk and took out the bottle and two glasses. "I don't like this ritual," he said. His new pup came over to grab his pant leg. Rosen shook him off and poured. "*Semper fidelis*," Sid toasted.

They drank without another word. The dog came over and sniffed at Rook. "Saw Marie from the old Ace of Hearts," Lucas said. "She must weigh two-fifty."

"How those knees of hers? Figured she'd have bad arthritis now from working on them. Occupational hazard."

Sid poured a second. "Tuze alright?"

"Had a bad tooth, which they were supposed to take out, but his face is still swollen."

"They treat you as bad up there as they do at the VA. You remember Dr. Jackson got pinched for signing in and not showing up." He picked up the bottle again. "Comes in threes."

"Two's my limit, especially after the other two I had over at the Ace."

Sid poured them each another anyway. "I meant Big Jim passing and Hy Gromek was just laid out."

Lucas Rook let the drink be and sat for a moment with a look in his eyes that he was seeing something very far away that was very bad.

He went back to the St. Claire to make some calls and check his messages. Maybe work on his report or whatever. First thing was to call Stevenson and put him on Donny Wagoner before the crip wheeled on out of there.

Tony and Leo were at it again in the lobby. This time Tony was doing the laughing and jiggling a shopping bag at Leo. "Got ya good. Got ya good this time, Leo. Got him good, Mr. Rook."

"It's not right, not right. You're not right." Leo's lips were wet with the spittle from his s's and t's.

Rook waved at them and went on by.

"It's not right," Leo called after him, "to be shocking a man's system with a shopping bag full of rabbits' heads."

"Got ya, Leo. Got you good," said Tony.

Rook rode up to the 10th floor. Somebody was coming out

of the dentist's apartment. Short, baseball cap, wearing glasses. He had work clothes on and a tool box. The only thing that was just as likely to be bullshit was a clipboard and a pencil behind the ear.

"Something I can do for you?" Lucas asked.

"Finished up, thanks."

Rook walked over. "Mrs. Abraham's TV on the fritz again?"

"Don't know nothing about no Mrs. Abraham," the repairman said.

"What do you know about?"

"Know I'm on my own time once I close that door, so I'd like to get to my next stop."

"How about you open up that tool box of yours?"

"How about you butt out. They tell me to make a stop, I make a stop."

"My guess is you got something in that box of yours don't belong to you," Rook said. "And you've been behind the walls. You got that all over you."

The repairman put his tool box down.

"You a cop?"

"You know the drill," Rook told him.

Rook patted him down. There was an asthma inhaler in one pocket. A pack of Winstons in the other. He opened the toolbox, which was filled with tools and tubing and some thermometer parts.

"What are you doing here?"

"I fix aquariums. Downstairs gave me the key."

"You tell your boss you can't make this stop anymore. You come back here, you're going back inside. Must've been rough for a little guy like you."

The repairman picked up his box.

"And I'm going to hurt you before I take you in. And you're not going to like it."

Lucas rode him back down on the elevator. Leo was alone at the front desk.

"While you were playing Abbott and Costello, this piece of crap got upstairs."

"You know me," the repairman said. "They called. Right?"

"I told you, you're not welcome here anymore," Rook said.

Leo wrote himself a note as the repairman left. "He was here to check the aquarium while they was in Florida, Mr. Rook."

"He's a piece of shit, you two. You just let one of New York state's foremost jewel thiefs into my building."

"I did?" said Leo.

"It was his shift," said Tony.

"Onto my floor."

Leo came out from behind his desk. "Jesus Christ, Mr. Rook. Anybody hears about this, I'll lose my job."

"Maybe I call them now." He moved out of spitting range.

"Christ, no. They'll crucify me," said Tony.

"That skel comes in this building again, him and you two are going off the roof. You understand that?"

"Right. And I'll bring your mail and papers up for a week, you don't say nothing to nobody," said Leo.

"Right," said Tony.

Lucas rode back up. Drinking on an empty stomach had gotten to his gut. He took some Tums and listened to his messages. Nothing that mattered a shit. Then he called over to the 20th. Stevenson and Nucifora were both out. He left any message that meant anything, it was likely as not, another detective would jump their play.

Rook fried up a couple of hot dogs and ate them on rye bread as he sat outside. They were washing the windows in the building across the way as the hawk went by looking for something to kill.

No way he felt like dinner with MJ O'Reilly, but work was work and a client like SDA certainly beat the hell out of running precinct jobs and looking over your shoulder that the bosses didn't piss on your parade towards pension.

The phone rang. It was MJ.

"I'm sorry, we have to reschedule," she said.

"I don't have my calendar handy," he told her.

"No, I mean tonight's fine, but not the time. How about eight o'clock, I'll send a car. You like Thai?"

"Locked him up a thousand times."

"I don't get it," she said.

"Police joke," he told her. "Thai-Ty-Tyrone."

"Now I do. Casual attire is fine."

"And I was going to wear my tuxedo, Ms. O'Reilly."

"So concierge," she said.

Whatever that meant, which didn't matter since he was getting paid for her cutesy shit. Rook made a note of her phone call so he could bill for it. If you're Warren Phelps, Esquire, you're charging a half hour for that call, and if the client asks you about it, it's going to cost him another hour to get an answer.

Rook grabbed a towel to go downstairs and hit the bag in the boiler room. He closed the door so he wouldn't have the super come in and bust his balls if the heavy bag jumping on the chains woke him up or disrupted the hand job he was giving himself. The left hook first, Philly style. To the body, then the head. You bothered with a jab in the real world, you could find yourself getting stomped to death.

Then the right hand, short and deep. That didn't take him down, you had real trouble. Lucas shoved the bag and slipped it coming back. He did that a dozen times and then worked his hands again. No gloves, no wraps. You didn't have them in the street. They used to go some rounds. Kirk could take a shot and had quick feet. Lucas had the heavy hands.

Thinking about his brother slowed Rook down. He pushed himself to work the body, then the head, the head as he screamed it out.

Lucas Rook went out into the basement hall. The air was cool. He toweled off his face and rode the elevator up. Mrs. Weiss got on at the lobby. Her husband had made a living selling stamps before he dropped dead of a heart attack.

"Have a nice run?" she said.

"Something like that," Rook told her.

16

Rook's phone rang while he was soaking in the tub. Lucas starred them back, but it was outside the calling area. Probably a dothead from New Delhi letting him know that he had qualified for something he didn't want. Whoever it was, they would call back if it was something worth talking about. Except for Catherine Wren. If it was her apologizing for going nuts on him about his private justice or whatever, ruining what they had, she wouldn't call back at all.

Lucas thought about calling her, but the phone rang. "Hold for Attorney Gavilan." It was the fag assistant with the chromed-up .380. Lucy calling for Ricky. But Ricky paid his bills.

"*Buenas tardes*," Gavilan said. "I hope I'm not disturbing you, calling you at your home and after working hours."

"Your checkbook gives you the right, unless you're calling about your calendars."

"Regretfully not."

Rook took an index card from his desk and started a file. "You're saying 'regretfully,' I'm thinking you're saying family business, which tells me your sister."

"The lovely Cielto. *Que lastima*."

Rook wrote down "Sky Alterstein, drugs." "You said 'how sad.' How bad we talking, counselor, other than it's your sister?"

"Bad enough, but I think resolvable if we act quickly. The life insurance proceeds on her husband's suicide were delayed. They do that when somebody leaves their brains on the kitchen table. Then the dope runs out."

"We talking the good guys or the bad guys, Felix?"

"Little of both. My sister's signing her deceased husband's name to some scripts and driving into Manhattan to get them filled. And she's running with some bad people."

"She get pinched?"

"Not yet. They talked to her twice. Detective Bobby Fusco. The second time was not nice, as in she doesn't help with getting her new friends, she's in for a hard time. Then she calls me."

"There's two Fuscos, counselor. They both work drugs. Big Bobby and Little Bobby. Big Bobby is 'NMI,' Northern Manhattan Initiative. That's okay. Little Bobby works NITRO. Narcotics Investigation and Tracking of Recidivist Offenders. That's career criminals. That's not okay."

The Atlanta attorney said something in Spanish to Miguel, then gave Rook Fusco's phone number.

"That's Big Bobby. Not so bad. I'll see what I can do."

"Send your bill to me, Lucas Rook. The usual rate."

"I'll get right on it, Felix. It may get complicated, counselor. But I won't jerk you off."

"Of course you won't," Gavilan said. "That's what I have Miguel for."

Lucas tried a pancake holster with his new suit. Looking prosperous would help with Big Bobby Fusco. Manhattan Borough had an NYPD "Initiative" which focused on narcotics enforcement through a command center coordinating narcotics investigators, detectives and uniforms. The fact that Manhattan North was where the Alterstein job was meant that it made the most sense to meet at the KFC in Midtown South.

Lucas had worked with Fusco on three or four jobs. He

called over to the 26th precinct and arranged the meet.

Big Bobby had already gotten himself a window seat and a bucket of extra crispy when Lucas Rook came in.

"Don't you look all elegant. Grab yourself a pail of grease and pull up a chair," Fusco said.

Lucas got some wings and a biscuit and sat down. "I do look pretty, don't I? Must be the suit. Got it from over at Sarkissian's."

The narcotics detective bit the gristled end off a drumstick and sucked the marrow. "My house grabbed the kid up early on. Can you believe it? His own father winds up taking him out. World is fucked the fuck up."

Lucas sipped his coffee. "Robert, I agree with that."

"No doubt." Big Bobby sucked the skin off another leg. "But you didn't ask me out just to chat about the Colonel's famous recipe."

"Somebody's asking about this *donnicciola*. Very stupid woman. All in mourning and what not, her old man does himself into his Cheerios. Cielito Alterstein goes on to some local CVS or whatever like she's a Barnard student, Columbia, or whatever, getting in because she's one of the ethnics. Shows a little belly. Hits them with her accent. Drops the bogus scrip on them, grabs her Percs and then out she goes."

"Sounds familiar," Fusco said.

"My friend wants to know if it's bad for his sister."

Big Bobby put his piece of chicken down and wiped his hands with a paper napkin.

Lucas bit into his biscuit. "Her brother is a dear friend of mine. He tells me you're squeezing her, she should get you to some people she doesn't know. He wants to know if it's a bad thing she moves out of state for permanent."

"You asking or he's asking?"

"I'm here, Bobby."

Fusco sipped his Diet Coke. "Nothing from nothing leaves nothing."

"Appreciate it," Rook told him.

"How about those Yankees," Fusco told him.

Rook went back to the St. Claire and got ready for his dinner date. Gavilan could wait for the call. As he came outside, MJ O'Reilly pulled up in a chauffeured black Town Car.

She opened her window. "Going my way?" she asked.

The driver began to get out, but Lucas let himself in.

"Decadent corporate indulgence?" she asked. "You would think so, but our cost analysis people actually ran the numbers and it's more cost effective to use a car service."

"SDA is a fine company, Ms. O'Reilly."

"MJ," she said. "Especially when the best Thai place is across the river. Mint Thai Garden is in Trenton. The *goong gan tiem* is to die for. Especially if I don't take my little purple pill."

The Holland Tunnel was backed up, and then the ugly stretch of road that took them to the Turnpike. The driver pulled into the last gas station and got out to check the pressure on the right front tire. "Sorry, Ms. O'Reilly," he said. "She was running kind of uneasy. Just wanted to make sure we didn't have a leak up front."

"That's very thoughtful, Jerry," MJ told him. She waited until he was outside of the car before she finished. "Waste of time. That's something that should have been checked before I got into his freakin' car."

The driver got back in and took them south, through the filthy air, where the Towers used to be and past the Newark Airport. MJ asked the driver to put some music on and talked about herself as Barry Manilow sang his greatest hits and Rook's meter ticked on at SDA's generous hourly rate.

She switched subjects from how she knew John Edgar Wideman as they crossed the bridge. "'Trenton Makes, The World Takes.' I love that. Let's see, Mr. Rook. New York Creates…"

"You tell me," he answered.

"Masturbates, I was thinking." She leaned forward to direct her driver. The Mint Thai Garden occupied the space of a failed Mexican restaurant. There was a large lot on the left. The driver let them out at the front door, then went around to park.

An unattractive woman in a Thai costume greeted MJ and Rook and took them to one of the many empty tables.

"Must have a candy store in the back," Rook said.

"I don't get it."

"Guy gets busted for the third time in a month for running a betting parlor in a storefront," Rook said. "Detective says to him, 'I don't get this. You can't be making it. We hit you already twice before and we're going to keep on doing it. I know you're hurting.' 'Don't worry,' the bookie says. 'We got a candy store in the back.'"

"I still don't get it, Lucas Rook."

"It's kind of reverse humor," he said. "See, you usually got the candy store in the front and run the gambling in the back."

The hostess came back with her husband. He saw Lucas Rook and stopped. He began to weep and his hands went to his face. Then he stood straight and nodded.

"You bring a great honor, detective. I thought I might never see you again." He took another step forward, then back. "I shall make something special for you. For you for whom there could never be enough gratitude." He bowed and took his wife back into the kitchen.

"Duly impressed, Lucas. Will you tell me about it?"

Rook picked up the menu. "I don't think you want to hear about it."

"I do," MJ said.

"You only think you do. You really don't."

The first of the Thai dishes came and the next. "I do want to hear about it," she said again.

He told her finally so she would shut up. "His sister was a nun. Her glasses were broken. She has to go to the eyeglass place to get them fixed, but she won't wear them the way they looked, broken and all. So she can't see and she gets off at the wrong floor. There's a half dozen homeless pieces of crap living there. They beat and raped her. Kept her there for seven days. I caught the case. I took care of it."

"You were right, Lucas. I didn't want to hear about it." She drank her tea. "You must have seen…"

"Lots of things the world is better off not knowing about? You bet, Ms. O'Reilly."

As they left the Mint Thai Garden, MJ O'Reilly took Rook's arm. The driver brought the black Lincoln around from the parking lot. The driver had Barry Manilow on and they went back up the turnpike to the city, MJ crossing and uncrossing her legs Sharon Stone style.

They stopped in front of her building on Sutton Place.

"This will be fine," she told the driver.

"I have those files for you, Lucas. The ones you asked Ellis Rayvitch for."

"I'm a committed employee, Ms. O'Reilly."

They went upstairs. "The files are on the coffee table, Lucas. Make us a drink, will you? Meanwhile, let me get these shoes off, they're killing me."

He picked up the files.

"Private Eye," MJ said when she came back. "It sounds so judgmental."

"I don't judge," Rook said. "What is, is."

"And how's that, Lucas Rook?"

"It's usually not very nice to look at," he said.

"I see," she told him.

"I hope not," he said.

Lucas Rook made some coffee when he got back to the St. Claire and spread out the files next to a tablet of graph paper. Yellow tablets were for lawyers and graph paper made it easy to draw straight lines. Seven personnel jackets of present full and part-time employees who had access to the bodies at the funeral parlor.

He propped his bad leg up on a chair and started a look-through of the first manila file. The end of the day or walking a lot, the leg was shot. Courtesy of Etillio's gang who beat him bad in their garage after he got the first of the pricks who killed his brother. They had meant to kill him slow, break him up and burn him and he would have wound up in plastic bags if Ray Tuzio hadn't come in with his riot gun.

Lucas planned to work an hour, charge for two and then he'd stretch out on the sofa. Maybe go down to the Jersey shore tomorrow, bring back some of that sweet white corn for the shineman and see how Duke was doing. He heard that he had opened up a pizza joint in Ventnor. Get back in time to pay one or two of the SDA employees a visit. Send out the alarm and see if anybody jumped.

He drew his columns on the graph paper and skimmed the files. There were two who fit the profile, a college graduate, Steven Winder, and Mark P. Breene, whose face had that look about it.

The black guy was going to get a look "because," and there was something hinky about the red bearded guy who was complaining about the thermostat. Rook took down their DOB's and operator's numbers from the copies of their driver's licenses and their socials from the first page of their file.

Winder had the color and age. Not married. Got his B.S. at CCNY at night while working as an orderly at St. Vincent's and Flower Fifth Avenue Hospitals. Had been with SDA for eighteen months and at Riverdale for half of that. His application said he wanted to familiarize himself with anatomy to help prepare for a career in nursing or medicine.

Mark Breene looked like the Dr. Mark Green on *ER*, who had died of the brain tumor. There was creep written all over him. He had worked at Riverdale for six years and "liked to work with people." Redbeard was Milton Bradley Foss. Something wrong with parents who name their kid after a board game. He'd once locked up a habitual mutt named Parcheesi Johnson. The black employee's name was Lonnie Richardson. There was a note that he'd adopted the Muslim name Bilal. Beats Parcheesi anyway.

Lucas Rook went over to his computer. He was by no means an expert or a wonk, but in his business being able to access info fast and cheap was an absolute necessity. He had public and private databases at his disposal, and like any decent PI who had been on the job, he had updated access codes to police department information.

Mark Breene "liked to work with people," but apparently only after they were dead. He had dishonorable from the Army after a ruckus or three at Fort Jackson, which meant he was a fag, a liar, or a thief. Probably didn't appreciate the age-old tradition of a blanket party.

BCI showed nothing, but the civil dockets carried a Protection From Abuse by Consent Order from a Lois Breene and in Surrogate's Court there was protracted litigation over the Estate of Lois Breene, deceased. A Petition for Accounting filed by a

Jennifer Pepper of Lauderdale Lakes, Florida, likely the sister.

Breene's employment history was spotty, with two years off after the settlement of the family dispute. He bought and sold a three-unit apartment house in Canarsie without making a dime and then rented out the Breene family home while he tried his luck in Carson City, Nevada, where he took a pinch for a bad check. Then welcome home, Markie Boy. A job at UPS and a collar for frequenting a prosty. Just the background for handling your dearly departed.

Redbeard was the son of Louis and Louise Foss, both psychologists, which maybe explains why they named their kid after a board game or whatever. Milton was a graduate of CW Post and had an MBA from St. John's University. He had been at SDA for ten years, was not married. No moving violations. No overdue taxes. Redbeard owned no real estate or motor vehicle. His name alone got him a second look.

Lonnie Richardson had a pedigree. Started out as a pee wee in the drug trade and worked his way up. Possession, possession with intent to deliver. Aggravated assault. He received his diploma and his jailhouse religion in a three-year bit at Elmira. Either Bilal had covered his tracks, or human resources at SDA had dropped the ball.

Rook's research came up with nothing to speak of on Winder, but the imperative of a hundred plus per hour and expenses was enough to justify a face-to-face. And at those generous rates he would throw Ellis Rayvitch into the mix.

It was too late for a run to AC. Lucas poured himself another cold one and surfed the channels. Bullfighting from Mexico on one channel, flyweight boxing on another. Maybe they should get together. *Point Blank* with Lee Marvin was halfway through, but he had seen it a dozen times so it didn't matter. The best detective gangster movie that was ever made, except like all of them it missed the charm of doing paperwork after midnight. Catherine said he was like Walker in the movie. Maybe he was, except his hair wasn't grey and he wasn't Lee Marvin and this was real life.

Lucas picked up his .45 and went in to brush his teeth. The phone rang. It was Catherine Wren.

"I couldn't sleep," she said. "You looked so unhappy when I saw you at Central Park."

"Cinderella?"

"And angry, Lucas."

"That's part of my charm."

He could hear her light a cigarette. "When did you start up again?" he asked her.

"Right after."

"It was your idea, Cat."

"I know it was."

"Show Derby Man the door and I'll be there in an hour."

"There's nobody here, Lucas. He's an interior decorator, anyway."

"I'll bring Chinese food in paper containers. We can eat in…"

"I'm not ready yet."

"Let me know when you get around to it." He put his automatic down. Catherine thought that was the funniest thing, the lady in Philly confusing Browning, the gun, and the poet.

"Good night," she said. "Good night."

Lucas unplugged his phone and slept as long as he could. When he awoke, his machine had a call transferred over from the business line from Mr. Sirlin's secretary to return the call. Maybe MJ O'Reilly had something not nice to say about him or SDA was pulling the job for another reason. In any case, the call would not be returned until he had another day's billing in. Since he would be getting his interviews after the close of business, Lucas went over to Rosen's garage to get a car to run down to Atlantic City to see the Duke.

Sid had Kirk's Avanti out on the sidewalk with the engine running. He had new pup on a short leash. "Got to teach them who's boss, Lucas boy. Otherwise it's worse than being a bigamist." The dog shied away from Lucas Rook. "Listen," Sid went on. "Fiberglass or not, you keep this indoors you're down there for more than a couple of hours. And wipe the chrome down. The salt'll pit her up."

Lucas nodded and got into his brother's coupe.

"I checked the thermometer and the radiator and replaced the ram arm."

"The ram arm?"

"The power steering box. She still may be a little stiff."

Rook gunned the big engine and headed off. The Studebaker coupe handled hard, but the Duke would get a kick out of it. He and Kirk were real motorheads.

Lucas took the Holland Tunnel and jogged over to the Garden State South. He rode with both windows cracked so he could listen to the engine resonate and the wind.

You could smell the ocean air even through the garbage heap that Atlantic City had become. Duke had moved down when the Burt Lancaster movie came out and his disability pension came through. Bad low back whatever, he could still deliver that right hand like a sledge. He was living over in Brigantine and going out for flounder twice a week, doing some security work at a titty bar until he had a crazy run at the craps table they're still talking about and bought his pizza joint.

Lucas came into town the old way. Swinging by the Avenue where Lou's used to be, the lines around the corner, from salami and eggs breakfast to ice cream sundaes after the movies. Now the theater was a Spanish furniture joint. "*Nuestros Muebles*" had replaced *Spartacus* on the marquee. Lou's was a water-ice joint with no sit down.

Two wannabe malos gave the forty-year-old fiberglass coupe an "Esse!" as Rook drove into AC. Then the Knife and Fork big family feud over the restaurant, you take the knife, I take the fork, whatever. And Perk's bar-restaurant on the first floor and gym upstairs. Lucas slowed down, he could see the old man upstairs still working his moves on the speed bag.

The temperature gauge on the Avanti was running hot again. If it didn't cool down, there was the Sunoco back in Margate. A tight parking spot opened in front of Duke's pizza joint. Lucas backed the coupe in.

"Bravo!" said Howie Pets, walking up like a picture from an old magazine. "Looks like we're in one of them time wharves. You being here in that rig. Me looking as fine as I do. You stopping by for them old times?"

"Come to see the Duke," Rook said.

"You looking for the Duke? He got the place up for sale

again. Me, I thinking of sprinkling a little of my vast financials into the place."

Lucas tried the door and looked inside. There was somebody sitting at one of the round tables in the dark.

"It's him," Howie said. "He won't be getting up or letting nobody in. Doc Kirchener went by, but Duke wouldn't even let him in since he said he got the cancer. Says he's just going to be eating tomato sauce and nothing else until he ain't sick no more." He brushed an imaginary spot off of his wide lapels and then started up the block on his platform shoes. "Some Japs gave me four mill for the Oceanaire. Going to take them another four to get the jit stains off the walls. Take it light," he said, tipping his purple hat.

Rook knocked on the door again and then called the neon number in the window. The figure inside didn't move. Lucas let him be. Everybody had the right to die as they wanted to, except pus bags like Etillo. Sid Rosen had given him a quote: "Revenge is a dish best served cold."

"Only in books," Rook said. Rook told him that was pussy shit. "You serve it smoking hot on a bloody plate."

Lucas pulled the Avanti out and headed to the Trop. Rook hit the buffet. Not like La Penta, but pretty good. A plate of shrimp and decent roast beef and then some salad like the magazines said. He waved goodbye at some chocolate cake and then walked the floor. Rook could see them like they were glowing in the dark: grifters, pick-pockets, prosties. He could also see security watching him on their closed circuit. "Who's that hard case walking around like he knows the game?"

The air was filled with the lacquer smell of stale cigarette smoke and counterfeit of fate. A fat woman in a sailor hat made the slot machine ring. Two others ran to the seat next to her as if her luck was catching.

Lucas went through the too-bright lights and the metal sounds. The opposite of the funeral home, but somehow the same. He went up onto the boardwalk where a running man headed towards the end of the pier in his rich sweat and the hope that he might catch the eye of a girl with low-riding shorts and a pierced tongue. A lone rolling chair laboring by carrying a Chinaman in a madras suit. There was a new sand dune piled up by the state engineers so that you could not see the surf.

Another rolling chair came by and Lucas flagged it down. "Off duty," said the tattooed Puerto Rican pushing fast.

"Slow down, Paco," Rook told him.

The chairman complied. "Twenty dollars a ride to the one end and back."

"I'll give you ten, you take me down to Steele's and back to the Trop and I won't be asking for your license or your green card."

"I'm a citizen," the chairman said as Rook got in. "And I fought in Desert Storm."

"I'm impressed," Lucas told him. "You got yourself a pound of fudge."

There was a tired-out woman at Steele's. Trays of fudge waiting to be cut, dark chocolate brown, with marshmallow veins, butterscotch with lumps of nuts, and one unearthly green.

"Two pounds of fudge," Rook said. "Mix it up."

"We mail," said the woman.

"I'm right here. Two pounds of fudge. You can give me the ones that are already boxed."

"We mail. No extra charge. I'm supposed to say that twice." She sighed and got the fudge.

He paid her and went back outside. She gladly sat back on her wooden stool. Lucas rolled back to the casino and paid over his ten and the pound of fudge.

The black Avanti coupe started running hot again, so he swung over to the Sunoco for them to take a look. The bays were closed. They were just pumping gas. "Myers around? He knows the car," Lucas asked. "Or the mechanic on duty."

"I'm just pumping gas. No self-service in the Garden State," said the man with the squeegee in his hand. "Ain't no Myers around. Nor mechanic neither."

Lucas popped the hood.

"I just pump gas," said Garden State. "And clean off your glass."

Rook checked for a leak or a bad rubber, then loosened the radiator cap. The attendant came over with a water hose. "I do that too," he said.

"I'm full," Lucas told him and rolled off. He called Rosen on his cell.

"Probably the gauge," Sid told him, "but she starts to boil over, pull off and wait for me. I'll be down. But I think you're good unless there's a pinhole somewhere."

Rook found a decent produce stand on the slow way home and got a bushel of the Jersey corn like he'd said he would. He ate a couple of peaches on the way back, sucking on the pits like they were wads of chaw.

Rosen had the garage door open and a bottle on his desk. He was over at the sink washing out two glasses as Rook pulled up. "Never too early for one," Sid said. "Never too late for two."

"Who said that?" Lucas asked.

"I did. Either me or Dean Martin. Could have been Dean Rusk." The pup trotted in, carrying a knotted sock.

"Pass, Sid, I got work to do." He handed over the keys and the box of fudge and went home to change his clothes. That started the client's clock running. Since there was no real threat to any person or significant property, Rook worked the list from the bottom up for billing purposes. You catch the bad guy too soon, you're catching yourself by the balls. Do Bilal Richardson first. Nothing better to start the shift than a dashiki-wearing ex-con, all militanted up with jailhouse religion.

Lucas waited for him to come out of the Riverdale Chapel and followed him over to the subway. Rook stopped him as he started down the steps. Lonnie, Bilal, whatever, gave him shit, he was going to take a tumble.

"Lonnie," he said. "We need words."

"I don't recognize your existence," Richardson said.

"You want to pay a return engagement to Elmira?"

"You an occupying mother-fucker?"

"That's more like it. Forget your posing until we get this done." Rook walked him back to the street.

Bilal Richardson smoothed out his tunic. "I did my time. I got nothing to say to the police."

"Then you can play me some jungle drums, Mustafa. We're looking at you for stealing from the dead where you work. Not very spiritual of you."

"Bullshit."

"We got you on videotape. Got you from the moment you walk in till the moment you walk out. In the men's room too. I guess that's a myth about black men."

Bilal took a deep breath. "You got the wrong nigger here. I do my job. I don't do nothing else. You got tape, it's another Bilal."

Rook leaned over and brushed Richardson's dreads aside. "What's this Lonnie boy? You catching the high hard one you learned to know and love at Elmira?"

"I got a hickey up on my neck, it's from this white girl at the Fashion Institute. She knows what she likes coming and going."

"Like a posing, phonied-up Afrocentric jitbag whacks himself off to dead white folks. I got my eye on you. A salaam and cheese, Lonnie. Have a nice day."

Rook crossed him off the list and went on to the next asshole.

19

Steven Winder fit the profile and had a pizza face. His app showed him working his way through CCNY as an orderly at St. Vincent's. His personnel file showed a decent address on East 12th,which meant he was either noted up or the building was rent control. "Apartment 5F" better mean he had an elevator.

The East Village: St. Mark's Place. Richie Havens. Blacklights. Dayglo. The Rook boys were there as teenagers looking for the Southshore girls coming to be Janis Joplin for a day. They were back a couple of times for NYU mixers after they graduated the Academy. Washington Square was half Richie-Rich and half Jamaican drug gangs. Three Rastamen picked the wrong two white boys over near the concrete checkerboards and got broken up by the Rook Brothers. Luke and Kirk back to back, playing cowboy games for real. For a moment Lucas Rook felt his brother was still there, next to him. Then there was nothing.

He walked up on the building as Pizza Face came out, stocky with a military haircut. Maybe National Guard or Reserve or a wannabe. Winder walked fast, with a cheap briefcase on a strap over his shoulder. He's walking with both hands free, he's looking for something.

Rook had learned to cover ground quickly even with his bad leg by taking long strides, and he got on to the F train right after Winder. Winder put his pizza face in a public health book.

Lucas sat down next to him. "Steve, right? We were in class together."

"I'm studying."

"You always were. Med tech, right? I got my RN, doing great," Rook told him.

"Is that right?" Winder answered without looking up.

"Right as rain. Working over at Gracie Square, which is why we happened to be on the same train, although I don't usually work this shift. Travel Nurses got me the gig. The hospital got more than a hundred beds, mostly psych and most of them are on cloud nine. There's one that looks just like Lisa Pilgrim, the porno queen."

"I'm happy for you," Winder said.

"You needn't be a dick about it, Steve. I just thought…"

Pizza Face closed his book for a minute. "You're right, I don't mean to be rude. I got a mid-term, I'm working full time. So thanks anyway."

"No, you're right, Steve. It's just there's going to be a job posted, so I figured we went to school and all."

Steven Winder went back to his studying. Being a rude prick was going to get his apartment rough-tossed just because. Rook got off at his stop and then crossed over for the subway ride back downtown. Lisa Pilgrim was a nice touch. He confiscated a bunch of XXX movies of her with dwarves and what-not when the world gave a shit.

There was a part of the *Times* on the seat next to him. New day, same liberal jism. The corruption trials in Philly were still going on. That whale of a prosecutor, Sharkey, and the FBI jitbag Epps, who were busting his stones for getting rid of a cop killer, must be happier than pigs in shit. A monster probe like that still going on was Thanksgiving, Christmas and Happy New Year all rolled into one. And with everybody's plates piled so high, it was less and less likely anybody was going to waste time bothering with a former gold shield from New York who had done the right thing.

A bunch of rich white kids in maroon blazers got on at the next stop. They were all talking street. "Don't be all up in my grille," said the one with a cigarette behind his ear.

"Give a brother some slide," answered one of his private school posse.

"Much love, much love," tried another.

An elderly couple came in from the next car, looking for a place to sit. The man had a hooked nose.

The tough guy walked over. "You Christ killers, best not be up in here."

"True dat," said the second preppie.

"You are mistaken," said the man.

"Going to bust a cap in your kosher ass!"

The woman crossed herself from right to left. "*Thoxa si o theos*," she said.

Lucas Rook leaned forward. "You're disturbing me reading my paper," he said loudly.

"I'm not afraid," the old man said.

"Then you'll be disturbing me too," Rook told him.

The white kids moved closer. The Greeks got off at the next stop. The prepsters high-fived each other as if they had done something.

The car got crowded. Lucas watched people getting on. Young execs talking on cell phones, some dotheads, a bum wearing one shoe. Two transit cops and a junkie in a mismatched suit. The subway was its own world, just the way each block above ground was. Rook got off and went to Winder's place.

Getting in the building was never a problem. He pressed the buttons on different floors until he was buzzed in. Somebody was always expecting Con Ed, a prescription delivery, or their girlfriend. They could be letting in the Boston Strangler, but that still didn't matter. Pizza Face had a deadbolt and a police lock, but like anybody worth a shit, Lucas had a pic-eze set.

The place was a mess. A pile of dirty laundry in one corner. The closet was jammed with crap. Books and a box of cereal on the couch. To the left was the kitchenette. Grease all over the stove and walls. One other room. The bed wasn't made, a small desk with one drawer missing. The other drawer was filled with more crap except for an address book. An incense burner on the night table. An unopened three pack of rubbers inside and a six-inch hunting knife. Maybe that made sense in New York. Or maybe it said something else, like a military haircut and no service-related material in the apartment.

Lucas tried the speed dial on the phone. He got a girl named Tina. Another pass at the kitchenette found a cold Coors that needed testing. He sat down and did that as he looked through the address book. A couple of the girls' names had stars next to them.

Steven Winder might be a jerk, but he didn't fit the profile. Rook stopped at his office before he paid the next employee a visit.

They had put a card swipe in at 166 Fifth Avenue and an intercom for customers or deliveries who came in after five. The little pirate who delivered the doll parts was coming out as Rook came in. "Where's your partner?" Lucas asked. Never lose an opportunity to show that you're the boss. He picked up a little plastic eye left behind from the delivery and went up to his office.

Rook's mail was sticking out of the slot. A cute hello card from Jeanie Oren, "Hoping to Z-Z-Z you soon," a cat dreaming of a bowl of milk. Another bill from Warren Phelps and an offer of free teeth whitener.

Lucas checked his message machine. An inquiry from possible new business if he was also licensed in New Jersey. If the price was right and the job wasn't shit, he could always work under Belasco's license. Another call from Sirlin.

The desk calendar had nothing for the rest of the week,

which was not a good thing. Monday he had the appointment to get another opinion on his leg. He wrote himself a note to cancel that. Tuesday he was supposed to get over to the range and make sure he could still hit paper, have them look at his Glock .40 that wasn't feeding right. And get over to see Tuze, see how he was doing with Big Jim gone. Grace had asked that he work a couple of fashion shoots with her and that was looking better and better, even if it meant putting up with that douche bag, Lawrence.

There were a couple of hard-boiled eggs and a bottle of seltzer in his fridge. What was he thinking? By the time his body got used to no carbs, he could be locked up for throwing somebody through a window. Praise Jesus for the pack of peanut butter crackers in the bottom of his desk drawer.

The looney next door was into his whooping noises, which meant it was time to leave and swing by the Stroll. Keep his info sources alive for when it meant something important and bill it to the file since Mark Breene had a prostie bust.

Big Leon was ordering two Sabrettes from Georgie boy's hot dog stand when Rook came up.

"You George's brother?" Lucas asked the vendor. "He told me you'd be here."

"I'm George's cousin. You still got to pay full price."

Big Leon adjusted the straps on his sundress. "You don't have to, sugarpie, the way you eatin' me up with your eyes."

The new Crystal Lee and Ms. Amy herself got out of a cab. They were both wearing black leather skirts and tops, except Crystal Lee was showing more flesh than anything else. "Well, don't you look just fine, Mr. Rook. You come by here for a dinner date?"

"I left my tux at home, Ms. Amy. Just came by to pay my respects."

"This is Mr. Sid's friend, Crystal Lee. Now go have yourself something cool to drink and read some magazines."

The whore did a little curtsy and then went up the street. The hot dog vendor gave Amy a Diet Sprite without her asking.

"Bought up a brownstone down the block," she said. "Let the girls put their feet up, read a magazine, douche their precious pussies and what-not. A regular dormitory." She gave George's cousin a hard look. He handed a soda to Rook.

They walked up the block. "Had to turn to real estate since that lazy, self-aggrandizing, stupid, no-good prick mother from Merrill Lynch fucked up my portfolio. Did I say half-a-fag?"

Lucas took a sip of his Coke. "I don't believe you did."

"My memory's not what it used to be," said Ms. Amy, "since I subluxed C-2, giving one too many vigorous blowjobs. You see I'm strictly management now."

"I missed your retirement party."

"Just trading chafing for agro. You got time for a bite, I'm eating seven meals a day. Seven days, seven meals, it's the calendar balance diet."

"Then I'd have to eat and run, Amy."

She finished her soda and handed Rook the bottle. "Used to be my job."

Shavon started over. "I got to pee, Ms. Amy. Again." Amy waved her off.

Rook showed her a photocopy of Mark Breene's driver's license and a twenty dollar bill.

"One of them looks like President Jefferson. The other like that doctor on television got the brain tumor. Never seen him around. I'll pass it along to my girls." She looked at her watch. "Time for my meal. Today's Wednesday. Lots of wheat. Toodles," she said. "223 around the corner. Top floor, if you ever need to put your feet up, use the can, whatever." Ms. Amy started down the block then turned around. "Bambi Cabresa, poor dear. Somebody put one in his head. Toodles."

Lucas walked back to George's brother, cousin, whatever and had one with sauerkraut and cooked onions. He drank a cream soda as he walked over a block to grab a taxi.

When he got back to the St. Claire, Leo was just coming in to start his shift downstairs. He had a goose egg on his forehead, but wouldn't talk about it. The big shot from NYU who always smelled like reefer got on the elevator. Last time Lucas saw him, he was being all cuddly with one of the students who looked young enough to be his kid. He tried small talk on the elevator, but Rook gave him nothing back.

His message machine was flashing as Lucas came into his dark apartment. The lights overhead were out and he had never replaced them. One of the standing lamps was on. It had been a long day and his leg was bothering him. Rook lay down on the sofa and listened to his calls. One was from Wingy Rosenzwieg telling him that Shirl Freleng took a pinch, and one was from Shirl herself. "It's about that thing you talked to me about," which meant the cigarettes without the stamps. She'd need Warren Phelps, Esq. for that. Lucas would call the lawyer first to see if he could earn some rhythm on his own bill for the referral.

Lucas Rook went out and around the corner for a mushroom and onion pizza made by Syrians hoping that they looked like Greeks wh were pretending to be Italian. He ate the pie in front of the tube and three beers later put his .45 on the night table and closed his eyes.

Ninety miles away in the City of Brotherly Love, Philadelphia Homicide Detective Jimmy Salerno lay in bed stone awake while the wife slept soundly, her breathing calm and rhythmic as the old music on their radio, Vic Damone, Sarah Vaughn. Maybe it was the no caffeine or his electrical system was misfiring from his heart.

Four-forty. He would hear the newspaper hit the driveway in another twenty-five minutes. Jimmy turned back to Carmela and waited for the time to pass. Then he walked down to the sidewalk, a cop's dream, nobody out and nobody coming. He read the local news first. Which pol was getting endorsed. Which one getting pinched. A bad wreck up on The Ridge. The sports: whining multi-millionaires, all roided-up. He met Bobby Shantz once at the FOP. About five foot six, maybe a hundred and forty pounds. A real ballplayer. In '52 he went 24-7. Finished thirty games. Shantzie said you found out you were going that day if the Skipper left the ball in your shoe.

Breakfast blew. Egg Beaters, decaf tea. Salerno went downstairs to ride the stationary bike as the doctor had ordered. The television was always the same, them trying to turn the news into some pirate movie. He pedaled for twenty minutes then went back upstairs.

Salerno put the coffee on for her and went out to hit some

balls. Jimmy and his partner used to go in and hit a couple of buckets after the graveyard shift. Now Chick's dead, some whacko kills him with a clothes iron. How's that for TV news?

He hit half a bucket. The seagull out on the berm still sitting there waiting to get conked, taunting and asking for a round in his little white head.

A blue and white pulled up. "You want to warm up before you shank a couple of shots?" the sector man asked.

"I want to warm my hands, Dickie Boy, I put 'em in your ex's blouse," Jimmy told him.

"Guy is teeing off at Torresdale. Girl pulls out of the lot at Holy Family College. The shot goes right through her windshield, girl runs into a tree, finito. I grab up the mope in the clubhouse. He's crying like a baby. 'What did I do? What did I do?' He's saying over and over. I says you're rotating your top hand."

Salerno was cold faced.

The sector man turned and went back to his cruiser. "You heard it before, right and you made me tell the whole story, Salerno. You're a pisser. A real pisser. Now don't be staying out in the rain. You'll melt or whatever."

"Like dogshit on the pavement," Salerno said. He launched another shot at the seagull.

Mike Kessler came up, looking skinny as a rail. He broke a piece of cigar off and put it in his pipe. "How ya doin'?" he said, dropping the ball towards the driving tee and hitting it deep and straight.

"I don't know how you do that."

"It sends itself," Mike told him.

"All that zen shit don't mean nothing to me," Jimmy said.

"That's right," Kessler said. He went to roll down the awning as the storm came up.

Salerno packed up as the rain slanted. He left a fiver as he always did and drove over to the precinct.

Big Joe Garrett was working the front desk. "Hi-dee-ho," he

said.

"Back at you, Desk. The boss upstairs?"

Garrett turned his attention back to the yellow pages. "Out and gone, detective. Did his do at roll call and went on out. You going out, bring me something back."

"Bring you back Halle Berry if I'm going out, Sgt. Garrett. Except I'm not."

"Cream-filled donut just as good," Joe said, rubbing the top of his big square head.

Detective Salerno went up to the squad. Somebody had forgotten he was back and put their raincoat on his desk. Somebody is out, you don't sit anybody at their desk, and no way it becomes a dump for coats, boxes of supplies and coffee cups. Somebody's back, light duty or not, you don't use his space for a coat rack.

Radicchio came over and took it off. "No offense, Jimmy," he said.

The firedoor opened and closed as Inspector Joe Zinn arrived in his running clothes: gray sweat suit, black knit hat. The Philly PD had given out sweats with the insignia on the chest, but that meant somebody was going to be asking you to get a cat down out of a tree or throw a rock at you.

Salerno waited until Inspector Joe Zinn was comfortably settled on his foam donut before he knocked and went in.

"How was your run, boss?" Salerno asked.

"Good, detective. How you handling things?"

"Nothing I like better, boss, than eating cardboard, drinking Diet Fresca and riding my desk to nowheres."

"I'm trying to be fair here, detective." Zinn adjusted his cushion. "Detective Moore thinks he's being given the short end."

"Hawkey still wants to be the Lone Ranger?"

"I don't want a grievance to deal with. From either of you. You two should talk things out. Clear the air," said the inspector.

Salerno remembered his blood pressure and took a deep breath. "He wants to grieve, it is up to him. Anyways, it's Downtown administrative horseshit that I'm on light duty, which is why I'm going to see the city's so-called doc again."

"Talk to me after you talk to Hawkey," Zinn told him.

Detective Salerno went back through the squad. His stomach was in knots. In a pig's eye he'd talk to Moore. He rode out to Wal-Mart and walked the aisles for a while.

Inspector Zinn was writing up a memo of the meeting he'd just had with Jimmy when the desk sergeant called. "We got a juicy one here, boss. Officer Macrel just took a call. Lady's dog retrieved a human head."

"This go to the XO?"

"Of course, Inspector," said Joe Garrett. "But I thought I'd give you a heads up."

Zinn let the joke go and called over to his executive officer. On top of the case itself was going to be the personnel problems he had just talked to Salerno about.

Captain Cisone knocked before coming in. "Looks like we got a red ball, boss," he said. "I just talked to the officer on the scene. Dog brings a head in and drops it on the kitchen floor is going to get a lot of people's attention." He rolled his shoulders like from his fighting days.

"Hawkey and Lefko are up, boss."

"Right, Guido, but Jimmy Salerno still thinks he should be in the catching order notwithstanding his light duty. Let's get our people together and make sure this gets off on the right foot."

"I'll take care of it," said Captain Cisone.

Detective Moore arrived first. He was wearing his Western clothes: boots, a string tie, and a hand-tooled belt with a turquoise buckle. Gene Lefko was a step behind. He did the little dance steps before he sat down.

Lieutenant Esposito came to the door. Hawkey got up and let her in.

"Chivalry's not dead yet," she said.

Moore tipped his imaginary Stetson. "All here and accounted

for," he said.

Jimmy Salerno came in.

Captain Cisone rolled his shoulders and started the meeting. "The Spence lady from Essex Avenue called in. The one calls that dog of hers that's always jumping in car windows, 'her little boy.' She says, 'Timmy,' that's the dog's name, 'My little boy,' he brings this thing in the house which he knows not to do, that's from a department store window or some museum or whatever. Officer Mackrel says that when he tells her what the dog brought in, that she gets this sick look on her face and throws up right there in the living room."

"Timmy clean it up?" Lefko asked. "Dogs do that."

"Thank you, detective," said Lieutenant Esposito. "I appreciate the image."

Joe Zinn got up. "I don't want the overtime getting out of hand," Inspector Zinn said. "And I want this quiet. We'll have every rag magazine and television station to deal with. Let's get the scene secured and see where the rest of the vic is.

"Anybody asks why we're digging up the yard," Cisone said, "Somebody's stealing utilities."

"Me and Lefko are up on this John Doe melonhead," said Hawkey.

"Or Jane," said Esposito. "From what I got the vic's head's in pretty bad shape, so…"

"Whatever," said Detective Moore.

"Nobody's running this case, but me," said Captain Cisone. "Hawkey, you and your partner get out to the scne."

Moore got the camera and Lefko got two pairs of gloves.

"This is fucked up," Hawkey said. "It is not right." He adjusted the silver buckle on his belt. "No way I'm not lead on this case. Meanwhile, let's see Poochie don't trash the scene."

"Who's Poochie?" Gene asked.

Detective Moore pulled the keys for an unmarked off the board. "Tell you later. Now let's see what the maggot farm's all about."

When the two detectives got to the scene, Officer Mackrel was parked in front of the Spence house. He had a piece of pizza in one hand, a bottle of Diet Coke in the other. There was a cooler on the seat next to him. "You want a piece of pepperoni?" he asked.

"You got an iron stomach, officer," said Hawkey. "I'm proud of you. Coke and a slice and you got some poor bastard's head on the seat."

Mackrel turned green. "Jesus, no there ain't…I mean…" He opened the cooler to show another soda and melting ice. "Christ, you guys are sick."

"The head remind you of anybody you know?" Hawkey asked. "Close relative or whatnot? Maybe some politician or criminal lawyer of note."

"I don't know, detective. It's all a mess and all. Can I roll?"

Hawkey Moore nodded.

"Appreciate it," Mackrel said. "Got to take my daughter to confirmation practice." He backed out of the driveway as the two detectives walked up to the house.

The crime scene investigator pulled up. He was a round man carrying his cigarette in a pair of tweezers.

"Make yourself at home here, Poochie," Hawkey said.

"Don't be calling me that, Moore. Told you that before." He took a drag from the smoke in the tweezers like it was a gold cigarette holder and he was the king of the world. "Who's babysitting you? You two are contaminating my scene while I am up to my ass in sepsis."

"Sepsis?" said Lefko, dancing a few steps back.

Crime Scene's formless face hinted at a smile. "Not that kind of sepsis, jerkwad. When I say sepsis, I'm talking 'Secure, Examine, Photograph, Sketch, Interview, and Summarize.' Keeps my eye on the ball, and the protocol in my head."

"I'll give you a *heads* up, when I can," said Moore.

"Let's *head* off any problems, detectives," Crime Scene said. "Let me do my grid and collect my samples. Don't be tracking anything in or carrying it out."

"Why don't you take your *head* out of your ass?" Hawkey said. "You do your CSI shit, Poochie. We're going to do our detective thing."

Hawkey Moore and Lefko followed the crime scene investigator into the kitchen. The lime green room was immaculate. There was a photo of the dog on the refrigerator. Timmy wore a tuxedo and a top hat.

"Must be the wedding picture," said Hawkey.

Iris Spence came into the room. Her clothes were neat, but her face was rumpled. "Timmy, he brought something inside. He doesn't do that. He's a good boy. The officer said it was not from a mannequin." She paled and sat down.

Moore patted her on the hand. "Sit down, Mrs. Spence. Take some deep breaths. I'll get you a glass of water." He opened the fridge. "What have we here," he said. "Maggots, decomp and Timmy have taken their toll."

"I think I'll go upstairs," said Mrs. Spence.

"That specimen is part of my scene," said Poochie. "I log it and it goes to the ME."

"Make sure it don't jump up and lick you," said Moore.

Poochie gave him the finger. "Sit on this and rotate. You want a prelim note, don't hold your breath." He went back down the hall. "Meanwhile, I got work to do."

"What was that all about?" Gene asked, doing his little dance steps.

"We call him Poochie, his first day on the job, college degree and all, he gets to the scene, the smell is awful. Poochie is too amped to know anything. He goes in, this collie dog comes up to him, wagging his tail like he's the happiest doggie in the world.

Jumps up, starts licking Poochie's face. He goes in the kitchen, the old lady's been dead maybe a week. Her face is gone. Lassie had a tasty meal and now he's licking Poochie's face."

Hawkey Moore left Lefko at the scene. Things were just fine. Working with Gene, he could move things around however he wanted. He stopped at Gladfelter's for a pot roast platter on the arm and on the clock. A sad girl with dark eyes offered him a menu at the counter, but Hawkey waved her off and sat himself at a booth. The girl came over. "Can I help you, hon?" she asked.

"I bet you could," he told her. "But your platter du jour will do for now."

She looked at him and fidgeted with her name tag.

"The pot roast, dear," he said. "Today is Tuesday."

"Chicken rice is the soup du jour, I know that," the waitress answered.

Detective Salerno arrived at the Spence place as Poochie was getting ready to roll. A little chit-chat about what a douche bag Moore was got him the privilege of delivering the severed head to the medical examiner. It saved the crime scene investigator a trip, and he was happy to give it to Hawkey where the sun didn't shine.

Jimmy Salerno had worked the medical examiner before, him and Chick Misher coming up on the ME parked in the police garage. Dr. Nessel had the seat of his big Caddy up as high as it could go and blocks on the pedals so he could drive his big boat from his ice boxes of stiffs to his fancy house outside the city limits. The Caddy had enough smoke to be the Chicago fire, and

Sam was lighting one cigarette after the next with one burning in the ashtray and just begging to go spill his guts.

Unfortunately, all he had to cop to was that he was moving the bodies around to pad his numbers. White collar bullshit stuff. Bullshit when Chick and him were looking at him for strangling little Heather Raimondo.

Even with that, it turns out to be the accountants dueling with their pencil points. Seems Doc Nessel had been skimping on his lunch breaks for years, so the city has to back off so they don't get the Department of Labor doing an audit for unpaid leave of all their administrative employees. And the little fuck just sits around swinging his little legs while somebody else does the dirty work until everything's straightened out.

Salerno took one of the little blue pills which was supposed to keep him from blowing a gasket as he rolled up on the ME's free-standing building with the three overhead doors. The same douche-bag intake man called him "officer" and offered up a red plastic token for his gun and a blue one for the cooler.

Jimmy ignored him and the lady with the beehive hairdo, who called twice for Salerno to come back and sign in. Sam Nessel was in exam room three, sitting on the stainless exam table and smoking a cigarette. He looked up as the airlock popped and the door opened.

"Detective Salerno, isn't it? You look absolutely svelte. Smart thing to do, you don't wind up on one of these tables."

"Dr. Nessel, isn't it?" Jimmy said. "You look absolutely lazy."

The ME flicked his ashes down the drain on the table. "Still the charmer. What can I do for you, detective? You bring me a picnic lunch in the department cooler?"

"Stop giving me shit, Sam."

Nessel snubbed out his smoke. "Sorry to hear about your partner. He was a good cop."

"I was never a patient man," Jimmy said. "But since my heart thing I'm a kinder and more gentle man, so's I don't blow a gasket.

I got the vic's melon on a hot case, unless you're not up to it."

The medical examiner slid off the table and opened up the cooler. "Now we're talking," he said.

"You'll call *me* first, Sam." Salerno gave the ME a hard look. "You'll do that."

"That I will, Detective Salerno. That I will."

Jimmy went back outside and the medical examiner got to work. His sharps were in the cold room like pieces of a broken mirror. The tape was running. The machines humming in the background for the living and the dead.

"Lord help my soul," he said. Poe's last words before he left this earth. Then he made his first cuts and pulled the head flap down across the dead face. A back flap made by his cuts behind the ear. He pulled that backwards to the neck. A handy dandy tool, the Stryker saw with its vacuum shroud for the aerosol of flesh and blood and little shards of bone. There was a sucking sound when he lifted up the top half of the skull. The cerebellum, the cerebrum, the dura before the connections to the spinal cord were cut.

Sam Nessel removed the brain and sliced it like he was making art. He put some pieces underneath a paper towel before he hung the remaining section by a piece of string and took pictures of it all.

The victim's head had been severed from its neck by hacking wounds cut clear through the muscles and the bone. The ME looked at the clock. The room was cold. His stomach rumbled, but there was the cleaning up to do. Formic acid as prophylaxis for the Creutzfeld-Jacob, mad cow disease. Mad men.

Detective Salerno drove over to Bill Higgins' place.

Sal Radicchio was poking at his stew. He slid over from Chick's spot near the window when Jimmy came in. "Needs salt or whatever," Sal said.

Another new waitress came over. She had a bracelet tattooed around her wrist.

"Our specials today are flounder florentine, Cajun meatloaf and homemade apple pie."

Salerno ordered eggs and a ginger ale. Radicchio pointed to his glass for another Dewars and water. "I wonder whether that bracelet jingles she gives a hand-job, Jimmy." He speared a piece of meat. "I got to ask her when she comes back."

"Big Bill hires them. His kid's wife chases 'em out, Sal. Except the girlie he gets the new headlights. She gets them double-D's and then she's off on her own."

Bill Higgins came in.

"Right on cue, Bill," Jimmy told him. "I was just saying 'double-D's' and you walk in."

"Coming from my accountant. Everything's ready to roll."

"Same accountant told you you could depreciate that girl's new hooters."

Higgins leaned in. "This is for real. That was nothing. My CPA, the credit union, they all think it's a go. How's the stew, Sal?"

"Meat's a little tough, Bill."

"That's an evil lie, Detective Radicchio, and you know that."

The drinks came over. "Hello, Mr. Higgins," the waitress said.

"Hello to you, Molly Kiley. No charge for my friends' two drinks here."

Salerno toasted with his soda. "Don't look like a 'Kiley' to me, Bill," after she had walked away.

"She married a Kiley. Maiden name's Celluci. Her dad was in Traffic," Higgins said.

"Does that bracelet on Molly Celluci's wrist give you a jingle when she's whacking you off?" Sal asked.

"It does not," Bill Higgins said. "She does, however, sing Tony Bennett when she licks my balls."

"I'll tip her extra," Radicchio said as he got up to leave.

Detective Salerno moved to the other side of the booth and

slid in towards the window where Chick used to sit, watching the things he used to watch. It was a hard thing not to get swirled in and sucked down the toilet. He was even reading his old murder books when he pedaled on his stationary bike. But all the slime was the good times too, and he was glad to be working a case again.

Jimmy looked at the menu. He'd order fish, his partner would've had something to say, fish eaters, muff divers, carpet munchers, whatever.

The medical examiner came into Higgins' place, smoking like a chimney and wearing a trench coat to hide the fact that he was less than five feet tall and walked crooked. Salerno wanted to just sit there, but the cop in his head clicked on.

"Doctor," he said. "Why don't you sit yourself down?"

"Figured you might be here, detective. I wanted you to have my preliminary report as soon as I was done." He took a double hit of menthol.

"Boycotted the place for a while until they put our sign back up." Jimmy pointed to it. "What are you drinking, Sam?"

Molly came over to tell the ME that where they were sitting was the no-smoking section. Nessel snubbed out his smoke and ordered a Johnny Walker on the rocks.

"Glad you could roll by, Sam," Salerno told him. The little guy loved cop talk.

Nessel took another cigarette from his shirt pocket and tapped it on the back of his watch crystal. All the masculine moves he could accumulate. "Your perp was a very angry man, detective."

Salerno sipped his ginger ale. "They usually are, they take off somebody's head."

The scotch came. "Hacked it off. No sawing motion at all. He hacked through the trachea, esophagus, the carotid artery. All the muscles, the scalene, splenius, stenucleidomastoid. Sometimes an autopsy raises as many questions as it gives answers. But not here. Killer wasn't trying to hide a neck wound of some particular type. And we don't have a trophy taken or somebody trying to dispose of the parts. They could have used Satriale's for that."

"What's that, Sam?"

The medical examiner realized he had made a mistake. Cops don't like to watch cop TV. "It's from *The Sopranos*. The missus watches it." He took a sip of his scotch. "It's like that case two, maybe three years ago. Muldoon and Radicchio had it. The lawyer chops off his secretary's head and puts it in the filing cabinet."

Salerno picked up his menu.

"Rigor shows up in the small muscles first, so we're alright we only have a head," Nessel said. "There was no rigor mortis at all, which tells me time of death's at least 36 hours. It usually disappears completely in that time period or up to a week. I have taken your variables into consideration, acceleration from heat, a struggle before death, or even if the DOA was running a temperature."

Jimmy nodded. Let the medical examiner feel all big and competent.

"The livor," the ME went on, "is consistent with a violent death. We've got Tardeau's spots. They're little hemorrhage spots caused by broken capillaries. These were on the neck, but not in the whites of the eyes, which would suggest your DOA was choked before your killer went to work. The wound hacked all the way through the arteries, the visceral column, the muscles, SCM, and the vertebrae." He exhaled as he went on. "We had exophthalmus, bulging eyes, hair slippage and marbling along the blood vessels. No parmesan cheese, fly eggs. The maggots had pupated…"

"Swell, doc. I was about to order dinner."

"Sorry, detective. So what I'm saying, preliminarily is, we have an adult, murdered by decapitation, approximately six days ago."

"You saidd adult, Sam. Any reason you're not giving me the sex?"

Nessel nodded and lit another cigarette. "Can't from the autopsy. Marilyn Monroe's brain weighed more than your average man's and the hair length doesn't tell us anything here. The atlas was pretty well smashed, so an image analysis of the vertebrae won't work. Best thing is the teeth. Odontology will tell. Better if you find me a tibia or a kneecap." He started to laugh. "Best of all, you find me a twat."

Detective Salerno put his menu back down. "I guess we're done here, Sam," he said.

The medical examiner swung his dwarfed legs out of the booth. "I recommend a forensic entomologist. If you don't have one, I can be of some help."

"I'll let you know, Doc. Good work," Salerno said.

The ME pointed to the sign on his way out. "It's us against them," he said. "Right, Jimmy?"

"Right," Detective Salerno told him.

Mary Zinn made ziti and meatballs as good as if she were Italian. She was adding a little raw egg to the chopped beef and pork when the inspector came downstairs. He was wearing a white shirt and had a furrow between his eyes, which meant there was something bad going on.

"I thought I heard the phone ring, Joe," she said. "The supermarket call you back?"

"It was work." He came over and stood by his wife while she began forming the meatballs. "Steak tartar or whatever they call it. They give you a piece the size of your little finger, they charge you eight dollars."

The oil was starting to bubble. The inspector went over and sat at the kitchen table, which was still as white as the day they bought it, but worn from where Mary pushed the chairs in when she did the floor.

He got back up and looked into the pasta pot.

"We going to Mary Elizabeth's, Joe, or do you want me to call over? I could take a casserole tomorrow."

"We're going. I want to see my grandson." The inspector looked at his watch. "The good with the very bad," he said to himself.

Mary Elizabeth was following little Tom down their short hallway when the front door rang. "It's Mee-mom and Pop-pop," she said.

Joe Zinn put down his bag of groceries and picked up the two year old.

"It's Pop-Pop," said Mrs. Zinn. Mary Elizabeth gave them both a kiss. "Let me take him, he weighs a ton."

Little Tom walked back down the hall, rocking back and forth like Charlie Chaplin to keep his balance.

"Big Tom's lying down," Mary Elizabeth said.

Mrs. Zinn went into the kitchen to keep the ziti and the meatballs warm and to avoid the conversation.

"His neck or the other thing, Mary Elizabeth?"

His daughter picked up the grocery bag. "He's tired, Daddy."

Joe Zinn straightened his tie. "I'll talk to him," he said.

"Don't…"

"His neck or them Percs, neither one shouldn't keep him from looking at his wife and son. He's not taking Oxys, is he?"

"No, Daddy, just what the doctor gives him when it's bad."

Mary Elizabeth had set the table in their little dining room. She moved the highchair at the table so it didn't show so much that her husband wasn't there. Then she brought in the salad.

The inspector led a quick grace and broke off a piece of bread.

"How's work?" Mrs. Zinn asked.

"Good," she said. "Dr. Zarro said I could have some more hours if I wanted."

"Not too many, Mary Elizabeth. A child needs to be raised by his mother."

"Big Tom helps out," she said, and then to change the subject, "I ran into Mary Pica at the market, she's going to have twins. Then the same day her mother comes into Dr. Zarro's for her diabetes. I haven't seen them two in a year, and there they both are."

Tom Schmaulke came out of the bedroom when he heard the voices.

"A man should eat dinner with his family," Joe Zinn said.

Mrs. Zinn gave him a look.

Big Tom moved the high chair so there was room for him to sit. Then he leaned over and kissed Mrs. Zinn. "Hi, Mom," he said. "Inspector," he nodded as he sat down. "Sorry I'm late."

Joe Zinn started to say something, but stopped. Mrs. Zinn and her daughter went into the kitchen to get the pasta and the homemade meatballs.

"You straight, Tom?" the inspector said.

"I'm doing good."

The little one threw his spoon, and Joe Zinn leaned over and picked it up. "Get straight or get out," he said.

Dinner came and there was no more talk of it. When they were done, Big Tom went in to start the dishes. "Your father has to go in to work," Mrs. Zinn said. "I'll come by on Tuesday."

"Tuesday's good, Mom." Mary Elizabeth went over to her father, who was putting on his coat. "He's trying, Daddy, he really is."

"Trying's never good enough," Joe Zinn said. "And certainly not when you've got responsibilities."

"You tell me if he's sleeping when you get there Tuesday, Mare," the inspector said. "This time of day a man shouldn't be sleeping unless he's pulling shift-work."

"He's hurt, Joe. Don't be so hard on him."

"I talked to him, Mare. He's got a problem with them Percocets. Meanwhile, he's driving, watching the boy, whatever."

Mrs. Zinn crossed herself.

"You're coming by Tuesday, Mary. I'm coming over there Wednesday. He's still not right, he's getting into a program or he's getting out."

Mrs. Zinn knew the talking was over.

When they got back home, Joe came inside, but only for a

minute. "Work," he said. "I've got to go in," he said.

"You've got gravy on your shirt. It must have been the baby."
He looked.

"It's just a dot. I'll get you another one and soak it out."

Inspector Zinn stood in his warm kitchen, thinking about his family and the world of blood he was going into. He kissed his wife on the cheek as she gave him the clean shirt. "Don't wait up," he said and left for the precinct house.

Inspector Zinn was looking at the week's numbers when Detective Salerno knocked on his office door.

"The decap job's running, boss. Nessel gave me his prelim. Time of death is hard to tell. He's saying we should get a look at the bugs and somebody to check the DOA's choppers to see whether our vic is a male or a female. And our bad guy is a very angry citizen."

"You working with Hawkey on this?" the inspector asked.

"Sure, boss, sure."

"I hope so, Jimmy," said Joe Zinn. "I'll see you in an hour."

The inspector had moved their meeting to the conference room on the second floor to accommodate them all. Executive Officer Cisone, Salerno, and Hawkey Moore, Lefko, Vanessa Esposito and Dr. Winokur, who had the bad news for them.

Dr. Albert Winokur had an enormous neck and was as bald as a cue ball, which made him look more like a professional wrestler than a forensic reconstructionist with a PhD in anthropology.

"People, some of you have worked with Dr. Winokur, some of you have not," Inspector Zinn said. "Listen to what he has to say. Save your questions for the end. And nothing leaves the room."

Winokur got up and loosened his tie. "We've been doing decent facial reconstruction for a couple of hundred years. Not me, but sometimes it feels like it. Actually, Kant and Schiller's faces were constructed by Welcker in 1883."

"Judge Schiller?" somebody called from the back.

"No, I don't think so," said the reconstructionist. "And Phillip II of Macedonia's face was reconstructed. Not to mention Joan Rivers."

A chorus of chuckles.

"All of you here have worked with sketch artists and the wireframe and clay reconstruction. Pretty good volumetric approach. But what we have now is state of the art. Stay with me here. Lights, please."

Esposito got up and hit the switch. Somebody whistled.

Dr. Winokur started the slide show. What appeared on the screen was a series of cubes.

"What we have here is called volume morphing. Actually, volume deformation, which defines a transformation of one geometric volume into another. Given a starting volume and a finishing volume, we can interpolate using a control database. Like CATscans in a way, or ultrasounds that your physician might use. What we have here is a skull of an average-size man. Now follow me here." Winokur ran through a number of slides and a face began to appear. "You see, what we have here is John Wayne."

"That's not right," Hawkey said, "to disrespect the Duke that way."

"I don't get it," Lefko said. "John Wayne's the DOA., that head or whatever?"

"Just hold on, people," Joe Zinn told him.

Then Dr. Winokur put in a slide of the skull the dog had brought in. "Va, Vi, Vz, Vn, Vb," he said as he clicked through a series of slides, each one producing a more identifiable visible. "Showtime," he announced as the last slide came up. A middle-aged woman with a calming face and smiling eyes.

"It's a woman," said Lieutenant Esposito.

"Jesus Christ," said Jimmy Salerno. "The lady from television. Kids used to watch her."

The anthropologist turned on the lights and packed up his case. "You find the rest of her, give me a call," he said.

Inspector Zinn stood up and waited until Winokur left the room. "We got ourselves a celebrity. Janice Shay, *The Little Red School House.* Which means we got ourselves a red ball with hair all over it. We're going to have the press, the Feds, and everybody else. You want OT, you got it. You want to be famous, find yourself another line of work."

"Me and Gene running this one, boss," said Hawkey Moore.

"In a pig's eye," Salerno told him.

"Not now, detectives," Zinn told him. "Right now I'm going to talk to Captain Cisone and our information officer. Meanwhile, there'll be plenty for everybody."

Moore almost bumped Salerno on the way out, but at the last minute steered clear. Heart attack or not, Jimmy would have called him out or thrown down right there, and either way would have put them both in the shit soup.

Hawkey and Lefko went down to the coffee room for things to cool down while Jimmy shuffled papers at his desk. "I'm passing my physical next week, I'm back to regular duty, and I'm the best there is, you all know that," he said.

Captain Cisone walked over to him. "We're running a team, Salerno," Zinn said. "Rivalry in the squad, it's never good."

Salerno walked back and forth. "No way that should mean I'm not working the case."

"The case is up on the board, and you're on light duty, Jimmy," Cisone said.

"So maybe we'll talk about your meeting with the medical examiner, Detective Salerno. Meanwhile, nobody's jumping anything. And I'm still the XO. And you're still on light duty, so I expect you to stay within those parameters."

Salerno left without another word.

Cisone rolled his neck and went in to see Inspector Zinn.

"Boss, I just got a rush prelim on the tape the vic's head was wrapped in. Run-of-the-mill, everyday you'd find in any shipping room or whatever, any office, the lab tells me." He looked at his notes. "Scotch 3850, 6 BD, 2 inches wide. It's clear, 3.1 millimeter thickness. 'Super strength' they call it, but it's an over-the-counter thing. The way the tape is cut is from one of them dispenser guns. The brochure I looked at says 'easily seals cartons with one hand.' But that's not going to get us anywheres neither. Any retail or whole office supply carries it. This is going to be a dead end until we find what we're looking for," the executive officer said. "What I don't like is there's no doubt we're going to have the Eyes all over us like the cockroaches they are."

Joe Zinn nodded. "The Feds will be around. I expect that and more. The newspapers will do their worst. Maybe we can buy some time so this case doesn't turn into a circus act. I'll have Lieutenant Esposito notify the next-of-kin and let them know to keep it quiet as long as possible so we can get our job done."

Lucas Rook had his first two cups of coffee of the day and took the subway to Brooklyn to scope out Mark Greene's situation. Brooklyn, home of the Dodgers, Duke Snider, Carl Furillo, Gil Hodges. Canarsie was for the Jews and the Italians. Now it was Tyronne and the Jamaicans. The 69th was over on Foster Avenue. There must be more OT in that precinct than they can handle with the drug trade and all the property crimes to support the customers.

East 101st Street wasn't bad, but the smell of weirdo got stronger. Living back where Mommy and Daddy did. The dishonorable discharge and then smacking Mommy around. Stealing from her estate. Mommy's not around to beat anymore, so I'll beat off on her.

Lucas took the clipboard from his plastic bag and put a pencil behind his ear. Greene lived on the top floor of the duplex. A woman with splotchy skin looked out of the front floor window. You're an owner, you don't live downstairs to hear all those footsteps overhead. Rook gestured a hello to her with his clipboard and then used his skeleton key for the side door to the upstairs.

The place was neat as a pin. All the drawers and cabinets were closed with labels on them. "Spoons, forks, knives." Who labels where they put their own stuff? The kitchen cabinets had dividers in them so that the Rice Krispies didn't touch the ketchup and so on. One of the cabinets had a padlock on it which took about a second to open. A cheap china set, two jelly jar glasses, one from *The Mickey Mouse Club* and one Roy Rogers.

There was no mess, no dust, no crumbs. The chair closest to the window was worn at the headrest. Maybe our weirdo spent his spare time looking at the world going by as he spanked his monkey.

The bedroom door had a lock on it to keep who out or who in. Lucas pic-ezed it open. Mark Breene's bedroom wasn't a necrophiliac's dream or Satan shit. Weirder than that. The wallpaper was all Dumbo with his flying ears. The bureau was Peter Pan, a Cinderella desk, and a four-poster Sleeping Beauty bed.

No bubblebath or Disney crap in the bathroom. Zoloft in the medicine chest and a Fleet's underneath the sink. Rook looked for Vaseline or Jergen's, a peenie puller's favorite, but there wasn't any. Maybe he liked to rub it dry or used one of the labeled jars of mayonnaise. A weirdo here for sure, and the type who'd be doing his nasty all over the dead bodies at the funeral home.

On the way to the subway, Rook called Sirlin back. The secretary said he wanted a meeting late that morning, but they settled on one o'clock so he could get a decent report. Breene looked like the one, but just as often as not, it was the chatty neighbor next door, which in this case meant he'd want to get up to the funeral parlor before meeting with Mr. Sirlin and see what kind of creep was coming off of Milton Bradley Foss.

Tony was back at the St. Claire's desk. "I'm sorry nobody was here, Mr. Rook. We had a mix-up, Leo and me."

"Your mix-up get him that egg on his head?"

The desk man looked away. "Don't know nothing about no egg on Leo's face, Mr. Rook. Me, I'm allergic. Anyways, sorry."

Rook rode up with the potted plant twins and the new actor wannabe who always wore shades so he would be noticed and kept waiter's hours. The phone was on its last ring as Lucas opened his door. He star-69'd it back and got Valerie Moon.

"I was hoping you could stop by," she said. "I'll make stuffed pork chops. You bring the beer."

"I'll bring the beer."

"And maybe you'll spend the night? I got tomorrow off," she said.

As easy as that, no deep introspection shit like Catherine Wren, but none of what Sid Rosen would call poetry either.

Lucas tried to get Warren Phelps on the phone to tell him Shirl was going to be calling, but as usual, he was told that his eminence was "in court," which just as likely as not meant he was at his tennis game or sitting in his office getting a manicure. Rook left the message that he was referring Shirl Freleng. They could work out the details later of what consideration he'd get on his own bill for the referral.

He worked two hours straight on his report, which he headed "Preliminary" as much to indicate that there was more to be done as to cover himself if he was off the mark. He put on the suit he had gotten from Sarkissian and a turtleneck to make himself look real "private-eye."

Lucas flagged a cab for the ride up to 42nd and 3rd. The hack was the Caribbean woman who had spent the whole time on her cell. She was back at it again, this time telling somebody named Riddick in ever-increasingly passionate terms that he was a no-good loser who could go fuck himself. When she dropped Rook off at Hugh Sirlin's building, she paused enough only to announce the fare and to add that it was nice to serve him again.

The dark-haired receptionist with the Canadian accent had been replaced by a stately woman with steel gray hair and a British accent. Somehow that was always supposed to mean class.

"I have an appointment with Hugh Sirlin," Lucas told her.

"Please be seated," she said. "Mr. Sirlin will be with you shortly."

There was nothing to read except the slick brochures that made it seem that it was half good to be put into a box and covered up with dirt. Fifteen minutes went by. Rook went to the Gent's room to make sure he looked *Spenser For Hire*. When he came back into the waiting area, MJ O'Reilly was waiting for him.

"So glad to see you," she said with the same combination of false commiseration and corporate formality that was the décor.

"Glad my primping was worth it."

They went back to Sirlin's office with the black wall. Hugh was in his golfing costume, which included a pair of plaid shorts he should not be wearing. He offered no apology for the informality of his dress, and the formality of his demeanor made it almost irrelevant.

The Canadian woman with the phony glasses, who had been the receptionist the last time, brought in two glasses of sparkling water. Ms. O'Reilly got the hint.

"Do stop by my office if you get a chance," she said. "It was nice seeing you again."

"You play golf, Mr. Rook?"

"Can't say that I do, Hugh."

"Just played a round this morning. Sorry I didn't have a chance to change, but traffic on the George Washington was terrible." He took a sip of Pelligrino. "You can do a lot of business on the golf course, and I must say there's something zen and aggressive at the same time about hitting that little ball. That mean anything to you?"

"I don't think you should ever try and hit something that's not going to try to hit you back. Besides, it reminds me of the white ball in the sing-alongs in the movie theaters."

Hugh Sirlin actually smiled. "You don't mind," he said. "I'm going to write that down and use it." He took another sip of sparkling water. "Well," he said. "It's gone quite well. You may submit your final bill."

"How's that?" Rook asked.

"Both matters have been resolved."

"I only gave you the car thief, Mr. Sirlin. You letting the other thing go?"

"Of course not."

Lucas finished his water. "Which means you do have closed-circuit surveillance in the mortuary."

"We keep an eye on things, Mr. Rook." He finished his Pellegrino. "And if you were to submit a report, whom would you say was doing those nasty things?"

Rook saw the look of the cat who had swallowed the canary. "I want to take a look at Milton Foss before I answer that, Mr. Sirlin."

"Exactly, Mr. Rook, Foss is no longer with the company. He submitted his resignation yesterday, which closes out the matter."

"Would you call that a 'seamless transition,' Hugh?"

Sirlin smiled again. "Indeed. Which brings me to our second item of business."

"And that is?"

"I like what I see, Mr. Rook. And I'd like to offer you another piece of business. A client of ours is the executor of the estate of a well-known person who met a very ugly end. Does that interest you?"

"It does," said Lucas. "It does."

24

You cast your bread upon the waters, the best you usually come up with is bird shit. But Rook knew that when a businessman like Hugh Sirlin referred you a client, it was going to mean something.

Philip First was waiting at the table overlooking his country club's eighth green. "You play?" he asked.

"Not really," Lucas said.

"Hugh gave me your line. 'I don't hit anything that's not going to try and hit me back.' Very clever, but certainly you'll have none of that in this matter."

Rook nodded. "Nice club you have here, Mr. First."

"I appreciate that. That's my wife coming up in the next four-some. The tall blonde woman."

"Very attractive."

"Here they all are very attractive. And everybody's blonde. You show grey, they drum you out." He called the waiter over. "A Cobb salad and a diet iced tea, Seth."

"Turkey club and a Heineken," said Lucas.

"Hugh speaks well of you, Mr. Rook," said Philip as he turned to watch his wife tee up.

She stroked the ball well and then looked over at her husband.

"Good job, honey," he said. Then he turned back to Rook. "A

Jewish girl's dream, to be blonde and play golf."

"And to marry a doctor?" Rook asked.

"That too. But a certified public accountant's not bad." He handed over his card. "First and Associates," he said. "You're 'Phil Feinstein' you're going to get who you got. You're 'Philip First,' you get clientele who'll never let you in the door." He adjusted the silverware in front of him. "I just have to remember not to try and 'jew them down' at the first meeting," the accountant said with a little smile.

Their drinks came and then he went on. "I am the executor of the last will and testament of a person of some means, a person of public stature." He sipped his drink. "There are some issues. If we have confidentiality, I'll be happy to elucidate. That's a complicated issue even with CPA's."

"Not with me it isn't, once I'm retained. Unless you have or are about to commit a felony."

The accountant handed Rook a retainer check. "Actually there is a crime involved. Somebody chopped the decedent's head off. I represent the estate of Janice Scheyman, also known as Janice Shay. 'Teacher Jan' from the TV show."

"I remember her," Rook said. "You were contacted by the NYPD?"

"Actually it happened in Philadelphia." The CPA looked at his file. "We were contacted by a Lieutenant Esposito from their police department."

"Vanessa. She's their information officer. How can I help you, Mr. First?"

"The 'corpus,' there's a joke there, Mr. Rook, the estate, is in New York and Hugh Sirlin recommends you highly. The Philadelphia police found her head and are working on finding Janice's killer." He folded his napkin. "I want you to find her body."

Rook finished his beer. "My fee is one hundred dollars an hour, plus expenses. No regular overhead or whatever."

Feinstein wrote himself a note. "That'll be fine, Mr. Rook.

Your fee and costs will be an estate expense, which means they will be subject to the scrutiny of the Surrogate Court."

"No problem," Rook said.

"I'm glad," said Feinstein as their lunches came. "I'm sure we'll work well together, but you'll forgive me if I eat and run so that I can join my lovely wife on the fairway."

The Merc that Rosen had picked up at the auction drove smooth, and the fuel gauge hardly moved on the way back to the city. Rook went to Sid's garage and then to the bank to deposit the check and to see if the hot chick was back from sick leave. There was another new teller at her window, sporting one of those concentration camp-chic shaved heads and a sleeve of tats showing through his shirt.

Lucas went up to Macy's to buy a half-dozen pairs of black cotton socks without elastic at the top. There was a sale on white dress shirts so he got three, a year's supply. He bought a quarter pound of almond bark and ate the candy on the way back to the office.

Going to Philly meant the Raimondo job, which was the last job he had worked down there. The killer was dead, and the US Attorney may or may not still be trying to squeeze his shoes for that. Inspector Joe Zinn was a stickler. Jimmy Salerno had gone down with a heart attack. The dwarf ME. Esposito, the good-looking information officer. And since then, all the indictments around city government. The rest of the world was getting more like New York every day.

First things first, he'd check with Attorney Warren G. Phelps on how to play working back in the City of Brotherly Love. Then give Jimmy Salerno a call. Maybe with some luck, he could use some extra scratch. And if Salerno was interested, it would save a lot of agro if he could bypass Inspector Zinn altogether.

While he was decent on the computer, Rook used it for

taking information out, not putting it in. He still kept his case information on index cards rubber-banded together.

Lucas took the cards he needed from the Raimondo stack and put them in a new pile labeled "Shay." Then he opened a Coors and went onto the Web.

Teacher Janice and *The Little Red School House* had begun on an Indiana public television network and then became a family favorite on PBS. With the show's success, commercial viability came and eventually, sponsors like Johnson and Johnson. The show ran for four years on NBC Sunday nights and for a year on CBS.

During the pinnacle of her career, Dr. Shay also appeared regularly on talk shows and had a "Kid's Spot" that carried thirty-second gems on radio, "reminding us about the vulnerability and magic of children." She appeared on David Letterman twice and got in a dispute with his producers over their proposed "The Top Ten Worst Things I Ever Told My Children" list. The *Times* reported that she put her hand on Dave's and told him, "When you say 'I'll give you something to cry about,' that is absolutely true."

While merchandising deals for lunch boxes, toothbrushes, and car seats were rejected out of hand, Janice Scheyman's lawyers and accountants negotiated her residuals so that she was able to live very comfortably in a little red school house in Rutland, Vermont. She ventured out only to speak at graduations, and then for no students over the age of twelve.

After some more web surfing at the very pleasant hourly rate, Rook found parts of four of her old shows. As the interior of *The Little Red School House* came into focus and the theme music came up, Teacher Jan took a step forward. The camera came in close and she said in the most calming voice, "Children are happy and successful when they feel safe."

Once each program, she also spoke just to the children: "It must be scary doing something for the first time." Later she would teach the parents the same lesson: "We must remind ourselves that all feelings are real."

When it was a particularly important lesson, Teacher Jan would ask the children to please leave the room. Then she would turn to the camera on her right. "This is Dr. Janice Shay. Please do remember that words are actions and that children believe the words we say. When we tell our children, 'Night night, Don't let the bed bugs bite,' we're warning them that something very scary is about to happen."

It was not good business when you're charging a hundred dollars per hour and you're talking to somebody who was charging you four times that. But Rook had put those two rounds into the murderer's head in Philly, and maybe the US Attorney was still trying to jam him for that. Therefore it was time to call Warren Phelps, Esquire at his exorbitant hourly rate.

"The law office of Warren G. Phelps, PC, a professional corporation," said the lilting voice on the other end.

"Lucas Rook returning his call."

"May I ask what this is regarding?"

"His dog keeps fouling my lawn," Lucas told her.

After a "One moment please," and thirty seconds of recorded music, Phelps got on. "I didn't know I had a dog, Lucas."

"I didn't know I was going to buy tickets for the Boston Pops."

Rook could hear the lawyer going through some papers. "Excuse me?" Phelps said.

"You're playing that elevator music at four hundred dollars per while I'm waiting."

"Four-fifty, but who's counting? In any case, I trust that you are not calling me about my health, which is excellent thanks to my young Brazilian wife. If you are calling about the Raimondo case, everything's still quiet on that front. Any particular thing to prompt your concern, or are you just updating?"

"Going back down to the City of Brotherly Love."

"Not to worry, Lucas."

"I appreciate that, Warren," said Lucas. "Just the way I do your recent middle initial."

"That's the kind of word that you pay the big dollars for. My marketing people believe it makes me sound royal somehow, as I deserve, Warren G. Harding and so on." Rook could hear the computer keys. "The 'professional corporation' is new. A recent Bar Association ruling says you can't say 'and associates' unless you have them, and the only associate I could ever brook in the practice of law is myself."

Lucas popped a beer. "Thanks for the update thing about your law practice, Warren. I hope you only charge me for half this call."

"If I do," Phelps said, "it'll be at twice the rate."

Rook did some more Internet research on Teacher Jan and took a look at Philip Feinstein-First. Nothing much of interest in Phil except that he was past president of the county CPA Society and of his country club. Lucas did pick up that the lovely Mrs. Feinstein was the former Phyllis Weinstein and in one local article about her work in the local leukemia drive was proudly referred to as Phyllis Weinstein-Feinstein.

Lucas heated some clams spaghetti and some garlic bread from around the corner. He should've known better, and it took a Zantac for his stomach to quiet down.

He turned on the TV and ran through the channels until he found one of those 1960s comedies, *A Guide to the Married Man*. Jayne Mansfield, her mouth looking all Marilyn Monroe-like and her tits like rocket ships and the day after that movie comes out she gets her head knocked off in a car wreck.

Rook went over his notes from the Raimondo case, Salerno, Inspector Zinn. Then he packed his bags for his trip to Philly. Everything that anybody would take on a business trip, including his carry-gun, ankle piece, plastic handcuffs, and enough pepper spray to stop a horse.

25

"We got a celebrity vic, we got to get working," said Detective Moore. "You know, Gene, like Lucille Ball and what's-her-name with them candies coming down the assembly line. before the Feds, whoever, interrupt all those hours we got coming to us."

"Wertz. Ethel Wertz, the other one was," said Lefko.

Hawkey turned left at the corner. "You don't seem like a happy boy, Gene. Thought you'd be dancing up a storm with the golden time we'll be pulling down." He cracked the window and pulled a Winston from his shirt pocket. "Anyways, it's Ethel Mertz. You're thinking about Vic Wertz, the guy hit the ball Willie Mays caught in the World Series." He adjusted his string tie. "Which is just what I'm talking about, the spade he catches the ball, helluva catch too, mind you, except that he almost falls down throwing it back in. Everybody remembers 'The Catch.' Nobody says nothing about Vic, who unloaded a ton on that bad boy."

Gene Lefko fidgeted, which is what he did when he wasn't standing up and he couldn't do his little dance steps. "I don't follow baseball that much, Hawkey."

"Right, right. '54 was before your time anyways. Mine too, really, except it was the Indians. You know, Rapid Robert Feller, whatever."

Lefko opened his window. "He just said it was a sin about Ali being at the All Star game, I read that."

Moore changed lanes without a signal. "Maybe it was, his being a draft dodger and all. He wasn't 'the greatest' anyways. Marciano would have kicked his pretty black boy ass."

"He wanted to be a baseball player, you know, Hawkey. A catcher in fact."

"You're shitting me, Gene."

"I kid you not. My family was from up in Brockton."

"No shit," said Hawkey.

"No shit," said Lefko.

They rolled up on the scene. Officer Barag was sitting in the cruiser, reading a racing magazine.

"Everything alright here, patrolman?" asked Moore.

"I'm holding down the fort now that Mackrel had to leave." He put his magazine down. "This Spence lady's driving me crazy. She must've been out here a half dozen times asking me about her frickin' dog, like I'm a frickin' vet or something."

"She got him dressed up in a tuxedo or what?" asked Lefko.

"You bustin' my balls, detective?" asked Barag.

"Nobody's busting nothing," said Lefko. "You got anything else to offer?"

The patrolman picked up his magazine. "I'm good," he said. "You fine gentlemen may carry on."

The dog started barking and running back and forth when they rang the bell. They heard the dog yip and a tall man with an aggressive comb-over answered the door. "What?" he said.

"These gold shields give you a hint, pal?" Moore said.

"You're the Lone Ranger and Tonto, you're late."

"Not too late to give you a world of shit behind you being a wise ass. You a wise ass?" Moore asked as he and Lefko went inside.

"I'm her brother."

"Great, brother Spence," said Lefko. "You can tell us all

about yourself and then we can talk to your sister again."

The terrier was barking and scratching at the bathroom door.

"Shut up, you little pissant," Spence said.

"You don't like dogs, brother Spence?" asked Hawkey.

"Fucking dog's a pain in my ass. Worse than a baby, the way she treats him. And I'm not your brother."

"Right, but you could be a collar for obstructing. Let's see some I.D."

Lefko sat him down at the kitchen table while Hawkey surveiled the refrigerator.

"My wallet's upstairs. I'll get it."

Moore opened up his jacket so Mr. Comb-over could see his .357. "Sit yourself down, Mr. Spence. My partner'll get it."

"Stephen," the man said. "I'm her brother, Stephen."

"Stephen? Not Steve, Steverino, Stevie?"

"Stephen Spence."

"And you married, Stephen Spence?"

Spence started to get up. Moore pushed him back down. "What do you do for a living Steve-O?"

"I got to go to the bathroom."

"Hold your water, Stephen, till my partner comes back down. You got a problem in the meantime, use the sink."

Gene Lefko came back into the kitchen. "Mrs. Spence's sound asleep, like a bomb hit her. There's a second bedroom, Arthur here had his wallet on the bureau."

"Arthur, partner? Our friend here said his name was Stephen."

"Arthur Stephen Spence. Arthur S. Spence. You want to go through life with the initials ASS? Now can I use the bathroom, please? I'm on a diuretic."

Lefko walked him down the hall. "Let's hope Timmy don't go all rabid on you when you go 'number one.' And don't let the critter out, Mr. Ass, he might get shot."

"I should live so long," said Spence. He opened the bathroom door a crack and pushed the dog back with his foot.

Gene waited outside the door and took him back to the kitchen. "We done playing games, Mr. A.S.S.? Tell us all about you."

"I'm married. My wife's name is Diane. I got two kids. My daughter's in the Air Force. I work night work for the gas company. I should be asleep now. My sister's nuttier than a fruit-cake."

Moore took a Diet Coke from the fridge. "Like how?"

"Like how? The fucking dog's like how. My boy's birthday party, she brings Timmy over and asks if he can have cake and ice cream. She sits him at the fucking table." He put his hand to his forehead. "I'm just here to calm her down. You staying here, I'm going home."

"Let's take a walk around your sister's spacious grounds, Arthur," said Hawkey. "While my partner calls in to see if you are who you say you are and you're no bad guy."

Stephen Spence shook his head and led Hawkey out to the backyard. It was a grass patch of approximately twenty by twenty separated from the adjoining yard by a fence on both sides and a hedge in the back.

"That's where the little fucker escapes. You let him out, he waits for you to turn your head and he's through the bushes."

"What's on the other side, Arthur?"

"Some poofy guy. His name's Maurice."

"Well, thank you, Arthur. But tell me, how does your sister keep the yard so neat? There's no dog shit, the grass ain't burnt from piss or whatever?"

Spence started back into the house. "If I told you, you wouldn't believe me."

"Try me," said Moore.

"She got the dog using the toilet. I swear."

When they got back into the kitchen, Lefko was standing with his jacket open so Arthur Stephen Spence could see his shoulder rig. "You've been a bad boy, Mr. Arthur Stephen."

Spence paled.

"Just kidding, Arthur. You're clean as Tuesday's laundry," said Lefko, doing his little dance. "Tell your sister we'll be back to chat when she wakes up." He handed over his card. "You think of anything yourself, you call."

The two detectives went back outside. "He had it coming, the little shitbird being all hard-boiled and all," said Lefko.

"Gene, Gene, my dancing machine!" said Hawkey. "Now let's go see what Maurice looks like."

They swung around the block and then up into the cul-de-sac. The three houses were all faux something, but the one that backed up to the Spence's had purple trim.

"Can you believe that?" said Hawkey. "Purple trim. I can't wait to see the inside of the place."

The door chimes played "Three Coins in the Fountain." The man that answered was wearing aqua pants, a matching silk shirt, and bedroom slippers.

Hawkey tinned him. "We'd like to ask you some questions. I'm Detective Moore. This is Detective Lefko."

"Of course, come in. I'm kind of in between now, though."

"Between what, Maurice?" asked Detective Lefko.

"Coming in and going out. Hence the odd costume."

The two detectives walked into the foyer and down into the hall. "Did you say 'hence'?" said Hawkey.

"I guess I did." He extended a handshake. "I'm Maurice Haynes. How can I help you?"

"We'd like to look around, Maurice, starting with your outside property. There's been prowlers in the neighborhood."

Haynes led the way to the French doors that led out on to the patio and then his roll of back lawn. "I'll have to remember to keep my alarm on. Maybe put in some motion detector lights."

"That's a good idea," said Lefko.

"Any particular worries?" asked Detective Moore.

"I'm a numismatist."

"To each his own," said Hawkey.

"I collect coins," Maurice Haynes told him. "The doorbell. By day I sell insurance, long-term care mostly, which I guess you don't have."

They walked out back. The lawn was pitted with patches of dirt.

"You have a dog, Mr. Haynes?"

"Not by choice," he answered. "Actually, I've already filed two complaints with Animal Control. That little terrier from next door gets through the hedges and digs holes in my ground."

"He ever find anything, the dog?" asked Lefko.

Haynes tamped down a loose piece of sod. "You mean like buried treasure? No, he hasn't. He digs the holes, I fill them up."

"Show me the most recent hole, Mr. Haynes," said Detective Moore.

"Really, or are you making a joke?"

"Cops don't joke, Maurice," said Hawkey. "Show us the hole."

Haynes started off the small flagstone patio.

"Hold on," Gene asked. "You've been out there since the dog dug that last hole?"

"I'm out back here pretty regularly and to fill it up, of course."

"Of course," said Lefko. "Just point out that hole. We'll go out there. You wait here."

Maurice pointed to a freshly planted piece of sod. "If that azalea directly ahead is twelve, the hole is at three fifteen."

"Three fifteen?" asked Hawkey.

"Three fifteen."

The two detectives worked their way towards the hole in concentric circles. Hawkey bagged a twist tie and a dime. Lefko picked up a day-glo orange sticker, a cigarette butt, a small piece of brown plastic. "You smoke, Mr. Haynes?"

"Heavens, no. It's poison. But I'm afraid Sondra does."

"Sondra?"

"A girl from work. She comes over every now and then. Parliaments, I think, the recessed filter."

"Funny thing for a non-smoker to know."

"Not if you're an ex-smoker, detective. I remember everything about anybody who I was ever around who smoked."

The two detectives went over and examined where Timmy had dug his hole. They knew enough not to re-excavate, but it looked big enough for the vic's head.

They took Maurice back inside.

"You got anything you want to tell us?" asked Moore.

"You collect anything besides coins?" asked Gene.

"Not really on both counts. Now if you don't mind. I've a dinner engagement."

Hawkey opened his jacket to show his service weapon. "You and I are going to sit here while my partner looks around. You've got a problem with that?"

Maurice sat down on the end of his sofa. "If you were to look upstairs, you might find a little weed."

"How much is a little, Maurice?"

"A couple of joints, that's all."

Lefko started upstairs. "For your glaucoma?"

"For Sondra and I."

Hawkey took out his pen. "Tell me everything you know about the neighbors, the neighborhood, Mrs. Spence, whatever. All my partner finds is a couple of joints, he flushes them, we're out of here."

Lefko came downstairs. He held up three marijuana cigarettes. "Three is not 'a couple.' Two is a couple. Three is a few."

"What are you guys going to do to me?" said Haynes.

"We'll see," Hawkey told him.

The two detectives left.

"We doing anything about the weed?" asked Lefko.

"Best I test it later, partner," said Moore. "You know, we're working a celebrity vic, I got to get into a celebrity frame of mind or whatever. Meanwhile, let's cruise the area while our meter's running."

26

The only thing Detectives Moore and Lefko discovered on their tour of the neighborhood was a middle-aged woman exercising in front of her upstairs window. They rode around the block twice and then were compelled to park across the street to determine whether or not she was wearing a bra.

"I swear to Christ, Gene, I'm seeing nippage up there."

Lefko squinted. "Could be you're seeing nip and could be it's one of them heart monitors."

"Right, right. I don't think so. You want to question the lady, maybe she knows about something."

The woman came closer to the window to do her deep breathing.

Detective Moore started the car. "My worst fear," he said. "We got definite saggage there."

"You know that's how this country's going to hell in a hand-basket," Lefko said. "People not taking care of themselves, like women not providing the support nature requires."

They drove out the Ridge and turned right on Bell's Mills Road. Halfway down they came to Forbidden Drive. "You worked that baby snatcher case with Salerno?" Moore asked.

"Right. Right," Lefko said. "He got his heart attack behind that and his partner getting his head burned off the way he did. Jimmy, he's a good cop."

Hawkey took them onto Henry Avenue and out to the Boulevard. "Stubborn, though, Gene. Stubborn makes a good cop, but it can get in the way. You want to stop at the diner or you going to eat at home?"

"Home's good," Lefko said.

Hawkey slowed as they drove past a group of high school kids. "Used to be the Northeast was 'Copland.' You were on the job or the FD, you lived in the Northeast. Now everywhere you look you got Jamal and Shameekwha and she's pushing her carriage and got another Jamal in her belly."

"Right," said Gene. "And her baby daddy and her other baby knocking down old ladies at the Roosevelt Mall."

Hawkey eyeballed a windowless van.

"You get a smell off that vehicle, partner?" Lefko asked. "Never liked them vehicles without windows. Half of them got kidnappers and rapists inside, half of them got illegal immigrants or whatever."

The back door of the van opened up and an orthodox Jew got out, complete with the beard and the big black hat. He had a basket of bread in his hand.

Moore pushed it to make the next light and then slowed for the one at Haldeman. "Chickie and Pete's. Lot of nice strange there you go the right time. Anyways, me and Radicchio were working this burglary ring some years back. I know they was Vietnamese or some other kind…"

"Right, right, Hawkey, because they were breaking in and doing the kids' homework and leaving."

Moore looked at his watch. "Math homework, Gene, you heard that." Hawkey pulled on to Lefko's street and stopped across from his house. He looked at his watch again. "I'll be back at one."

"One's good."

"Get some rest, partner," Hawkey said. "You look like shit."

Detective Salerno was working through a stack of papers when the two detectives got back to the precinct. Lefko sat at his desk to return phone calls while Hawkey went over to the boss' office. The blinds were pulled and nobody answered his knock. "Whatever," he said and went down to the coffee room.

He came back and took the unmarked keys back off the board. "Some genius unplugged the coffee pot. Maybe they can't drink the stuff no more."

"It wasn't me," said Gene.

"Your partner's a dick," said Salerno.

"He's a good cop," said Lefko.

"Gene, Gene, the dancing machine. He's a good cop. We're all good cops. He's still a dick.

Anyways, my glorious light duty is done for today," said Salerno. "And fortunately for the City of Brotherly Love, it's about over altogether."

"You going to see the doc this week?"

"Right, going to see my cardiologist tomorrow." Salerno put on his coat and signed out. "Then I'm back like I was never gone."

Moore was just getting back to his desk when the blinds to the inspector's office went up and the door opened. Inspector Zinn called Hawkey in. "What do you have, detective?" he said.

"Not much, boss. We located where the pooch dug up the vic's melon. Talked to the guy who owns the property. Name is Maurice Haynes. He filled the holes. Tells us that little Timmy's been digging up his yard and he's made two complaints to Animal Control. We'll check that out. He looks okay the first go around. Told him there were prowlers in the neighborhood."

Zinn made some notes and adjusted himself on his foam donut. "Phones will be lighting up like a Christmas tree. Get your canvassing done, Hawkey. Salerno knows he's to back you up, working from his desk the way he is. You need Radicchio for your canvassing, let the executive officer know."

Moore nodded. He didn't want Salerno in it at all, and his involvement could be minimized by using Sal.

Hawkey took Gene Lefko down to the coffee room. Radicchio was playing solitaire.

"We got some OT, Sal. You good with that, then saddle up," said Moore.

Radicchio put his cards down. "A cow got teats? My kid needs braces."

As the three detectives were leaving the squad, a tall black woman wearing shades came in with a golden retriever.

Lefko held the door for her and her dog. "Can I help you, Miss? Right this way."

She laughed. "You think I'm Ray Charles or somebody. I'm Human Remains Detection, and this 'seeing eye dog's' name's Tubbs and he's the best cadaver dog in three states. My name's Sonny," she said.

"Like *Miami Vice*?" Sal asked. "You know, Sonny Crockett and what's his name Tubbs?"

"You mean, Mr. Tibbs," said Lefko.

Sonny Hicks took off her sunglasses. "Sorry you dinosaurs were expecting some big white guy with his K-9. Well, you're behind the times. Tubbs here's the best sniffing dog there is, and I'm just the best handler. Now after I check in with your XO and Inspector Zinn, I'm going to get to work."

"I'm lead on this job," said Moore. "You the best in three states?"

She scratched her dog's head. "We got a 70% recovery rate, more or less. We get a hit, we flag it and make an oral and written report. So do me a favor, don't be planting no ham sandwiches or road kill to mess up Tubbsie here. The only scent he'll possess is homo sapiens, the dead kind."

Sonny put her shades back on. "Now that we've met, detectives, I'm going to work."

"Ain't that some shit," Hawkey said. "Got to be some of that affirmative hiring that she comes in all haughty and damn sure of herself."

"Probably for the dog too," said Lefko, doing his little shuffle.

Guido Cisone brought the HRD and her dog into his office, then came back out. "Now, now, girls," he said. "Let's not get our bowels in an uproar. Everything here is going to be just fine."

"No doubt, XO," said Hawkey. "It's just that we got Ray Charles with attitude on this case."

"The boss says she'll run the grid a day, two days tops. Meanwhile, I heard they're taking role call at Higgins'. Save me a seat at the bar."

"Very good," Detective Radicchio announced. "Gentlemen, Gene Lefko is buying."

Cisone briefed Sonny Hicks and then went back in to see Inspector Zinn. "She's good to go, the HRD, boss. And the squad's calmed down. Nothing better than lying over a couple of cold pitchers to increase morale."

"That's positive on both counts, Guido. We do not need backwash. This job's likely as not to be a mess. Esposito's dodging the media, and I just got my first call from the Bureau."

"Epps?"

"Dellum. He's the ASAC now. They just bumped him up. Which is no better." Zinn looked out the window. "Him and Salerno have history on the Raimondo job. Which reminds me, Jimmy doesn't get the clearance to return at his next physical, I'm going to be talking to him about going out."

"I hear you, boss," said Guido.

Joe Zinn looked at the clock on his desk. "Meanwhile, I got to get by Genuardi's. Mary took a leg of lamb back there. They gave her a hard time."

"That's not a good thing."

"No, it isn't. Tell the boys to have a cold one on me. And let's see if the HRD comes up with something."

"Right, boss," said Guido Cisone. "She's supposed to be good people. Not like them at the supermarket not treating your missus right. Used to be a butcher had pride in his work."

Tony DeAngelis became Detective Salerno's cardiologist the afternoon they brought him in with the elephant sitting on his chest. They told Jimmy he had gotten there just in time. So maybe Lucas Rook had done him a solid by calling it in, but somehow it didn't matter him getting saved while his partner, Chick, was getting murdered.

Dr. DeAngelis had cathed Salerno and put in drug-coated stents and everything was fine. Now Jimmy had only to pass the stress test, which the Doc told him was cake since he had had the procedure and had lost the weight and was living right with his diet.

"You doing this test yourself, or you passing it down to the college kids?" Salerno asked Dr. DeAngelis.

"The technician will administer the test, detective. I'll be right there to monitor everything."

Salerno pushed back the sleeves of his Eagles sweatshirt. "Is that a 'just in case'?"

"Standard procedure, James. I'm sure you'll be just fine. I'll see you when you start the stress test."

The technician was named Boyce, a thick man with a goatee. "Any allergies, Mr. Salerno?"

"Other than creeps and hospitals, I don't think so, but anyways, you're supposed to have my paperwork."

"It's protocol to ask again, Mr. Salerno. As your instruction sheet said, the entire procedure will take four hours. I'm going to introduce a chemical, thalium, into your bloodstream by an injection. We're going to take some pictures of your heart, then get you up on the treadmill and see how everything goes. Then we'll take some more pictures."

"Who's the 'we'?"

"Doctor DeAngelis will be present while you're exercising." He swabbed Salerno's arm and inserted a small IV and then the thalium. "It will take a while for the agent to circulate. If you want to go out of the hospital for a bit, you can. Nothing to eat or drink except water. No coffee."

Salerno went downstairs and out onto the new plaza the hospital had put in between the heart center and the administrative building. A couple of nurses were out catching a smoke, something he never did. His heredity and agita were enough, not to mention the thirty-five extra pounds he had been carrying, though as far as he was concerned that weight thing was bogus. Even at his heaviest, Jimmy could play eighteen holes carrying his own bags without his heart skipping a beat. He missed that, playing golf with Chick and busting on each other over a cold pitcher at Bill Higgins'. Life was tough, all the things he'd seen, dead kids, bad murders. Your partner dying in the street. Life was tough, but Detective Salerno knew that he was tougher.

There was a *Daily News* box on the square, but a doc in his scrubs and a Princeton baseball hat came and took the last two papers. The prick probably only paid for one, but Jimmy took a deep breath and counted to ten so as not to mess up the test. He went back in and shuffled through some magazines until they called him again.

The tech got Jimmy on the table. "This is like a mini-MRI, Mr. Salerno. There's nothing to be concerned about, just a little noise."

The machine did its business and then Boyce injected another tube of the thalium. "We'll call you in another hour, Mr. Salerno. There's some magazines."

"It's Detective Salerno. And the magazines are from six months ago."

In exactly sixty minutes they sent Salerno back in to see the tech. This time they hooked him up to an EKG and ran a baseline resting test.

Dr. DeAngelis came in. "Ready for a little exercise, detective? We're going to get you up on the treadmill here, the speed and incline are going to increase. And we're going to watch your heart work. Any discomfort, pain, dizziness, just sing out. But I'm sure everything will be just fine."

Salerno got up on the ramp and the technician increased the speed to 4.0 and then the incline. Then they ran some more pictures and did the scan again after he sat another half hour in the waiting room, watching the old and the fat come in and wait their turn.

When the test was done, Jimmy went out to hit some golf balls, thinking about taking the wife out to Reading for the outlets, he had promised her that. When he got home, Mrs. Salerno was folding clothes in front of the television set.

"Hi, hon," she said. "It go alright?"

"Good," he told her. "I see you're watching that English show where the fruits come in and change your house all around while you're food shopping or whatever."

She put the pile of towels on the sofa. "I wouldn't like it one bit, their coming in here. I like our home just fine."

Jimmy tried to fold one of the tee shirts, but it didn't exactly work. "I'd only change one thing."

Mrs. Salerno turned away from the laundry. "And what would that be, James Joseph Salerno?"

"I think you need them extra settings of the china and the two serving bowls you've been talking about. How about we run up to Reading, stop at the outlets?"

She held up a blue bath towel. "And you need undershirts."
She set the laundry basket aside. "Unless you're too tired, after the
test and all."

"I'm good to go. We can stop for dinner on the way home."

They took 476 North and were at the outlets in a little more
than an hour. His underwear, towels, and she got herself a
matching hat and glove set and the dishes she had been talking
about for three Thanksgivings.

Dinner was at Matts' right outside of Morgantown. They
even had a glass of wine and split a dessert of apple brown betty.
When they got home, she went upstairs and waited for her
husband to come up, but as she had come to expect since the
heart attack, Jimmy found things to do until she fell asleep.

In the morning, he got up while the wife slept in. Going over
to the Ridge Diner for breakfast and the paper. His cell rang. It
was Dr. DeAngelis.

"This can't be good news," Salerno said.

"It's not terrible either. Why don't you stop by my office at
say eleven, we can go over your test results."

"So?"

"Nothing to worry about, detective, but I've got to go. See
you soon."

"You got to give me five minutes, doc. What are you talking
about?"

"The stainless steel stent we put in to provide structural
support for your artery elutes sirolimus to prevent…"

"Elute? Sirolimus? How about you talk English?"

"The stent is to keep your artery open," DeAngelis said.
"The drug is to keep the tissue from overgrowing it. As I
informed you before we inserted the stent there is functional
success in two-thirds of the cases. The other third can be caused
by failure of the stent, human error, there's even some indication
that taking B vitamins…"

"I take those, doc."

"That's okay, detective. What we worry about is acute coronary syndrome. I see no evidence of that."

Salerno popped some Tums off the roll in his pocket. "What do you see?"

"We change the stent, a minor procedure. You're as good as gold."

"Good for what, doc?" Salerno asked, but Dr. DeAngelis had hung up.

Jimmy Salerno knew not to go home. It was one of the first things you learned on the street, you don't bring the shit home. Santa doesn't come down the chimney with a bag of crap.

He drove over to Kessler's to hit a bucket of balls. Mike was not there. A skinny blonde girl was working behind the counter, skinny as a rail. Skinnier than Kessler even, but with eyes that looked like opals. Jimmy put a five down.

"I'm supposed to say 'your money's no good.'" She took a 3 x 5 card from under the counter. "I'm supposed to say 'you can hit all the buckets you want for free as long as you want or until you hit that seagull out there.'"

"Where's Mike?"

The skinny girl shrugged her shoulders and tried to get at the cigarette that she had knocked from under the counter. "My Aunt Mickey comes by and picks me up."

Salerno took back his twenty. "Mickey, Mike's sister? You're his niece?"

She took a drag on her Marlboro Light. "Yup," she said.

"You know anything about golf, Mike and Mickey's niece?"

"Nope."

Jimmy felt angry and weak at the same time. His drives weren't for shit. By the time he got his anger into his swing, the mechanics were all a mess, which only made him more pissed. The only cure was a visit to Bill Higgins' place and more alcohol than was necessary.

Lucas Rook was at the bar when Salerno came into Bill Higgins' place. Salerno went by him and sat in his booth. What he didn't need was another weight dropped in his stomach full of acid, and that was the best thing that the out-of-state prick had ever been.

"Cutty and milk," Jimmy told the waitress.

Rook walked over. "Howya been?"

"I just got worse, New York. Don't ask to sit down."

"It's your town, Jimmy. I'm just visiting."

"You got that right." Salerno loosened his collar. "You got something to say, Mr. Rook?"

Lucas let the reference to his being a civilian pass by. "Maybe I do, maybe I don't. Depends on whether you're going to be busting my balls non-stop."

The scotch and milk came.

"Most likely, New York," Salerno told him.

"Suit yourself. You want to make some side money, you can reach me on my cell." Lucas left his business card with the chess piece on it and went on out.

Salerno ripped up the card and used the pieces as a coaster for his drink. It didn't change things that Rook killed the fuck who killed Chick or that he'd called in the heart attack. He was still a meddling out-of-town prick working off the job for the big bucks.

Jimmy had two drinks without a word to anybody and left.

The tank of his Town Car was three-quarters full. No cop worth anything leaves any vehicle without at least a half a tank. Right. For what? Hit another fucking bucket of balls. Balls is right. There ain't no easy way to give up the job unless you've already given up on it. No way was he going to spend his life paper shuffling and they put another hole in his chest so maybe he can shuffle some more.

Salerno drove until he got tired of the Lasix making him stop for a piss. Then he headed home. Like always, Carmela had tried to wait up for him, but it was almost twelve. He had driven out the Expressway and then the long way back. Helluva trip it had been, from his first day on the job finding little Helen Kucinzki frozen in the doorway with blood on her legs, and the rats running from off of her. And getting his gold shield. Doing right. Making a difference. Then his heart going bad on him and Chick getting all burned up.

Jimmy went down to the basement and took out his murder books. The Ratner brothers, Mandelker, the big shootout with the Black Muslims that never made the paper. And the Heather Raimondo job that wound up with his partner dead.

He went up to the kitchen and popped a beer. No way was he going to hang around the squad and hope they gave him a couple of ground balls, at best clear a case a beat cop could do the first day on the job. He went back downstairs and looked in the Raimondo book for Rook's cell phone number.

Lucas was sitting at Bonatelli's watching the middle-aged women in capri pants and the fags walk by. It was the place he had jumped on the two muggers and convinced the lovely Catherine Wren that he was a nut job.

"You got two minutes to tell me I'm not wasting my time, New York."

"You want to sit down, Jimmy?"

"Depends on what you're selling."

Rook sipped his Heineken. "Client of mine had a loved one

get their head whacked off. Esposito from your precinct called the next of kin."

"I'm interested," Salerno said. "I'll see you at the Peacock Lounge in forty-five minutes."

Salerno was parked up the block so he could watch Rook arrive. He waited until Lucas was inside the Peacock for ten minutes, then followed him in.

 Connie Small was behind the bar, looking like a queen from Africa with all the silver she had on. Rook sipped a draft in a front booth.

Jimmy walked by him and into the empty back room. Lenny came over with a coffee. "I'm sorry," he said.

"Not you, Lenny."

"I'm sorry, I'm sorry," the waiter said as Lucas Rook sat down.

Salerno poured a little bit of cream into his coffee and two Sweet N' Lows. "What are you looking for, Rook?"

"A little help."

Salerno tasted his coffee and then lightened it some more. "I ain't no welcome wagon," Salerno said.

"I don't need anybody to hold my hand, James. And I don't care who gets to clear the case. I just want to do my job."

"Spare me the soap opera, Rook."

Lucas called the waiter over.

"Sorry, sorry," Lenny said.

"Another draft," Rook told him.

The waiter offered another chorus of "sorry's" on his way back to the bar.

"You want a piece of this or not?" Rook asked.

Salerno sipped his coffee and put it down. "He should be sorry. The cream must have been bad or whatever."

Connie Small came over to the table. "You shaking your

head, Mr. S, something's got to be wrong. Leonard put his sorry-ass thumb in your cup or whatever." She sniffed the creamer. "That's not right. Leonard, he's supposed to take care of that. Since he got out the joint, he's not right."

"Friend of yours?" said Rook when she walked away.

"She ran the best cat house in Philly until the city got all moral or whatever. Now all her clientele going to them Asians with their 'washy-washy' or the she-males on the street."

Connie Small came back from the bar with a Crown Royal for Salerno. "I don't believe in new friends," she said as she walked away.

"What you got your 'private eye' on, New York? Last time you're here, it was a cluster fuck."

"Just trying to reunite the DOA's head with the body."

"Don't sound kosher, New York."

"That's just what it is. Jewish funeral, you got to have all the parts or something." Rook called for the waiter, who was too busy apologizing to notice.

Salerno sipped his drink. "So you know who it is?"

"Janice Shay. The old television teacher. The family don't want it turned into a freak show. If you want, I'll 'go back on up the Turnpike,' as you used to say, and wait for your call. You're in, we both get paid."

"I'll think about it, New York. Don't call me, I'll call you." Jimmy got up and left.

Rook stopped at the bar on his way out and handed Connie Small a twenty.

"Now, Thomas Jefferson," she said. "He is my friend."

Lucas drove back to Manhattan, the Grand Marquis running smooth and his client's meter running serious dollars. As he came up to Exit 7A, he thought about Catherine Wren. The last time he was there, she held the door with her foot so he couldn't get into the place where he had almost lived, and she had smelled like lemons. Maybe she was right that he fed on all the evil in the world, but there was plenty of it.

The houses had black poles with iron arms out front and the windows had boxes that stuck out like mechanical eyes that hummed and hummed when the sun beat down. The maple trees up and down the block had huge arms and the shadows of the leaves were like hands on the house where the Watchman lived.

In the coolness of his basement room, Delbert Fine watched endless rolls of celluloid that told him all was well, while outside there were a hundred thousand million mouths moving closed and open, open closed, with teeth so perfectly all alike. He had her words to keep them all away and stop the rutting noises that came from their moving mouths and the cries in strangers talk and the squeaking of their shoes.

The Watchman was safe downstairs with Teacher Jan's magic words and the rooms upstairs boarded shut. His sister was safe inside her bed, while Daddy smoked a cigarette and Mom was in her dress that shimmered when she walked.

29

Sonny Hicks took her cadaver dog to the Rittenhouse Hotel first because the more time that passed, the greater overlay of scents and the more cleaning would be there. She found a parking spot for her Explorer on 18th Street and walked Tubbs over to the little park for him to take a leak.

There was a fountain and a rectangular pool in the middle of the park and a bronze animal with kids climbing on it. An empty kiosk for the beat cops. Nannies with white kids. LPN's with rich folks on oxygen. Maybe when they came back out from the hotel, Tubbsie could get a jump in that pool.

A lady with a bag of poop called out as the cadaver dog lifted his leg on a locust tree. "We curb our dogs here," she said.

The HRD ignored her. As she crossed the street, Hicks saw a red-haired woman coming out of the hotel with an Irish setter. She held Tubbs off to the side and then went to the concierge.

"The PD sent me," Sonny said as she showed her ID.

"PD?" asked the man behind the desk.

"The police department. I'm here to check the room where Janet Scheyman stayed. The roof, the basement, the stairs. Maybe some other rooms, depending."

"I'll have to call my manager," said the concierge.

"We'll wait," said Hicks.

The manager came over. "We've been expecting you. A

Captain Cisone called. The detectives have already been here and we've turned over our surveillance tapes, but you're welcome. I just need to know where you'll be and for you to be mindful of our guests."

"Agreed," said Hicks.

The HRD took off her shades and she and Tubbsie went to work. They had worked buildings before, from abandoned crack houses to the rubble of collapses and Ground Zero. Inspector Zinn had arranged that Tubbs get a scent off the cadaver's head and if there was anything at all in the Rittenhouse, they would pick it up.

By agreement with the hotel, there was no crime tape up, but the room had been sealed as soon as Lieutenant Esposito learned from the next of kin that Teacher Jan had been staying there. What made this job tough was that there had been ten or so other occupants since the vic had been discovered. The room had been cleaned and deodorized regularly and Crime Scene had been in. But Sonny Hicks and her dog could work a scene.

Because there was only the one room and the bathroom, the handler worked her dog off the lead. They came up cold. Then Hicks put her cadaver dog on a six-foot leash to work the halls, the roof, the elevator and the basement. There was a restaurant on the second floor and another on the first. They both gave her shit about the dog, but she worked them anyway. Except for some raw pork which gave off a scent much like human flesh, there was nothing of interest to the cadaver dog at all.

Sonny Hicks looked at her watch. It was time to give her partner a break. They went over to the park again. Some art students were doing bad watercolors. A cop was reading the paper in the kiosk. Tubbsie pulled to get into the fountain's pool.

"You get us an 'alert,' boy, you can frolic to your heart's content," Sonny said.

They worked the shrubbery near the parked cars, the alley and all the area around the hotel, but came up empty.

Hicks had a turkey and cheese in her cooler, and she ate it as she drove to the spot where the DOA's head had been buried. As she rolled up to the property, she reminded herself as she always did before she worked an area, "Take the same path out that you took in. Don't add anything to the scene. Don't take anything away from the scene."

She called Maurice Haynes from the car. He was not happy to hear from her and insisted that he receive prior notification.

"This is 'prior,' Mr. Haynes. Or if you prefer, we can have an excavator out here and take up your whole property. But that would be a shame with all the care you expend on your land-scaping."

"I'll need some confirmation that you are who you say you are."

The handler parked in front of the house. "We're right outside. Give me a minute and I'll have Captain Cisone confirm that to you, or if you wish, I can have those two detectives out here again, but that will just mean four more feet on your plantings. On the other hand, we can get this over with. I'm here in front of your lovely home."

Maurice came outside. He was wearing white duck trousers and a linen shirt.

She got out of her SUV and did her demure approach without her shades and the dog still in the vehicle. "So nice to meet you," she said. "I'm Cassandra Hicks."

Haynes smiled. "Would you like to see the house before you begin?"

"Perhaps after." She went over to her vehicle and let Tubbsie out.

"Another dog? My landscaping certainly doesn't need that."

"Tubbsie here's perfect for the job. We won't be long, Mr. Haynes." She attached her dog to a ten-foot lead. "And we'll pay particular attention to your lovely plantings. The azaleas are magnificent."

"'Fleeting passion,'" Maurice told her. "Azalea means 'fleeting passion.'"

The handler and her dog went to work down the perfect path between the Japanese maples. There were trimmed hedges on the perimeter of the property and, except for one giant oak, all the trees in the yard had been cut down so that the lawn that sloped down to the Spences' looked like the fairway of a golf course.

As the crime scene drawing indicated, there were a number of places that had been resodded. The cadaver dog alerted on the spot that the head had been buried in and then again at another spot closer to the edge of Haynes' property. Hicks flagged them.

The Spences' dog came barking at the hedges between them, but Mr. Tubbs sat down quietly as the dog dressed in a hat and tie tried to get through the green wire.

Mrs. Spence came out. "Now what are you doing to upset my little boy?" she said.

"Police business," Hicks told her.

"Why, he's done nothing wrong."

Sonny took her dog back to her vehicle as Maurice Haynes came out with a tray of tea and something. "That's why I prefer dead folks to live ones, Mr. Tubbs," she said. "And you to all of them." She drove back to her office to write up her report. On the way, she called in a verbal to Cisone.

"There's a second spot, Captain. I've marked it with a yellow flag. Either you got remains in the second spot, or your perp buried his package then changed his mind and moved it to where the Spences' dog dug it up."

"Good job, Ms. Hicks. You'll be forwarding a formal report?"

"By tomorrow morning, Captain, but you can get your people out now. And thank them for not burying any tampons or whatever."

Gerry Doto was giving his grandson a bath when the phone rang. Mrs. D said he'd call right back. Over sixty and still working like he was thirty.

"I had the little one in the tub, Captain. Jesus," said Doto. "I just can't get used to that name. Who calls their son 'Lafollette'? Anyways, what can I do you for?"

"Hicks, the HRD came up with another scent."

"Sonny Hicks? Good people. Where we talking?"

"The Haynes property where the vic's head was."

"I turned the dirt and sifted it, Captain. I do my job. Maybe the dog got it wrong. Dogs aren't people, you know."

"She's marked it, Gerry, and we got a red ball on this job."

"Golden time is golden time," Doto said. "Anytime a boss tells me I got to work at double rate, I jump. 'Honor, Integrity, Service.' I'll get right on it."

Thanks to a McNaughton Grant, Doto's minivan was a high-tech lab on wheels. Fingerprint equipment, casting material and tools, enough cameras and lenses to shoot a year's worth of *Playboy* centerfolds, and all the biochemical detection apparatus you could dream of.

Doto checked his PPE. You don't use personal protective equipment, you're inviting some scumbag to walk. Since he only had one hole to check, the time gowning up would take as much time as the job itself unless Haynes was going to break his balls. There was a party going on, and Maurice did give it a shot. "I appreciate you're having festivities or whatever, Mr. Haynes," Doto told him. "But I'm not only a scientist, I'm a police officer, so I can really mess up your festivities."

"I have already tolerated police, detectives, digging, a Negro and her dog, and now this."

Crime Scene started back to his van.

"Thank you," called Maurice.

"You're welcome, but I'm just going to my van. Inside my van I'm going to change into my jumpsuit, gloves, boots, hood, mask and respirator, and then I'm coming back in with the most unpleasant piece of equipment you ever saw and tell your honored guests I'm testing for Ebola virus."

Maurice Haynes came down the driveway. "You're killing me. I've got clients here. What do you want?"

"I'll park around the corner. I still have to cover my shoes and put on the jumpsuit, but you can tell them I'm your gardener or whatever. Your 'horticulturist.' I'll be out of here in less than an hour and I'll be as quiet as a fucking mouse."

Maurice lit a cigarette. "I have no choice here."

"Correct, Mr. Haynes. You don't."

Doto moved his minivan to the side of the house and changed into his protective suit. The flagged spots were easy to find. The new hole came up dry.

He redug the yellow-flagged hole and made a note that it was now the third time it had been dug, maybe the fourth depending on the re-sodding job. All of the grass and dirt was screened and examined. He bagged and labeled his samples.

Doto dug another six inches down from his initial look the first time out. Then he took a pack of gelatin lifters from his bag. He removed the clear polyester cover sheet and laid the thick gelatin layer against the bottom of the hole. When he examined his lift under his work light, Gerry Doto found a sliver of a bloody tooth.

"He must have had an awful burn or allergies," said the lady across the street when Delbert Fine came out in his gloves and scarf and the black woolen hat he always wore.

"Must have," said the man sitting next to her. He tamped the tobacco in his pipe. "Must have, Patti, dear. I can see your saying that."

Delbert Fine went down the block and across the street to the drugstore to get his pills. There was a new man there from time to time and once a girl with a dot painted on her face.

He took the white bag from the man in white that covered up his neck and ran the back way home. Down to his basement room in his black trousers tucked into his socks and in his long black sleeves. And there he sat safe downstairs, the TV on. Teacher Jan saying it was all alright, that he was safe, her words going deep inside of him through the eyes that he had carved into his skin.

Lucas Rook went back up the Turnpike. He was going to be running the job in Philly with or without Salerno, which meant a car with Pennsylvania plates. No need to advertise you were from out of town or to put miles on your vehicle when somebody else was picking up the tab.

He pulled the Grand Marquis into Rosen's garage.

"She runs like a dream, don't she, Lucas boy?" said the garageman.

"Like a dream, Sid."

"I'm reading this book a guy gets stuck in somebody else's dream and can't get out." Rosen wiped his hands on the towel he had hanging from his belt. "Or maybe I'm talking about marriage."

Rook sat down and stretched out his leg. "Going down to Philly, so I won't be needing the Merc."

Rosen joined him at his wooden desk. "You return that book I loaned you, I got another one for you."

"I'll do that, Sid."

Rosen's dog barked from the back room.

"Bear, he got to go out."

Rook stood up. "I'll be leaving, Sid."

"You're wondering why I call this dog Bear, too. Continuity."

"Never gave it a thought, Sid. I'll drop that book off before I roll."

Rook went to his place. There was a black man working behind the desk of the St. Claire. "May I help you?" he asked.

"Where's the regulars?"

"Sir?"

"Never mind," Lucas said. "I'm 10 B. Rook. You got any mail or messages?"

"I'm supposed to ask for I.D., sir."

Rook tinned him. "How about yourself?"

The deskman reached for his wallet. Rook unzipped his jacket.

"My name is Winston Thomas. Leo and the other man got in some altercation and…"

"My mail and messages, Thomas?"

"Winston is my first name." He handed over Rook's mail. "I'm here for three days."

"Three days," said Rook. "That's nice."

He went upstairs. There was a note under his door from Grace. "Buy me dinner," it said. The answering machine was flashing. Two calls from Leo asking if he knew a good employment lawyer.

Lucas called over to Dr. Hepburn.

"Hello, hello," the shrink said.

"Since when do you answer your own phone?" Lucas asked him.

"Busier than the lube concession at a Christopher Street bathhouse."

Rook put his .45 on the mantelpiece. "You got an hour?"

Hepburn lit a cigarette. "Personal or professional? Personal, I always got time for you since you saved my ass. Professional, maybe we can do a phone thing. I got a catatonic coming in and they're hard to reschedule."

"Professional."

"We talking litigation here?"

"Doubt it."

"Well, there goes my prep time, deposition, and so on. You going to need a report at least?"

Hepburn's doorbell buzzed. "Got to go. Somebody's here that thinks being depressed is abnormal."

Rook went in and fried some eggs and the scrapple he had brought from Philly. Somebody told you you were serving them corn mush with pig ears and what not, you'd book them. But scrapple was a good thing. "Everything but the Squeal," the wrapper said.

He turned on the tube. "Boxing's Deadliest Fights." Emille Griffith was just getting into the ring. Rook showered and shaved and went around the corner for some Camay soap and a coconut cream pie for Tuze. Then he dropped off the book he hadn't even cracked and ran the Avanti out to the policemen's home.

Ray Tuzio was wearing dress shoes and his Aviators with his pajamas.

"How ya doin' partner?" Lucas asked. "Brought you some coconut cream pie."

Tuzio lifted his shades. "We'll eat it in the unit. We take it inside, every flatfoot in the precinct going to glom a piece."

Lucas put the soap in Ray's dresser. There was only one other bar. He hoped the staff was enjoying it, like everything else that they could carry off. "You good, Tuze?"

"I'm good. Better off than the newbie over there. First day away from home. No way he's going to get them paratrooper's wings unless he straightens up."

"I'll be back, Tuze. Take it easy."

On the way out, Lucas let everybody know he'd be back on Friday. At least they'd keep Ray Tuzio alright until then. Alright while Tuze thought it was fifty years ago.

Lucas looked at his watch. Plenty of time to head across the bridge and get his pipes cleaned. He called Valerie at her apartment and tried the restaurant. No luck until he was already on the West Side Highway.

"I was in the tub," she said.

"Hopefully alone."

"As a matter of fact, I was just laying around getting soft and sweet. Although to tell the truth, I did rub one out while I was soaking."

Rook slowed the fiberglass coupe as a fat man in a vintage Corvette pulled alongside and revved his engine. "Asshole," said Lucas.

"Only on special occasions, dear," said Valerie Moon. "You coming over?"

"Affirmative," Rook told her.

"Bring some cold beer," she told him. "And maybe something to eat. Anything but Chinese."

Rook exited the West Side Highway and went back uptown to the GW Bridge. When he got to Fort Lee, he stopped at a corner deli for the beer and two subs. Tomorrow, he'd be saying "hoagies." "Heros, subs, zeps, hoagies, poor boys." America, the melting pot.

She met Rook at the door. "If your belly can wait," she told him, "you can keep your socks on."

They did it on the sofa with the TV playing *Stargate*. She got up to get a towel and came back with two bottles of beer.

"You don't mind we drink out of the bottle, Lucas? I hate doing dishes."

It was ten of five. "I got to make a call, Valerie."

She went into the other room. "Whistle when you want dessert," she said.

"Detective," said the shrink. "My meter has just begun."

"I hear you, doc. What I got is the bad guy grabs up this old TV celeb and whacks off her head."

"That's not very nice. Can you tell me who the victim is?"

"Janet Shay. Teacher Jan."

"You're shitting me. Jan Scheyman, Jesus Christ. I worked with her a couple of times on panels. Jesus, this world is nuts."

"You got that right."

"I'll be happy to help you catch the crazy fuck who did this," Dr. Hepburn said.

"Just trying to give Teacher Jan an honest burial. I need your help in trying to locate the rest of her."

"Call me back in an hour, Lucas. Meanwhile I got to tell this forty-five-year-old fireman not to feel guilty that his parish priest used to suck him off in the rectory."

Rook went into the bedroom. Valerie was sitting on her bed reading a dictionary. "The whole world's in here," she said. "Now how about you come over here and give me another…" She turned the page. "…jumble, jumbo, jump."

Lucas Rook drove back into the city and let himself into Rosen's garage. Sid came out from the back.

"You were a bad guy, you could've gotten shot, Lucas boy."

"You're right, Sid. And I would have deserved it. You need me, I'll be in Philly."

"The City of Brotherly Love," Rosen said.

"Not now, Sid. My guess is it never was."

Rook went back to his place. There was another call from Leo. Something was up more than he was looking for a shyster. The phone book was filled with them.

At exactly six, the shrink called back. "Sorry, Lucas. Where were we?"

"Teacher Jan."

"Right, right. Listen, you hear any odd noises, it's me on the stepper. Give me what you got."

"I got Janet Shay's head. The family wants her buried in a

Jewish cemetery, so they need the rest of her. The bad guy took her head off and buried it."

"He saw it off, chop it off or hack it off, detective?"

"I don't have that yet. But then he buries the head in some-body's yard."

Cholly Hepburn put a piece of chaw in his mouth. "You're telling me he chops it off or hacks it off, something violent like that, I'm telling you where he buries the head means something. He does it nice and surgical, it means something else, especially if it's buried real shallow, he wants you to know what a good job he did."

Rook started to pack for Philly. "Like the cat bringing the mouse in and leaving it on the kitchen floor."

"Correct-a-mundo. The guy who hacks it off is trying to say something about who he killed rather than himself. The nexus is going to be where he buried it."

"Nexus, doc?"

"Right. That's one of those expensive litigation terms. So I suggest you look at what the burial location signifies, either in the real world or in the perpetrator's head." Dr. Hepburn spit. "And I wouldn't be surprised if he brings another mouse in. Now let me towel off and get ready for my next client. Poor dear flushed her newborn down the crapper."

"Appreciate it, doc. Send me your bill."

"Count on that, detective."

Lucas wrote a memo to the file and went down to the base-ment to do a load of wash.

The television set in Delbert Fine's basement room had an old "rabbit ears" antenna that hardly worked, but he did not mind as he watched the endless tapes of Teacher Jan. Delbert turned his TV off and put on his black clothes that covered up the eyes that he had carved on all the places he could reach and the ones drawn in for him in Chinatown. The eyes could see inside the night as he went down the alley dressed in black.

The train that took him into work clanked and banged above the stores and houses until it went underground where it belonged. The obese man at the all-night stand said, "Paper, paper. How ya doin'?" as Delbert and everyone else walked by. Two pastry chefs in tall white hats came along. An old lady playing a banjo and singing a song. A man with a sign saying The World is Lies.

The Watchman went behind the parking lot where the black man lounged and through the square park. In through the basement door to make his rounds. Check the doors and the lights. And always Delbert's eyes to see the truth. Where the trash was left and why. What the arrangements on the desks meant. The shining paper clip and silver dime left as a message for him to read.

Twice there was a man who was working late and a girl with long black hair he could see in the shadow on the wall. The blue lights of the computer screen were tunnels to moving lines and cartoons. Mouths moving upside down and secrets coming out.

Lucas Rook cabbed over to the Port Authority. Still the armpit of the world, vagrants, thieves and hookers. He bought a one-way to Philly and got on early to find a seat with a little leg room.

The bus driver was a stocky woman with a platinum dye job. Rook sat in the back right corner. A family of Mexicans with cheap suitcases moved to the rear of the bus, but gave him wide berth. "*Policia*," the father whispered.

The little boy was crying. "*Hijo mio*," the mother said to comfort him.

The driver got on her PA system. "This is not the 'Wayward Bus,'" she said. "New York to Philly. Non-stop. Smoking, loud music and foul language are prohibited by law. For your traveling comfort, a rest room is located in the rear. If you light-up in the bathroom, an alarm will sound and you will be asked to debark."

The bus driver closed the pneumatic door and they headed down the Turnpike, past the Statue of Liberty and the Newark airport. There was a back-up at the Carteret exit and she swung into the passing lane, which she held to make up lost time.

Traffic slowed again at the juncture with the Pennsylvania Turnpike, but she pushed it to Exit 4 and across Route 38 to the Ben Franklin Bridge. They arrived at the 10th and Filbert Terminal with two minutes to spare.

She reminded the passengers to take all of their carry-ons and to enjoy their stay. Lucas waited for the family of immigrants to leave for their dreams in the dung of the mushroom farms in Kennett Square. An ugly man in a denim jacket lit his smoke while still inside the bus.

"Extinguish all smoking materials," the driver said.

The smoker ignored her.

"Extinguish your smoke until you're off my bus," she told him.

The ugly man took another drag. "You ain't got nothing to say. The trip's over."

Lucas nudged him out the door. The smoker turned around but Rook was right in on him so he moved on out.

"Why, thank you," the bus driver said. She shook her long blonde hair like a movie star.

Rook crossed Market Street and walked south to 10th and Walnut. Tex Cobb's place was now part of the Tex's Steak House chain since Cobb's film career had gotten going again. Leon Spinks was behind the bar. The gapped-tooth ex-champ had beaten Ali for the heavyweight title, and Tex had beaten him.

Rook had a draft and a cheeseburger. "Another cold one, champ," Lucas said as he looked at his watch. Enough time to get up to 30th Street. The Budget Rental at 22nd and Market only had compacts. No way you can show up with anything smaller than a Taurus.

At the rental place he tried for an upgrade, but the girl behind the counter didn't get it when he showed the NYPD gold shield. Two salesmen in drip-dry shirts and matching ties were behind Lucas.

"We got a meeting," the first drip-dry said.

"How about letting us check out, buddy?" the other drip-dry said.

"I'm not your buddy," Rook said.

The first salesman started to say something again, but stopped when Lucas amped up his glare. The girl behind the counter finally passed over some keys and Rook was on the way.

Lucas had no appointments so he rode by what had been the roadside monument for little Heather Raimondo. There were no flowers there and one of the arms was broken off.

He stayed at the Embassy Suites near the airport last time he was in Philly, but this job wasn't going to take that long and they weren't giving law enforcement discounts anymore. Their loss.

The Holiday Inn people didn't have their heads up their asses, and you could get a decent room for under a hundred with what they were giving off and bill the client full boat. He took a room at the one on City Line, which was right off the Expressway "Schoolkill" he had learned to say a while back. Like if you say "Avenue of the Americas" instead of Sixth Avenue, everybody in New York knows you're from Kansas or whatever.

His bad leg was stiff from the bus ride, but the tub was only big enough for that dwarf ME, Nessel. Lucas took some Advils and stretched out. He called for his messages, but there was nothing doing. Maybe get a beer and then grab some winks.

There was a knock on the door. Rook answered it with his .45 behind his back. It was Jimmy Salerno.

Lucas put his gun in the waistband of his pants. "Well, if it isn't the Welcome Wagon," he said.

"Can't help but crack-wise, can you, New York? And I didn't bring you no cookies."

Rook stepped back to let him in. There were two chairs in the room and he sat down. Detective Salerno didn't.

"You here to roust me, James? I didn't even watch the in-room skin flicks."

Salerno took the newspaper off the bed and put it on the chair before he sat down. "You don't know who's been in these rooms, do you?" he said.

"So you're breaking my balls," Lucas said. "This part of your business negotiations, or is it just the same-old same-old?"

"You talk, I listen, Rook."

"About what?"

"About whether we got anything else to talk about."

"I can live with that." Rook stood up. "Over some breakfast." He picked up the coupons for Denny's off the nightstand.

"There's a deli across the road. You can follow me," Salerno said. "And I didn't see that .45 you're packing without no PA license, I'm sure."

Rook led the way out. "The world is full of bad men," he said.

They went across the county line into Lower Merion and parked in the lot behind the restaurant.

"Two," Salerno said. "In the back."

The hostess was a short blonde woman whose chin had dropped. "In the back?" she said.

"In the back," Salerno told her.

"It'll be just a minute."

He gave her his mean cop look and she called for the busboy to come over and wipe the table down.

"I figured you'd feel right at home at this deli place, you being from Hymietown and all, Rook," Salerno said.

"And we're not in Philly anymore, so you're off the chart."

"Smart man for a smart ass, Lucas Rook."

Rook picked up the menu. "So anyways, what's good here?"

"Don't go by me, I'm still eating cardboard and shit." He ordered a decaf and a corn muffin.

Lucas had two eggs over and corned beef hash. Then he called the waitress with the bad dye job back. She sighed.

"Order of scrapple," he told her. "I appreciate your hospitality."

"We aren't talking here, Rook."

"Right. And what aren't we talking about?"

Their coffees came. Salerno put in three Sweet 'N Lows. "You don't get anything off of before. You putting down the fuckbag that killed my partner, I appreciate that cop to cop. The US Attorney called me in, I gave them nothing."

The waitress came over again, but Jimmy waved her away.

"Now calling in my heart attack. Maybe that was a good thing. Maybe it's not."

"Which is why we're having this chit-chat."

"Smart man for a smart ass from up the Turnpike."

Rook stirred his coffee one way and then the other. "All I'm after is to bring the DOA's body back. It's a Jewish thing, they got to bury it all together."

"Got to be more than that. Off the fact she's a celebrity, they don't want the tabloids getting shots or whatever. For which they got to be paying you the big bucks."

The waitress came over again and put their breakfast down.

"Maybe I put you in a position. Maybe I don't," Salerno said.

Rook ate a forkful of eggs. "Business is business."

"If we do any, we do it the right way, New York." He reached across the table and speared a piece of scrapple. "And if anybody gets jammed up, it ain't going to be me."

Detective Salerno sat at his desk figuring out his leave for the tenth time. He had two weeks annual and the maximum sick. After that, there was Family Medical Leave Act. He had an appointment with Benefits, and then he'd go back over to the union rep to make sure he knew just how to play it if the operation went south.

Captain Cisone came out of the boss's office.

"How ya doing, Jimmy?" he asked.

"I'm fine, Guido. All of a sudden everybody's taking an interest in my health. I'm fine. I just caught Dillinger and I'm about to drop the hammer on Willie Sutton."

Cisone rolled his neck. "Just a manner of speech, detective." The executive officer sat on the edge of Salerno's desk. "I'm not busting your balls, detective, so how about you don't bust on mine. I'm asking if you want to do some police work."

"Somebody's cat get stuck in a tree?"

Cisone got up.

"Sorry, Cap. I'm not so good at this," Salerno said. "Just cause I'm on light duty doesn't mean I got to break faith on a case."

"I hear that, detective. You up to some good old-fashioned spade work on this decap job?"

"Hawkey's running that case," Jimmy said.

Captain Cisone rolled his shoulders. "Last time I checked,

I'm the XO and we got some celebrity's melon and nothing else but bullshit. Find out everything you can about the Spences' and the neighbor, Haynes."

"And you want this when?"

"Yesterday would be good," said Cisone.

"Sorry for being a prick, Guido. And speaking of pricks, here they come."

Assistant Special Agent in Charge Renaldo Dellum and Agent Eileen Handler came into the squad from Inspector Zinn's office. Dellum walked over. "Looking forward to working with you, Captain Cisone."

"Sure you are, Dellum. Too bad your boss climbed his way up the ladder and found himself in Baghdad."

The new ASAC turned toward Salerno. "Sorry to hear about your partner."

"Don't you say nothing about him, Renaldo. Nothing at all."

Dellum smoothed the lapels of his charcoal grey suit. Agent Handler walked up. "In any case, we do look forward to working with you again. Have a nice day," she said.

"In a pig's eye," Jimmy told them. "In a pig's eye." Salerno did some deep breathing and went in to see the boss with Captain Cisone.

Inspector Zinn had changed into his running clothes. "You alright, Jimmy?" he asked. "You look pale."

"I'm good," said Salerno.

"What did the Eyes want?" asked Cisone.

"The bad news is they just lectured me up on how they have jurisdiction under the expanded kidnap law," Zinn said. "The good news is they got enough on their plate with the trials here and Jersey on pay-for-play, not to mention making sure that nobody makes off with the Liberty Bell." He double-knotted his running shoes. "We've agreed, our information officer is to see they get face time with the media, and I'm to keep them advised and to provide complete access to case materials."

"Sure you will," said Cisone.

"Meanwhile," the inspector said, "I've got to take my run." He looked at his watch. "Before I tell Lieutenant Esposito she's going to be baby-sitting those college boys."

"I'll walk you out," said Cisone. "I could use the fresh air. No way the Eyes don't hijack this case we come up with anything good."

Salerno went back to the squad. Hawkey Moore and Lefko came in looking like they just solved the Lindbergh case.

"Hey, Jimmy," said Gene Lefko. Moore didn't say anything.

"Well, if it ain't the Lone Ranger and Tonto," Salerno said.

Gene, Gene, the Dancing Machine did that little shuffle with his feet.

"You working OT, Salerno?" said Moore. "Half a day's overtime on light duty, right?"

"Overtime in not asking you to step outside," Jimmy told him.

Lieutenant Esposito came into the squad. "Boys, boys. I could hear you in the stairwell. If you're fighting about who gets to take me to the prom, my dance card's full."

Jimmy got up. "Now that the Bobbsey twins are back, I've got some police work to do. Boss is out for his run. He said he'd fill you in about the Feds when he got back." Salerno gave Hawkey the finger on the way out.

He was feeling better and drove over to Higgins'. Big Bill himself was there and came over and sat in the booth across from Jimmy. Bill called the waitress over. Another new girl. This one had the complexion of a redhead, but she had dyed her hair jet black and she had a diamond stud in her nose.

"Can I be of assistance?" she asked.

"We're okay, hon," Higgins told her. "She dresses like some rapper or something. 'Hip-hop,' my young Billy says, but she's polite as hell. Looks are deceiving they say."

"Not to us, Bill. Beauty's in the eye of the beholder only if you've never worked the streets."

"You got that right. How about I pour us both a drink?" Big Bill Higgins got up and came back with a shot and a beer chaser for each of them. "Thirteen years here, and I ain't spilled a drop. Maybe that's why I'm thinking of getting out. You know, leave while I still got the gift."

"Getting out?"

"Selling to my kid. I work part-time. My lawyer says to have him and his wife sign a note, do it kosher. Plus the sign stays up."

Salerno sipped his whiskey. "You got to do what's best for you, Bill. Before you know it, they're cracking you open like me."

"You doing alright, Jimmy?"

"I'm doing alright. They're going to put another stent in, like a twenty thousand mile tune-up or whatever." He lifted up his glass. "It's Us Against Them," he said.

Jimmy drove over to the driving range. Kessler was back, but there was something hinkie about him. A pretty lady was teaching her daughter how to hit a ball.

Kessler gave Jimmy a bucket of balls without a word and set the two up down at the other end. Salerno remembered to exhale as Doc DeAngelis had told him and drove the ball good. His last shot came within fifteen yards of the berm where the seagull landed.

Salerno put his empty basket and a five on the counter. "He's mine next time," he said.

Kessler looked away when he spoke. "Better make it soon, Jimmy. I'm selling out."

"You're what?"

"I'm going to Florida, Jimmy. They're going to put a Toyota dealership in. They gave me an offer I couldn't refuse."

"When's this?"

"I'm closing up next week, but they won't be doing nothing

for six months or so." He took a key off the ring in his pocket. "Meanwhile, you play whenever you want." Kessler pushed the five-dollar bill back across the counter.

"Keep it," Jimmy told him. "Buy yourself some suntan lotion."

The world was going down the shitter. Salerno stopped off at the bank to check his safety deposit. On the way home, he called Rook from the car. "Meet me at Connie Small's," he said.

Lucas Rook's twenty-dollar tip the last time in got him some courtesy from Connie, but little more.

"What can I do for you?" she said.

"Here to meet my friend." He put another twenty on the bar.

"Now there be my friend." She called the waiter over. "Lenny, you show this fine gentleman a booth in the back."

There were only three "sorry's" on the way to the booth. Rook ordered a Coors Light and called in to pick up his messages.

One from Tom Bailey looking for work and one from a divorce lawyer. Maybe he'd put the two of them together. Two calls from Grace Savoy singing in a country-western voice that she had a shoot for that evening at the usual rate. Rook wrote himself a note to figure that loss of revenue somewhere into his billing to Philip First.

Salerno came in.

"You drinking?" Rook asked.

"Not with you," Jimmy told him.

"Sorry, sorry," said Lenny.

"That's twenty-three since I been here."

"I guess he's sorry, New York. You want to talk business, let's talk."

"You called me," said Rook.

Salerno took a deep breath. "Right. Here's the deal. I give you some stuff to do. Nothing that's going to get in anybody's way. You report to me. You bill your client. You give me a piece."

Lucas sipped his beer. "I can live with that, provided you give me the word when the Philly PD finds the rest of Teacher Jan."

Salerno nodded. "We wouldn't be here if I wasn't getting another procedure on my heart."

Rook wrote down the information Jimmy gave him, adding one digit to each number and advancing each letter of the Spence and Haynes addresses. Then he balled up the napkins underneath and put them in his pocket. "The heart thing, Salerno," he said. "I didn't know you had one."

In the old days you walked into City Hall with a couple of tens folded up small, shook a couple of hands, and you got whatever you needed. No way you did that in Philly now. The building looked like a birthday cake, but you took a nibble, you were going to show up in somebody's surveillance.

So Lucas let his fingers do the walking until the phone book gave him a title company that would provide verbal property information and charge it to his credit card and send the hard copy to his office for billing purposes. The Spence property was purchased originally in 1957. Refinanced once. One lien for unpaid school taxes.

The Haynes piece was more complicated. It was purchased cheap from an estate five years ago as three separate properties: 711, 13, 15 North Swain Street. Two mortgages; the second was five times the first, which probably was for new construction rather than refinance, since the loans were against 1101 Blueberry Hill Lane, formerly known as 711-15 Swain. Then one home equity loan for twenty-five that was marked satisfied.

It didn't matter that Salerno was running some Tom Sawyer game, getting paid for the privilege to do his work, because he also had the privilege of billing Mr. Feinstein. The public library was next to the juvenile court. The buildings were twins, but it was easy to tell which was which. The library had the street bums going in to use the toilet and take a nap. The court building had the thugs coming out with smirks on their faces.

There were no parking spaces, so Lucas drove into Center City and found a lot that wasn't going to rape him. He walked down Walnut Street to the ING at the corner of Seventeenth. He bought a non-caramel, non-French cup of coffee and computer time and ran "Maurice Haynes" and "Spence." Nothing to speak of, except Mr. Haynes won a Rotary "Man of the Year" award three years ago. He also was a sixteenth-century duke and a bit actor in four 1950s Westerns. There were hundreds of references to the Spences. Nothing relevant to the case except the billing.

Lucas crossed Walnut Street and started down the block to the Corned Beef Academy. A real beauty came out of a French restaurant and asked a crud to get his feet off the outside table.

"This is a free country," the dirt bag said.

"Please," she said again.

"It's the people's sidewalk," he told her. "The streets belong to the people."

Rook grabbed the laces of both of the bum's shoes.

"Police brutality," the man cried.

Lucas dragged him off the chair. "Get walking and keep walking. You come back and I'm going to throw you into traffic."

"That was pretty rough," said the beauty. "But appreciated. My name's Daisy. Can I get you anything? A glass of white wine?"

"Not unless it's part of a corned beef on rye."

"Corned Beef Academy's closed. So's Pickles Plus. I think you can get one in the food court at Liberty Place."

"Mysterious men of action do not frequent food courts. Street vendors, I'll do. Food courts I won't."

He stopped at a vendor on 19th Street and got a sausage with cooked onions, which he took across the street to Rittenhouse Square. Lots of dog walkers picking up shit in little bags.

Rook got his rental at the parking lot. Paying twelve bucks for less than two hours was crazy, but in New York it would be twice that. Then again, you wouldn't have to pass on a deli when you needed one.

He drove back out the Ben Franklin Parkway. Go back to the room. Write up his notes and give Salerno a call. Then, depending on whatever, he'd go back up the Turnpike or maybe see what else he could pick up tomorrow morning.

Jimmy Salerno was in the basement counting the money from his safety deposit when Carmela called down the steps to him. "It's Tom Sawyer from up the Turnpike, hon."

"Tell him to hold, Carm." He put the cash in the little safe under the floor. Then he smoothed out the rug and put his exercise bike back on top.

"What you got, Rook?"

"Haynes and the Spences don't look like much. I'll run NCIC tomorrow."

"I already did that. One of them had a beef down the shore which is all. You bill your client for that."

"That's what I do."

"You got anything else, genius?" Salerno asked.

"Maybe grab a cold one or three. You allowed out of the house, Salerno?"

"I never mix business with displeasure, New York."

Jimmy hung up. Maybe he'd go back to Higgins' place before they turned it into some disco bar. Things weren't going the way he'd planned, the way he wanted it. His partner dead. Working light duty until they cracked his chest open. The driving range going to be a car dealer. The bar maybe gone. And doing business with that wise ass from Jew York.

He went upstairs. Carmela was at the stove. "I made some nice 'scarole soup. A little pastina," she said.

Jimmy sat down while she served him. "You know, I dreamt I was smoking again," he told her. "Camels. It's been years and I still could taste it."

She patted him on the shoulder. "I know you won't."

Right. No smoking. Eat like an old man. Sitting on his ass while Moore and Gene-Gene work the case for all the OT it's worth. Detective Salerno called into the inspector to let him know he was still a gold shield detective.

Joe Zinn answered his own phone. For a while when women were first being stuffed down everybody's throat, the inspector had a receptionist. But even with her movie star figure and big blue eyes, it didn't justify the waste of manpower.

"Just an update, boss," Salerno said. He gave over the spade-work that Rook had done for him. Then he couldn't resist, "The Lone Ranger and Tonto find who kidnapped Lindbergh's baby yet?"

The inspector adjusted the foam donut on his chair. "What we don't need is disharmony, detective. It's counter-productive."

Jimmy took a deep breath. "I didn't mean nothing by it, boss, like you were putting me in the bag or whatever."

"Right, detective. You just get yourself back in shape. The circus'll still be here. Captain Hadley down at the 92nd gives me a heads-up they just found a pair of legs on the River Drive."

Detective Salerno took a nap, then drove out to make a house call on the medical examiner. Sam Nessel's stone colonial was in a cul-de-sac out in the suburbs. His Caddy with the official business and handicap plates was in the driveway. Not bad for a thieving pain-in-the-ass dwarf twitch.

Virginia Nessel answered the door. A black puppy ran between her legs, but Jimmy scooped him up.

"Bad boy, Connor," she said.

"Your husband's expecting me," Jimmy told her.

Sam came up behind her, walking odd the way he did. He had an unlit cigarette in his hand. "Detective Salerno's a friend of mine," he said. "We're going over to the shop."

"So I save your poodle and now I'm your friend?"

Nessel lit up and took a double hit of the menthol smoke. "Bouvier. He's a Bouvier. You know, like the Kennedys. I named him 'Connor' after Arnold in *The Terminator*. You know, John Connor." He unlocked his garage.

"You got them photos, Sam?"

"Sure I do, like you said."

The detective leaned against the band saw. "Sure beats the hell out of the last time, don't it, Sam?"

"You liking me for killing kids, detective, that wasn't right."

"Neither was you double-charging the city, whatever, moving them corpses around the way you did."

Nessel handed over the envelope. "I took these shots of the DOA's legs on my own time, so I'm not turning over city property."

"How thoughtful, doc. I can find my way out. Regards to the wife."

Salerno hopped back onto 476. They had been building the Blue Route for a hundred years, but it was a beautiful thing not to have to take West Chester Pike to City Line.

The desk clerk at the Holiday Inn was either stupid or had something to hide. Jimmy badged him.

"I ask you if Lucas Rook checked out, you don't tell me, I figure you got something to hide. You running some cootchie on the side, Tyrone?"

"It's Kwame, accent on the second syllable, officer. Mr. Rook is in 317."

"It's 'detective,' Jerome. And don't bother to ring him."

"Shall I get my manager, detective?"

"I don't think so, Kwame. Now have a nice day."

Salerno went to Rook's room. "Open up in there. We're investigating somebody impersonating a cop."

Lucas left his newspaper and .45 on the bed. "Welcome Wagon remember to bring them cookies?"

"It's time they note us up pretty good. Maybe five grand," Salerno said.

"I told you," Rook said. "I get paid, you get paid. That's how this runs."

"This ain't on spec neither." He held up the envelope.

Lucas sat back down and picked up the sports page. "The suspense is killing me."

Jimmy Salerno handed him the photos. "Looks like your celebrity is coming up dead in pieces."

"Looks like it," Rook said.

Salerno pulled at the elastic of his black socks. "Complicates things, don't it?"

"Complicated is good," Lucas said.

"For once this don't make me sick," Salerno said. "At least nothing I can't wash off." He left and went out to his car in the Holiday Inn parking lot. Then he turned around and went back. "Welcome Wagon," he said when he knocked.

Lucas was packing his bag. "You forget something, James?"

"Just one thing, New York. You fuck me and I'll kill you."

Rook called Feinstein from his car. He got an automated voicemail system with not a lot of options. Maybe Phil wasn't doing all that good. He got his return call as he passed the Bordentown exit.

"Mr. Rook. I hope you have some good news for me."

"I'm on my way," Lucas said.

"My club at five-thirty?"

Lucas checked his watch. "Fine," he said. Everything has half of something else. Five-thirty means you're out of there before the dinner crowd shows up. Like he wore his watch on his right hand, so half the bad guys would think he was a lefty.

Philip Feinstein First was enjoying his Cosmopolitan when Lucas Rook arrived.

"Right on time," he said. "I appreciate that."

"Well, you're a very busy man, Mr. First. I'm wondering if we might have a moment in private." Lucas held up the envelope.

There was a smoking room down the hall, where two lawyers were showing off their fat Hondurans.

"Let's get some fresh air," said Lucas.

They went outside. Rook showed him the photos. His client took a step back.

"I never actually saw the other pictures," Feinstein said. "Or anything like this."

The accountant sat down on the white wrought-iron bench. "Terrible. Terrible. And disgusting, Mr. Rook."

"And much more complicated, Mr. First."

"Is it her?"

"I believe so, Mr. First."

"And that means what, doing what?"

"Right now, Mr. First, it means an additional five. Things just got way more complicated, Janet Scheyman coming up in pieces. And it means there's more to come."

Feinstein looked off in the distance. "Part of me understands. The accountant in me says you're trying to take advantage."

Rook leaned forward. "Let the first part write the check, Phil."

"It's a legitimate estate expense." Feinstein got up. "You can stop by the office tomorrow morning or I'll put it in the mail."

"Nine o'clock tomorrow is fine, Phil. Just fine."

34

A cop starts drinking alone, it's right around the corner that he starts thinking of swallowing his gun. But Lucas Rook knew he wasn't going to be able to sleep. He never could after he was thinking about his twin brother the way he did on the way back to New York. Rook poured himself another Jack on the rocks and went out onto the patio. Manhattan still looked good at night. Nobody could take that away.

The building across the way had its lights on every other floor to save on the electric, and there was the glow from the street. Rook looked out to where the night wasn't all broken up. The darkness and alcohol. He stretched out his bad leg and took another swallow of the Tennessee whiskey.

Grace Savoy came across from her place as easy as if she wasn't blind at all. As she got closer, he could see the puffiness on the side of her face.

"You alright?" he asked.

She felt for the other chair. "Why whatever do you mean, neighbor boy?"

"You tell me."

Grace gestured with her cigarette. "I discern the sound of ice cubes in the night. And my super olfactory senses detect Mr. Jack Daniels' finest."

He got up to pour himself another drink and make her one.

"I'm drinking green label, neighbor girl."

"Whatever makes a good Manhattan, Lucas." She had said that a dozen times before and he gave her back the same answer: "What makes a good Manhattan is flushing the bad guys."

"Right," she said. "And you don't make mixed drinks."

Lucas poured her a Jack on the rocks.

"Nice of you to put a piece of lemon in," she said as he came back with her drink.

"You got a great nose, Gracey, but no way you're smelling that from where you are."

She started to vamp for him, doing a little Tallulah Bankhead with her cigarette. Then she remembered the bruising on her face. "You forget that I can hear a pigeon fart a mile away, Lucas Rook. The sound of the knife on the cutting board."

She took her glass and offered a toast. "Here's looking at you, kid. Like I should have been looking for that door."

"You want to tell me who smacked you around, Gracey?"

"Nobody…"

"Whenever you're cracking wise about being blind, I know something's not right. Plus your face is puffed up and you got extra make-up on. So something tells me you didn't run into a door."

"I forgot my neighbor boy's a detective, didn't I?" She lit her cigarette. "Could you knock out Larry's teeth?"

"Little Lawrence, the dictator of the fashion shoot. It would be my pleasure."

Grace reached out with her glass. "Let's clink a toast to your knocking Larry's teeth out. Then I can open a bottle of *Shiraz*, or would you prefer *Charaz*?" she said.

"I don't get you, Grace."

"Precisely. *Shiraz* is red wine. *Charaz* means stringing pearls. It's a biblical reference. I was asking if you would like a pearl necklace?"

"Not tonight," he said.

"Then goodnight, sweet prince," she told him. "Call me when you've whacked him good."

The phone woke Lucas up at three o'clock in the morning.

"I'm downstairs," she said. "But they won't let me up."

Lucas recognized her voice. "I'll be right down," he said.

Jeanie Oren looked wasted. "I don't know what to do," she said. "I don't know what to do."

Rook took her back upstairs. "What happened?" he said.

"I don't know what to do, Uncle Lucas Rook. I was at this party, and we were drinking beer and all…"

He tried to sit her on the couch, but she wouldn't let go of his hand. "And then what happened, Jeanie girl?"

"People were doing X, I think."

He sat them both down. "What did the pills look like?"

"They were white with a smiley face like little boys."

"MDMA, ecstasy. How many did you drop?"

She looked at him.

"Drop, take, Jeanie. How many?"

"I don't even know that I did, Uncle Lucas. I kept thinking they were Sweetarts and I don't eat them because they're bad for my teeth. But I feel so weird. And scared."

"Your heart pounding or anything like that? You drink a lot of water?"

She shook her head.

"You having any hallucinations or whatever?"

She shook her head again.

Rook got Wingy Rosenzweig on his cell phone in Oahu. "Sorry to bother you on vacation," Lucas said. "But I got a young girl here who thinks she might have OD'd on Ecstasy."

"I won't ask how young," Wingy said. "Adam, bean, roll, E, M, a complicated drug. Does she know how much she did?"

"She's not even sure."

"Okay. We're looking for overheating, nausea, vomiting. Her eyes twitching?"

"No."

"Then assuming she took the usual recreational dose, the URD, we're calling it. You have a three-to-four hour-effect, and then two to six hours coming down. She can look for a crash afterwards if she's not lucky. Anything from sadness to terror, then a hangover, maybe some post-MDMA depression. But that's her problem. You look out for inappropriate bonding and an uncontrollable desire to hug."

"I can handle that, Wingy."

"The mortality rate is usually about 1 out of every 50,000, unless they're mixing their drugs, which they usually are. Also watch out for tongue and cheek chewing-hers, not yours. Have a good night. I'm about to go catch me some big-ass fish."

Lucas took Jeanie Oren into the bathroom. "You're feeling alright, maybe you should take a shower. I'll wait outside."

She said okay and after, came out with her hair up in a towel. "Do you have a sweat suit or something for me to sleep in, Uncle Lucas?"

"I think we should watch some TV until I know you're good. You know, 'pull an all-nighter' like you college kids do. You hungry?"

"I guess so," she said.

"Let me make you some eggs for a change. In the morning, I'll drop you off at school."

"You won't tell my dad, will you?"

"Of course I will, Jeanie, but we can talk about what I'll tell him when you're not stoned or whatever."

Lucas found something for Jeanie to watch on cable. He did some paperwork and then put some coffee on as the sun came up behind the office building to the east. He took her back to her dorm to change her clothes so she didn't smell like dope. Then he took her to the restaurant.

"We didn't discuss what we were going to say, Uncle Lucas."

"I'll leave that up to you," he told her.

Joe Oren was in the kitchen with Sam unclogging the drain when they came in.

"I got something to tell you, Daddy," she said.

"Is it bad?"

"It could have been," she told him.

Rook nodded and went back to his apartment. The bank didn't open for another two hours, and he could use the sleep.

The phone woke him again. "I'm thinking of taking her over to St. Vincent's for a check-up," Joe Oren said. "I just wanted to say thank you for looking after my little girl."

"Sure," Lucas told him. He turned the ringer off, took a Benadryl and set his alarm. It would be good to get back to work.

Detective Salerno sat in the back booth of the Dunkin' Donuts on Cottman Avenue.

"Excuse me if I don't get up, New York," he said. "These dot heads pulling down three, four hundred thou, I'm entitled to service or whatever."

Rook put his coffee and three donuts on the table.

"You got something else for me than a couple of glazed?"

"That I do, James." He handed over his newspaper with the envelope inside.

"I get my stent replaced next week," said Salerno. He wrote down an address and handed it over. "In the meantime, here's something else to run. I'm sure you'll do a fine job."

Rook's keycard did not work when he got back to his room at the Holiday Inn. His knock brought a priest with a dangling collar and a French accent.

"Can I help you?" said the priest.

"I don't think so," Lucas said. He went back down to check-in, where a Hispanic woman and a black man were trying not to look silly in their uniforms. "There's somebody in my room and he's either early or late," Rook told them.

"Excuse me," said the man, whose name was Clothier.

Lucas held up his plastic entry card. "I was here. I am here. And someone else is in my room."

"Can I help you?" asked the woman. "My name is Hilda Vasquez and I am here to serve you."

Rook took a deep breath. "Last time: I am registered in 317. You got somebody else in there."

She nodded. Clothier worked the computer screen and pointed to the information. "Father Phillipe is in 317. He has the reservation now. Are you his brother or something?"

"Not hardly," Rook said. "Where's my stuff?"

"You must have taken it with you," said Hilda Vasquez.

He leaned in. "I did, did I?"

"That's what people do when they check out," said Clothier.

Rook leaned over the counter. "Could be check-mate if this

conversation goes any further, pal."

"I don't get it," said Clothier.

"Of course you don't," said Lucas. "Now I'm going to walk over to the Adam's Mark and check in. When I come back, you better have my stuff."

"I'm sorry, sir," said Ms. Vasquez. "The hotel no longer is."

"No longer is what?" Lucas asked.

"A hotel. It's going to be a Target," she told him.

He thought of telling her that she could expect a similar fate, but let that pass. He had his weapons with him, but there was his change of clothes, shaving kit, and two pages of notes. "Find my stuff and call me on my cell," Lucas said. "Or you'll both be looking for jobs."

Rook made some calls from the Denny's. There was a motel up the road, but it was jammed.

He called back to the Holiday Inn. Clothier answered.

"Let me talk to Ms. Vasquez."

"I'm sorry, sorry, sir. She be on break now. Can I be of assistance?"

"I don't think so," Rook said. "I'm coming back for my stuff in an hour. It better be there."

There was a Dunkin Donuts down City Line. America at its best. You spend a million bucks, go to Donut College, and then make 400k a year selling product that cost you 9 cents to make and clogs the arteries worse than a glass of bacon fat.

He took a seat at the window with a cup of black coffee. The sector car pulled up and the p/o came in, talking on his cell phone. He loaded up for a trip back to the precinct without giving Rook a once-over. Bad police work all around except for the donut run.

When Rook got back to the Holiday Inn, Mrs. Vasquez had returned from her break. Hair neat, new lipstick. She probably was a looker twenty years ago.

She handed over a Holiday Inn folder. "I'm pleased that

we've located your property, Mr. Rook." She pronounced it as if it rhymed with "kook." "But I am sorry that the room is no longer available." She offered a discount ticket. "We can, however, offer you another room on the fourth floor. Housekeeping is in there now. And a discount on your next stay."

Rook looked at the coupon. "Not valid if combined with any other discount." It wasn't worth the paper it was printed on because it meant his law enforcement discount didn't apply. No way he was going to stay there.

There were two other places that would work. The Holiday Inn up at Penn. Two years ago he had worked a civil suit at Penn involving some allegations about their admissions policy, so he knew the locale. Too much cooz walking around the college in belly shirts was not good for the prostate. He drove back down to the Korman Suites where he'd stayed when he was working the Raimondo job.

The parking lot that was spread out like a fan was filled up. The small swimming pool off to the right still had a black tarp on it. Lucas swung around again and grabbed a spot as a '67 black Camaro pulled out. No antique plates. You got to spend a lot of coin on your vehicle to drive a classic every day. Or maybe he was just some rich dipshit who didn't care.

The only room available had a three-day minimum stay, with a "price upgrade" for early check-out. They're putting their hand in your pocket and they're calling it an upgrade. Beautiful, but that was Philip Feinstein's problem. Lucas had the address that Salerno had given him and a thirst for a cold one. He checked in. Then he made a quick tour of the building to see if there were any changes and went out after that beer.

Rook rode back in towards the two new stadiums so he could get a look. Now there were four sports venues in South Philadelphia. The Linc and Citizen's Bank Park were empty, eerie. They were supposed to be in the heart of town, like Baltimore, but Penn and a politician blocked that and then the Chinese were able to block the next move.

Rook found a bar near the off-track betting parlor. The beer was cold and the bartender had a great rack. He showed her the address. "You know where this is, hon? I'm going to look at a '67 Camaro." In Philly you said "hon" or "Howya doin'?" you could have two heads and nobody'd notice. You said, "Go Iggles," you could have three.

"Virgil Street. Never heard of it. You got a phone number or a zip code, I could help you with that a hundred percent."

A guy in construction worker's clothes, but clean shoes, sat down.

"You know where Virgil Street is, Norm?" She put his Coors up on the bar.

"Virgil Street," he said. "Virgil Street," as if he was contemplating the universe.

The bartender pointed to Rook's glass.

"I'm good," he told her.

"Virgil Street," said Clean Shoes. "I'm saying it's in the Northeast. Not down near Oxford Circle, that's all PR's now, or Trevose neither. Somewheres in between."

"Zip code's 19154," she said. "Maybe 19152. You could take 95."

"I was coming in that way, Theresa. It's a parking lot from Academy Road. I'm saying the Blue Route to the Turnpike. Second exit is the Boulevard."

"Appreciate it," Lucas said as he put another dollar down. "Go Iggles."

Route 476 North was jammed too. Maybe he should have taken the Expressway to Route 1. Maybe it didn't matter since he was being paid by the hour. He put the radio on. All news, sports talk from has-beens or never-was's. He worked the dial until he got WFAN from New York.

Traffic opened up and he got on the Pennsylvania Turnpike East. Easy Pass saves all that time waiting for the toll booths, but then somebody can tell where you've been and where you haven't. He drove Route 1 South until the crocodile's clock started ticking. Rook pulled into an Amoco for a fill-up, a Clark bar to stop that clock, and directions.

"Old Virgil Street or New Virgil Street?" asked the cashier.

Rook told him the number, but changed it by two blocks.

"Try Cottman or Disston. I think it's near the playground or the MAB."

Cottman Avenue was 73 East. Passed small shopping areas, a Krispy Kreme, a high school. There was an MAB Paint store and playground on the left. Rook made the turn and followed it to Disston Street. A short muscular man with a thick Jewish accent told him he didn't know from Virgil, except if it was Ozzie Virgil, the catcher. Lucas went back out to Cottman and drove until the candy bar wore off and the Country Club Diner appeared.

Two eggs over corned beef hash. Then a second cup of coffee and the newspaper. Not a bad way to make a living. The new directions took him to Burholme Park and then onto Virgil Street.

Lucas followed the numbers down, but then they stopped. The street name changed and the row houses were replaced by new single construction. There were four houses and then three lots.

He went back to the first house and rang the doorbell. "Three Coins in the Fountain." An older black woman answered. Frank Sinatra she wasn't. Or Rossano Brazzi.

"Haynes residence," she said.

Rook asked her about the Virgil Street address.

The woman shuddered. "I know that place. Or knew it. Everybody did, not that I knew anything about it firsthand. I'm from North Philly and proud of it."

"So what happened, dear?"

"I ain't no dear. And I don't want to talk about it. Burned to the ground. To the ground. And with them in it. And all the houses on the row got messed up, which is how they got torn down and Mr. Haynes he got this big beautiful house which I am responsible to care for and I don't like strangers up in here when he's not at home."

Rook went back to the car. Jimmy Salerno had him on a wild goose chase or giving him the long version so they both could get noted up by keeping the meter running. He swung back out to Cottman Avenue for another cup of coffee and one of the pieces of cheesecake that turned like art in the plexi-glass carousel. Then he drove over to the library in the 2200 block of Cottman Avenue.

Rook looked through the magazines until a computer opened up. That and the *Philadelphia Daily News* microfiche took him to the story of the woman who burned her house down with her invalid parents locked in their bedroom. A neighbor was quoted as saying it smelled like a barbeque for weeks.

Rook's examination of the microfiche confirmed what every cop knew, that reporters were right in the middle of the shitpile. The only worse things were the politicians, the lawyers, and the skels. The story about how Lyna Fine burned her parents got all the play it could handle and then some. The *Inquirer* tried the more subdued version, so *The Daily News*, which was owned by the same company, could run the bad stuff. There were articles on the front page for the first two days and plenty of grisly photos. Then the story worked its way back to the middle of the paper, where it got lost in the ads for cars and cheap furniture. Both rags dragged the story out again when the trial started and five years ago when the murderer was streeted and told to go out and have a nice day.

Rook took down the bylines along with his notes about how Ms. Fine burned the house down with her mom and dad inside. Naughty girl. Maybe that's what they got for not giving her a "d" in her first name. Daddy was on oxygen and Mommy in a wheel-chair when they caught fire. A brother, Delbert, had not been heard from.

Lucas went to the investigator's most trusty tool, the phone book. No Lyna or Delbert Fine. Then he went back to his room at the Embassy Suites and called the newspapers. The investigative reporter at the Inky was "no longer employed." The one at *The Daily News* was deceased. Rook hung up and then looked at his notes.

Lyna Fine, the poor dear, murdering bitch, served seven years in Muncy State Correctional. Not a nice place. He had been up there once before, about fifteen miles from Williamsport. The joint was where they housed the female capital cases and it looked the part. After graduating Muncy, Lyna was transferred to Cambridge Springs, the SCI in Crawford County. Cambridge Springs was a little more than ten years old at the time, and the newspaper took pains to inform its reading public that it was "a minimum security facility for women, the majority of whom were nearing release from prison." Important to know as well that it was located on the campus of the former Polish Alliance College. Thanks for the tasty piece of news.

The article on Lyna Fine's release confirmed she had probation to serve. Rook called over to the Philadelphia Adult Probation. PO's liked to think of themselves as cops so it took only a couple of calls to get to a probation officer who knew the case. The guy's name was Flowers and he sighed a lot.

"You don't like your job, Officer Flowers?"

"Oh, sure I do. Nothing better than to listen to the pieces of garbage sit here and lie to me about why they're not doing what they need to do."

"Big surprise," Lucas said.

Flowers sighed again. "The only surprise is I don't violate them all. Now how can I help one of New York's finest? We don't got another McFadden here? Board of Probation and Parole gave that scumbag a pass, he was a very convincing fellow, and he goes up your way and offs some old lady."

"Affected your governor's race or whatever?" Rook said.

"Right, right, but Ridge was the right man anyway. The other guy was a lightweight. He just got sued again or something."

Lucas looked at his watch. "I'm looking for the lovely Ms. Lyna Fine. Her aunt in Manhattan, an old spinster-type, left her some money."

The probation officer took a bite of his lunch. "I remember the case. She was transferred over to the Psych Unit." He mimicked an official voice. "Building a trusting relationship that includes accountability to the court."

"How thoughtful."

"Right, she knows enough to fry up her own parents, and now we're supposed to tuck her in." He took another bite of ham and cheese and popped the top of his Diet Coke. "I know the PO who handled her over there. Said she was a nut job. He's retired. The city got this drop program. I'm out in three with a roll big enough to choke a horse."

Rook doodled some dollar signs. "I'm sure you earned it. You got a number for me?"

Flowers barely stifled his belch. "Not really. Plus I don't know what he could tell you, them HIPPA rules and all. More paperwork bullshit. His name's Kozolewski, Murray, like 'Murray the K,' the old disc jockey."

Rook threw him a bone. "Lock 'em all up, pardner," he said.

36

The phone book didn't have Murray Kozolewski and neither did information, but for twenty-five bucks that he could bill as an hour, he accessed an Internet source that gave him a Turnersville, New Jersey address.

Lucas took a Coors Light from the small refrigerator in his suite. Not too many things had to suck worse than living on the road, unless you were a ballplayer, which meant you got all the poontang you could handle. Of course, sitting in a cold unmarked and peeing in a jar while you eyeball where some jitbag's holedup sucked bad too.

He drove over the Walt Whitman Bridge and off to Route 42 and 55. Murray the K lived two blocks away from a decent-looking crab joint. The houses were close together, but singles. A POW-MIA flag hung outside.

Murray answered the door in his bedroom slippers. He had a Kool in one hand and a hammer in the next. Rook flashed his NYPD gold shield.

"So?" said Kozolewski.

"I got a couple of questions for you. Then you can get to your redecorating or whatever."

Murray took a drag on his smoke. "It's for strangers. I don't like strangers."

Rook took out a fifty.

"Him I like," said the retired PO. "What do you want?"

"Lyna Fine."

Murray took another drag as he sat down heavily. "I can't talk about that unless you got paperwork on an open case."

Lucas handed over the money. "President Grant is telling me it's alright, detective."

"You were her PO?" Rook asked.

"Actually they had me as her 'case manager,' like she was some neurotic housewife who needed midlife counseling rather than what she was." He snubbed his cigarette and lit another with the hammer still in his hand. "That's important, what she really was."

"And what's that?" Rook said.

"Arsonist. Murderer. And filled with rage even after she done them. Not that I can blame her."

Lucas waited for him to go on, but he didn't. Rook sat down. "I'll wait."

Kozolewski got back up. "I told you I don't like strangers in my house." Then he realized what he was doing and put his hammer down on the end table. "Her father used to fuck her since she was a little girl. Her mother used to watch." He picked the hammer back up. "And help."

"Lyna Fine got an address?"

"Mt. Lebanon Cemetery," Murray said. "She shut the garage door on her head. One of them big overhead ones that weigh a ton."

"How long ago?"

"Year or two ago. She was done with reporting to me and all, but I used to get a Christmas card from her. Can you believe that shit?"

Lucas got ready to leave. "The brother, Murray. What can you tell me about him?"

Kozolewski picked a piece of tobacco off his tongue. "Half a weirdo himself, distant. But he held a steady job, which was important for her profile. Downtown, I think."

"Appreciate your help, Murray. Enjoy your retirement."

"Sure I will, detective. Let the good times roll."

Rook drove back across the bridge without stopping at the seafood place and called Phil Feinstein from the car. Mr. First was not in. Lucas said he'd call back at three rather than leave a message on the voicemail. You're going to nudge somebody for another couple of thou, you want to hear their voice when you tell them.

Telephone information produced a "David Fine," on Lombard Street, too rich of an address. "Donald Fine, CPA," and two "D. Fines." Usually it's a woman using the first initial behind not wanting some perv to get the first step at being familiar. The first one had an unlisted number. Lucas played good-cop, bad-cop to get the address from the phone company.

Sedgwick Street meant nothing to him, but the cobblestones and trolley tracks on Germantown Avenue did. It was one thing to go for the quaint "Battle of Germantown" thing, even if he had to drive by some high school with students pushing baby carriages and not a book in sight. But it was another thing to be playing havoc with his vehicle's suspension, even if it was a rental.

There was a Rite Aid drugstore on the right. Physician, heal thyself, or whatever, the Rite Aid bigwig doing a significant federal bit for trying to make his sick balance sheet look good. Sedgwick Street was not far up Germantown Avenue. There was a playground on the right, a new supermarket on the left. If you came to the Trolley Stop Diner, you'd gone too far.

Lucas Rook went back down Germantown Avenue and made his turn at Sedgwick. He took his Fed Ex cap and clipboard from the trunk and knocked next door to D. Fine's address.

A stringy white man with his hat on backwards answered the door. "You want D. Fine? That's next door. Besides, what you want Miss Diane for? You got a package for her, I takes her things and brings them to her."

"Sure you do, pal. But company rules say I got to deliver to the named recipient. Besides, the addressee here looks like a man's name, not Diane."

"Must be her cousin or whatever, because he don't live up around here, but I hold it for him."

"Appreciate, neighbor, I really do, but I can only leave this package with the named addressee," Lucas said. "Now have a nice day."

The next stop was in Upper Darby. The garbage smell got stronger. He'd take a run by Olympia Street, get a good look, then decide whether to pay Mr. Fine a visit or play it kosher and give what he got to the Philly PD.

Rook drove by the Holiday Inn that had double-booked his room and lost his stuff. City Avenue was an old combination of the fancy suburbs on one side and what looked like it was changing on the other. Then St. Joseph's University and the Cardinal's residence. A little down the road, St. Charles Seminary on the right. With all the bloody clothes being dragged up from the Church's basement, maybe they should have some good PR, like "The Church That Doesn't Love You Back" or whatever.

Lucas took a left where US 1 became Township Line. Familiar turf. Not far away he had walked where the murderous fuck had dropped Heather Raimondo like a bag of rocks. Down Lansdowne Avenue and then left at Garrett Road. What a long-ass route, but with the mileage and the clock ticking, he could forget it made his head spin.

Olympia Street was behind the Tower Theater that had an Oren Evans concert coming up. Lucas found the street and address. Delbert Fine's house was dark. There was a row of black lampposts outside. A thin back alley. Little traffic on the block. A curtain moved across the street.

Clipboard time again. Rook walked down the alley and up to the back door. He could not see the interior, but the television was on. No bars on the windows, the locks were old, no indication of alarms. A car pulled in the alley. Rook walked slowly by each garage, doodling as if he were taking notes. Then he drove the short way back to his room.

As he expected, there were no messages on his room phone. He called back to his office and his apartment. Tom Bailey asking if any work had turned up, a call from the Yellow Pages about renewing his ad, and Catherine Wren. Maybe she had come to her senses that he was not some monster. Maybe not.

Rook was writing up his notes when there was a knock at the door. He put his .45 in his back waistband and answered it. It was the Feds.

"What a pleasant surprise. You two the Welcome Wagon?"

"Still a wiseass," said Assistant Special Agent Renaldo Dellum.

"And I'm still Lucas Rook. Agent Handler, you have ginger snaps or whatever for me?"

"I do not," she said. "I hope you have a Pennsylvania permit for any weapon you're carrying."

Lucas sat down on the bed and picked up his Coors Light. "Sorry," he said. "This is my last one. If I knew you were coming I'd've been more hospitable." He took a slow drink. "To what do I owe this honor?"

"Time to pack it up and go back to where you came from," said the tall black man. "Maybe find some transom to crawl through."

"And why should I do that?" asked Rook. "Last I checked, guys like me were still free to travel."

"Because this is our matter now, and you don't want to be obstructing a federal investigation, now do you?" asked ASAC Dellum.

"Why, heavens no. I don't. But do tell, is Uncle looking for some easy pub?"

"The Bureau does not need any publicity, Mr. Rook," said Agent Handler. "What it needs is anything you have on the murder of Janice Scheyman. And then you can get yourself back to New York."

"Somebody got some juice or fame gets dead and like usual, you wait until the real cops do the dirty work and then you come waltzing in."

"Wrong as usual, Mr. Rook," said Dellum. "The Bureau is investigating the work of a serial killer." He smiled his best Ivy League smile. "And the last time I checked, you weren't a real cop anymore."

Lucas finished his beer. "I got nothing and you're not even getting that. So how about you go be 'Federal' somewhere else and I'll catch up on my beauty sleep."

"You can expect a formal invitation," said Agent Handler. "You can count on that."

Rook fluffed his pillow. "I wouldn't miss it for the world," he said.

The two FBI agents left, leaving the door open behind them.

The knives lay sharp in the cold, cold room. First to the arm and when that was done, deep into the chest until the sternum cracked.

Rook let his thoughts settle before he placed his call to Warren G. Phelps, Esquire. You better know what you're going to say before you dial up a five-hundred-dollar-an- hour conversation or when the Feds are going to be listening in. An even more aristocratic voice answered the phone than the last time, a sure sign that the hourly rate was up again.

Phelps put him on hold for thirty seconds. "I'm sorry for that, but I simply cannot resist the opportunity of billing multiple clients for the same time."

"I'm working that job in Philly we talked about. The Feds pay me a visit about how I should keep my hands off."

"They mention anything about the other matter?"

"They didn't, Warren. Just the usual 'don't be obstructing while we're doing God's work.' But it's Dellum and Handler, who 'happened' to be on the Raimondo killings."

"Right, right. Epps has moved on up the line. Not bringing up the Raimondo case could be a lot of things, none of them to be concerned about. My educated guess is that the underlying civil suit has settled and the US Attorney's got so much on their plate, you're not even on their radar. I'll take a look at the dockets on the civil rights claim."

"At four-fifty an hour, I'd appreciate your paralegal or what- ever take a peek. Some world, isn't it? I kill a baby killer, a cop killer, and somebody files a suit for damages."

"Section 1983 is often a lucrative means to recover damages," Phelps said.

"Damages? You're kidding me, right, counselor?"

"A man has to make a living, Lucas, but if you have any questions about what may or may not constitute 'obstruction,' call me before you act. I always get back to you."

"At your rates, Warren, so would I."

"I like that, Lucas, and thank you for the referral of Shirl Freelang. I'll make a note not to charge you for the memo to the file that I was about to dictate. Now let me go. I've got a stockbroker on the line who just got a federal subpoena. I like them to sit in it for a while after they shit themselves."

The Feds weren't still running that bag of crap case against him, there was no way they'd be running a tap on his phone. But he placed his next calls to Salerno from a payphone anyway. Lucas got an answering machine at home and the cell phone didn't answer. Then he called up to the squad.

Rook said he was an appliance repairman calling about a dishwasher complaint. Gene Lefko took the call and told him that Detective Salerno was not in.

"My wife had the same problem," said Lefko. "They said the drawer was too long and we had to use this additive."

"That is a problem on some models, sir. I'll try Mr. Salerno at home."

"It's Detective Salerno, sir."

"I'll remember that," Lucas said. He had work to do. The Feds tell you they're investigating a serial killer, there's information to be picked up all over the place. But Lucas knew he had to work fast. You got a killer with an appetite, everything can be pulled into a bloody whirlpool, including his fee.

He tried Salerno again on his cell and at home. Then he wrote down the mileage from his odometer and started back to town. First Lucas swung by the driving range. Nothing doing there except a big seagull sitting on the sign like he owned the place. Rook leaned on the horn and the bird flew out and settled on the berm at the edge of the driving range.

Rook drove by Bill Higgins' and the Dunkin Donuts near the precinct. Nothing doing.

"Telegram, telephone, tell-a-woman." He rolled up on Connie Small's place with a folded twenty in his left pocket and a Grant in his right. She was behind the bar in an elegant dress.

"You look like you came right off a birthday cake," he told her.

"As long as it's double chocolate fudge." Connie poured him another glass of last time.

"Miracle what they can do you get to the right doctor," he said. "Like with Jimmy."

"True, true," she said.

Connie Small poured a Hennessey for a black man with a shaved head, who was none too happy to be sharing a bar with a white man.

Shaved head gave him a hard look. Rook motioned for Connie to come close. "Send your hard-looking friend a drink on me and tell him to save his wolfing for somebody who gives a shit."

She poured the drink and took it over to her patron. "Now, Jerome, don't be eyeballing my friend. He's my financial advisor."

Jerome finished his Hennessey and took the other one to a table.

"Financial advisor?" asked Lucas.

"Yes, you are. You're about to advise me I'm going to get some finances or you're about to pay for your drink and say goodbye."

Rook put the twenty on the bar. "I'm working on a murder case, an ugly one."

"So you figured I'd know about whatever's going down ugly in this here City of Brotherly Love. You pour people whiskey, you hear a lot of things." She walked down to the end of the bar, then came back. "But what makes you think I give you anything, you coming here alone?"

"Our friend could be here, he would be," Rook said. He put the fifty up. "String of murders, Miss Connie. Real ugly, which is why they haven't hit the papers."

She poured Rook another drink. "Onliest thing I got outside of the normal shootings and stabbings in our fine city is they find some lady's legs. That do it for you?"

He wrote his cell number on his business card with the chess piece on it and handed it to her. "We got that. You come up with whatever else going down here, give me a call. It's going to be some kind of freaky stuff like that, somebody chopped up or whatever, but not this lady's head shows up. Jimmy and me already got that. What Salerno and I are looking for is another victim." Lucas got up to go. "Killer got an appetite for the cruel and unusual."

"Like that Jack the Ripper dude?" asked Connie.

"Could be, but I believe he's been dead for quite some time."

She poured herself a shot of Crown Royale. "Is that a fact? Well, I'll be crossing him off of my list."

Lucas wanted to pay Salerno a call to get a line on the Feds before he went after Lyna Fine's brother. You find the brother, you find the corpse, you find the bonus at the end of Philip's rainbow. But you don't go barging in when the Feds are around and get yourself jammed up like last time down in Philly.

Salerno was nowhere around, meant maybe he'd had that operation. He called around to the hospitals until he found him. Patient Information will tell you anything. Salerno was still in intensive care, but was doing good. The charge nurse bought his bullshit that he was Salerno's boss and gave up that he'd be in a regular room tomorrow.

Rook drove back to New York for the night, thinking about Catherine Wren again. Him the rough one, her smooth and finished. Like playing the piano with a fist, Catherine Wren had said, but making good music somehow. Then the Raimondo case and his need for private justice showing more and more, she said. And she had shut him out.

Lucas was just passing Exit 6 where the PA Turnpike crossed into the Jersey when he dialed her number. Her machine picked up. The same intelligent voice with just a hint of tomboy. He remembered the way she'd go out for a run and come back still smelling like lemons.

She picked up. "Yes?"

"I'm a mile down the road," he told her.

"I was just going out, Lucas."

"On a date?"

"For a run."

He pulled into the middle lane. "You going to take that stun gun I gave you?"

"That and a 78 or whatever."

Rook laughed. "You mean a .45?"

"I knew it was some kind of phonograph thing. Are you asking me to invite you over, Lucas?"

"Is that an invitation with or without your foot in the door, Catherine?"

A sixteen-wheeler came up tailgating him. Rook put on his headlights so the trucker thought he was hitting the brakes. Then he turned hard into the passing lane.

"Coffee. No bedroom," Catherine told him.

"I can if you can," Rook said.

They couldn't. And they spent the night sleeping like lovers who had never left. She cried in the morning when she made him breakfast. "I don't know," she said. "I just don't know."

"That's alright," Lucas said. "I know enough for both of us. I know more about the bloody shit in the world than any ten men should and that makes me a hard case, I know that. But like I know about all the bad, I know about good when I see it."

She raised her glass of orange juice. "To the good," she said. "Let's see only that."

Rook stopped at the hospital gift shop and bought Jimmy Salerno a box of hard candy. The nurse was just leaving as Lucas came in.

"You don't look half bad for a heartless prick who just had heart surgery."

Mrs. Salerno came out of the bathroom.

"Carm," Jimmy said. "Could you run down to the gift store and see if *The Daily News* is in?"

"Pleased to meet you, Mrs. Salerno. I'm an old friend of your husband's. A fine man and a fine detective."

Mrs. Salerno smiled and went on her errand.

"The missus knows bullshit when she hears it, New York. You here to buy me off with them stale candies or whatever?"

Rook sat down. "Things are getting complicated. I had a visit from the Eyes. The big colored guy Dellum and the half a dyke, Handler."

Jimmy took a mint. "Nobody likes it. Nobody gets it neither. My boss tells me them Feds dropped off a bunch of them VICAP questionnaires, almost 200 questions or whatever, looking for a serial killer. And Joe Zinn says since when do we have a serial killer, for which you got to have three murders, for which maybe we got none at all. Maybe abuse of a corpse or whatnot with the lady's head and them legs."

Lucas fished out a lemon candy. "Who called in the college boys?"

Salerno took another mint. "Some nervous Nellie legislator hears that in the Sixth they found somebody's prick in a trash can. Then the phone starts ringing and up pops the Feds. The Sixth

Precinct is Center City, so more than anything we got some fag love triangle from one of them bathhouses or whatever." He took a sip of water. "You got anything for me off that address I gave you?"

"The Feds being around makes it complicated, Jimmy. That's good and bad."

"How's that?"

"Good for our pocketbooks, bad for my client's."

Salerno reached for the button to call the nurse.

"You alright?" Lucas asked him.

"You're making me sick is what I am with all this New York, clever ass shit. So how about we skip the twenty questions? You get anything off that address or what?"

Mrs. Salerno came to the door. "Are you okay, hon?" she asked.

"Give us a minute, Carm. My friend here was just leaving."

"I'll see about that ginger ale," Mrs. Salerno said.

"Trying to get some ginger ale for an hour, Rook. Like I'm trying to get a straight answer out of you. You get anything or not?"

"I got the Feds up my ass like last time I was there, James. That's what I got," Rook said.

"In a pig's eye you do. First, they're just pushing paper behind some politician's complaint. They got the towelheads to worry about. Also that redheaded ballbuster Epps ain't around. More than that, no way I'm putting my own self in the nutcracker. So what did you get off the address I gave you?"

Lucas took another candy. "I ran the address and came up with the sister who barbecues her child-raping parents. With my excellent detective work it leads me to the brother, and you can bet your pension when I get to Delbert Fine I get the rest of our celebrity."

"You get the body, we split the bonus. But it's my case. I'll be out of here tomorrow, the next day at the latest. Make sure that freak don't go nowhere."

"I'll do that," said Lucas Rook. "I'll do that just fine."

38

Rook checked his phone messages as *Man On Fire* came on the Embassy Suites pay-per-view. Good flick. Half *Training Day*, half Clint Eastwood. Good except for the line, "trained, not tough." You're in the real streets, you sure as hell be both.

Grace Savoy was blind, beautiful and crazy as a shithouse mouse, but she also hired him on those modeling shoots. He'd need that work when things were slow, so he returned her calls.

"Gracey, you call laughing or crying, doing your musical comedy, I figure you're bored, but you leave me three messages like that, I figure the drama's real."

"I knew you'd call me back," she said. "I knew you would." She lit a cigarette. "You're not in your apartment."

"That's right. I'm here. Something's wrong?"

"I saw that stalker again, the one who was around my shoot."

"No you didn't," Lucas told her.

"No I didn't."

Rook froze the picture on the pay-per-view. "Do you want to tell me about it now in twenty-five words or less? Or I'll be back in a couple of days."

She tapped her perfect nails on the dressing table. "Remember that beautiful red bird that flew into my mirror? That beautiful cardinal? A whole bunch of them flew in. There were dead birds all over my room like dried flowers."

He started the movie again. "No there weren't. Do you want to tell me what's going on?"

"Is there somebody with you?"

"Just me and Denzel, Gracey. I'm going to hang up now."

"I fucked him once."

"No you didn't."

"No I didn't. He said he's a family man."

"Goodbye, Grace. I'll be home on Wednesday or Thursday."

"They asked me to go to Australia to do some commercials. Only I have to go with that wretched little Lawrence. Will you come with me and knock his teeth out?"

"We'll talk about it."

"I love you, Lucas. Tell me you love me."

"Of course I do."

"Say it," she said. "Just for now that you'll come with me."

"See you soon, Gracey."

"Me too," she said.

The conversation with Hugh Sirlin from the funeral business would be a relief after that bullshit. He got one of those "I'll see if Mr. Sirlin is available" when he returned the call.

Sirlin kept him long enough to let him know who was boss. "How's the matter going that I referred to you, Mr. Rook?"

"Everything is under control, Mr. Sirlin, but I always can handle more work."

"Mr. First called me," Sirlin said.

Rook waited for him to go on.

"He's getting apprehensive, Rook. The time, the expense. It reflects on me."

"I expect things to be wrapped up in a few days, Mr. Sirlin. I was going to return his call after yours."

"That won't be necessary," Sirlin said. "I'll relay the message."

A call like that meant watch your billing and the clock, which meant he'd eyeball Delbert Fine, then close the case as soon as Salerno was out of the hospital. Being out front was a bad idea with the Feds around.

Lucas put the volume on the TV back up and called Catherine Wren. A man answered the phone. "Right," he said.

"What's 'right' about it?" Rook asked.

"Yo, pal, I'm just calling out for trouble on the line."

"You found it," Rook said.

Catherine took the receiver. "Lucas, is that you?"

"How could you tell?"

"The repairman looked like somebody…"

"I didn't…"

"Of course you did," Catherine said.

"I'd like to take you to dinner, Catherine. Tell the phone guy I didn't mean whatever."

"I've missed you," said Catherine. There was a pause. "And there's been no other."

There were two other calls. One from Feinstein, which he didn't have to return anymore. And another call from the dentist's office.

Rook went by Delbert Fine's place that afternoon and again about seven. No activity. No lights.

Loud Latin music came from two houses up the block. Lucas rang the bell. The music kept on. He rang the bell again.

Somebody inside turned Tito Fuentes down. "Jesus Christ, I'll be there in a minute," they said.

An old man in a gaucho outfit answered the door. He was about eighty and had sneakers on. "Jealous prick neighbor complain about the noise again?"

"It's pretty loud, Fernando."

"Jealous prick bastard. He should keep his yap shut. I don't say nothing about what he's doing."

"And what's that?" Lucas stepped inside.

"Being a jealous prick bastard, fucker. And all he is jealous that he's all shriveled up and I'm two full years older than him. Mrs. Dowd from across the street, she don't mind I do my 'gauchocize.' She even took a class once up at the Y. Is it that nosy slut from next door? She's not complaining I hear her say 'give it to me, give it to me' over and over while she's diddling herself day and night."

"Delbert Fine," Rook said.

Gaucho shook his head. "I knew who it is, that weirdo up the block. Always wearing black and so forth, the creepy nightcrawler son of a bitch that he is. Rattling around the alley the way he does, I'm the one who should be making the complaint."

"You got any more specifics about this 'rattling around'?" Rook said. "I talk to him about it, he goes away about your flamenco or whatever."

"Creep works nightwork and he's using the back door half the time. The other half, he's running out the front all dressed in black and covered up like it's Halloween." He felt his pulse. "Fuck it, fuck it. Now my pulse is all back to normal, goddamn it. Now I'm going back to my gauchocize. And I don't give a flying flaming shit fuck what you do."

The old man started his cha-cha down the hallway. Rook closed the front door. So the murdering creep worked the night shift. If it was graveyard, he wasn't going to wait four more hours for the vermin to surface.

Lucas was getting into his rental when Delbert Fine came out. He was all blacked up, watch cap, collar up, black gloves, even though it wasn't nearly winter yet. Another psycho murderer walking around the city. Every city had them, active psycho murderers walking around between the next horror they had in their heads. If the citizens knew, they'd move to some island or whatever.

Delbert Fine looked lean and strong. Long strides, but his arms in close to his side. Rook drove around the corner and picked him up again. A teenager was walking a black lab. The murderer crossed the street with his head down and took a circuitous route to the subway.

Lucas Rook had enough info to write another report, "with a reasonable degree of professional certainty…" But with Sirlin and Feinstein busting his balls, somebody was going to have to grab the bad guy fast so he could retrieve the corpse. If Jimmy Salerno was still out of commission, Inspector Zinn or whoever in that precinct would have to move on Delbert Fine so he could do what he had to do.

In the meantime, it was back to the Embassy Suites for another evening with Denzel, maybe stop along the way to see whether the food and service at the Hard Rock was as bad as in Baltimore. Or be the relentless, but irresistible sex machine he was.

Lucas called Catherine Wren from the Jersey Turnpike. "Italian or Chinese?" he said.

"Is this how you invite a lady to dinner? Are you in the car? It sounds like you're under water."

"I'm inquiring of your availability to dine, Miss Catherine. Tonight."

"There's a Northern Italian place just opened up. Chinese food is something you eat in front of *Casablanca* or in bed."

There was a place three blocks from her place, and Rook stopped to get the white containers. Tofu lo mein and orange peel chicken.

Catherine was on her cordless when he got there. She was not happy.

"Everything alright?" he asked her.

"He was 'busting my balls,' as you would say. My friend in the derby hat."

Lucas put the food on her breakfast room table. "About what?"

"I handled it, Lucas Rook. You're not the only tough guy here." She kissed him on the forehead.

"About what?"

"About covering my eight o'clock class tomorrow. So we can sleep in."

Rook got Salerno on the phone. "You good?" he asked.

"I'm good, New York. I didn't know you cared."

"We got to close this case, detective. You got a murdering fuck walking around free and my client is squeezing my shoes."

Salerno took a deep breath. "It's my case."

"You good to go?" Rook asked.

"I don't like dealing with outsiders, Rook."

"And I thought we were partnered up, James."

"In a pig's eye, New York. Let's get two things straight or we're done right here and you can get back to where you belong. One, this is Philly PD's job and always been. Second, you ain't my partner."

"No problem. Meanwhile, if you want to do this thing so there's something at the end from my client, you can buy me a cup of coffee."

Salerno took another breath. "Right. Outside the colored bar in an hour. Not Higgins'."

Lucas Rook waited until twelve-thirty. A cop is that late, he's not coming at all. Salerno pulled up as Rook was leaving.

"Get in," Salerno said.

"You look like shit, James."

Jimmy Salerno made a U-turn. "I feel better than I look, but the wife hides my keys. Isn't that some shit?"

"We all care about you, James. Now are we going to be able to run this or not?"

Detective Salerno spoke without turning his head. "This could get ugly, and I don't got the muscle. I make sure our bad guy is in there, I call for back-up, but I still get a bounce out of it on the job. The body's there, I call you on your cell. Then you can call your people. We get paid…"

"If it's just eyeballing, I want to eyeball the scene," Lucas said. "I have an interest to protect here."

"And I got an interest he doesn't chop somebody else's head off, Rook."

"Don't guilt trip me, Jimmy. This is your city. You remind me enough."

"And I'm right, New York. You want to eyeball this whole piece of shit world, be my guest, but stay out of the way. You got me?"

"Careful, Jimmy. You'll blow another gasket."

"Fuck you," Salerno said as he let Rook out.

Lucas followed three cars back and waited in the coffee shop across the street as Salerno sat in his unmarked outside of the Kennedy House. "Black, two sugars," he told the college kid behind the counter.

Jimmy Salerno went inside the Kennedy House. Lucas took his coffee across the street and drank it leaning against the detective's unmarked. Fifteen minutes Salerno didn't come out, he'd go in after him.

Fifteen minutes passed. Rook put his cup under Salerno's car and went in. He flashed his NYPD gold at the front desk. "I'm with Detective Salerno. Where is he?"

The desk clerk had thick glasses and a tattoo of a clown on his neck. "He went up to the mailroom. That's where Del has his little office."

"Del?"

"The goth dude who's the night watchman and all. That's where he went. You need me to get him?"

"Don't do nothing. You do, I'm going to run you in for obstructing, drugs, all kinds of shit." Lucas leaned across the counter. "And I'll beat the hell out of you."

The building was mixed use, mostly residential tenants, but there also were offices: a dermatologist, dentist and lawyers. The mailroom was in the rear of the second floor.

Rook unzipped his windbreaker and went into the room at an angle with his .45 at his side. No Jimmy Salerno, but there was a strong vibe. A killer's vibe, two rolls of packing tape and a heavy-duty paper cutter. Dollars to the donuts he didn't have with his coffee, you test the blade on that paper cutter, you're going to find he lay Teacher Jan down and hacked her head off.

An empty closet and a drop ceiling. Maybe the fucker was up in there. Lucas grabbed the pushbroom from the corner and lifted up one of the foam tiles. No murderer waiting to jump on him, but two spots of dried blood. Another look in the closet showed a thin red rivulet.

Rook heard somebody coming down the hall. He opened the closet door and stood behind it. If it was the Watchman, he'd take him down if he could, take him out if he had to.

Detective Salerno came into the mailroom. Lucas announced himself before he pushed the door aside.

"You could've got your ass shot, New York."

"You too, James. Our friend?"

"Not here or in the bathroom. What are you doing here anyway? You get involved it's a cluster fuck for sure."

Rook nodded.

"Appreciate it, though, New York. The desk clerk said he was here, I couldn't just sit on the place, heart job or not. There's too much bad coming off this fuck. Anyways, I'm fading." Salerno sat down on the table with the paper cutter. "I figure he brought her up here. There was blood in that closet."

"And up in the ceiling." Rook pointed to a roll of packing tape. "Bet your pension that's what he wrapped her in. And that he knows we're here," Rook said.

"Likely as not." Salerno took out his cell phone. "I'm calling all this shit in. Hawkey, Lefko, the boss, I don't give a fuck whoever grabs him up. I call it in and this place'll be locked down in fifteen minutes. In the same fifteen minutes I'll have a search warrant issued for the residence. I'll call you as soon as we get him."

"You'll call me?"

"That's right, New York. I'll call you. Nobody wants to explain why you're in the mix. And nobody wants to fuck you out of your fee neither."

"Or yours," Lucas said.

"They won't. And this job's got 'Salerno' written all over it now."

Rook went down the elevator and waited in the coffee shop for Jimmy. Two patrol cars came and then a third. Detective Salerno gave a sergeant what he had, then drove away in his unmarked. Lucas followed two cars back until he was sure that Salerno was on his way to Olympia Street. Jimmy was right that if he was caught up in the mix it would be a cluster fuck. But no way in the world was he going to let anybody fuck up his job either.

Lucas Rook followed Salerno to Delbert's house and circled the block where the air conditioners stuck out of the windows like ugly eyes and the black poles stood with black arms and the leaves like faces fell down.

In his black clothes the Watchman waited in the dark until the detective got out to search his house and Rook's car drove by. Then he hid in the back seat of Salerno's car and waited. When the detective got back in, he looped a noose of packing tape around his neck and pulled it tight. Delbert Fine wound the adhesive tape around his head, sealing closed his nose and mouth. Jimmy struggled, reaching up to his face, back behind him, then trying for his gun, but the madman ran and ran the packing tape so that Salerno could not move, could not breathe.

"I see it all," said Delbert Fine, "I see it all," as he took off his clothes so those eyes could see. Then he ran back into his house to hide where it was safe.

Rook was not far behind as he rode by again. He saw Salerno's unmarked and that something wasn't right. Lucas double-parked and came out fast. Then he saw Jimmy wrapped in a big cocoon. Lucas pulled at the packing tape and then tried to cut a hole. He grabbed at the dash for the lighter to burn a hole so Salerno could breathe. The fumes of burning plastic came up, but it was too late.

"God damn it!" said Rook. "Delbert Fine, it's time to die." Lucas took the front door with his .45 and maglite out. No one there or in the rooms above. The basement door was bolted shut. Rook took that too.

The steps were turning, narrow. His light cut the basement's darkness. A sofa bed across from the hot water heater. Dishes in the laundry sink. An old television showing an endless tape of Teacher Jan saying it was safe, "Goodbye, dears, good night."

Lucas called out, "Come on, you crazy fuck. I'm waiting here to kill you."

Nothing. Nothing until Rook turned to go. Out of the dark came the killer covered in his hundred carved and tattooed eyes. Eyes that watched the TV box that gave him warmth as he sat with the slab of flesh that had been Teacher Jan. Eyes that had seen her lie to him by walking from that big hotel when she was at home with him in his basement room. Eyes that watched him cut away her head he left to watch his mom and dad and her legs that tried to run and her arms that told him no. And that awful serpent between her legs thing like his father's that he threw into the trash so it could not be seen.

Out sprang the Watchman to kill all that he saw with those hundred eyes. Lucas grabbed at the noose as Delbert Fine tried to strangle him and wrap him up like he did to Salerno in his car. Rook tried for his gun, but Delbert got to that arm with his ropes of packing tape. Lucas hooked him hard to the body and the head with his left hand over and over, but the killer would not fall. He kneed the Watchman in the groin and thigh as Delbert Fine kept coming, snarling, screaming, "I see! I see!" They both went down. Lucas rolled to reach his ankle gun, but Fine broke free, running into the dark.

"Good night, good night," said Teacher Jan. Rook used his light to search for the killer marked up like a circus freak. "I'm not going anywhere, you psychofuck," said Lucas Rook. "And there's no place you can hide. From Daddy or Mommy. Or from me!" The Watchman rushed out, bellowing, screaming with the antenna he had ripped from the TV set, slashing, slashing back and forth.

Rook emptied his .38. Delbert Fine fell, then rose, then fell again, the carved and tattooed eyes watching through all his blood. "I see, I see!" he screamed. "I see it all!"

Lucas took the broken antenna from the bloody hand. "I'm the last thing you'll see," he said as he drove it deep into the Watchman's eye.

The Philly PD came rushing in. "Another mess?" said Inspector Zinn.

"Detective Salerno made your case before this fuck killed him too. Delbert Fine whacked Janet Scheyman and cut her up. I was only here to clean things up," Rook said.

"You can discuss that with whoever is paying your bill," said Joe Zinn. "Meanwhile, we need your statement. You can take your car. I'll follow you in."

Lucas Rook went back to the precinct and they wrote it down. Then he went back up the Turnpike and sat in the night with Grace Savoy.

- END -

Mark your calendar...

Lucas Rook faces his most terrifying adversary in *Hell's Redemption*.

Available Summer 2006.